OVERKILL

A MAGGIE RYAN MYSTERY

Susan McBride

Mayhaven Publishing

This is a novel, a work of fiction.
All characters, scenes, and events were created by the author.

Mayhaven Publishing
P O Box 557
Mahomet, IL 61853
USA

Cover Design by Aaron M. Porter
Copyright © 2001 Susan McBride

First Edition—First Printing 2001
1 2 3 4 5 6 7 8 9 10
ISBN 1-878044-87-7
Library of Congress Number: 2001 135136

Printed in Canada

Dedicated to my mom,
who always believed.

Also by Susan McBride:

And Then She Was Gone

Winner of Mayhaven's Annual Awards for Fiction

Acknowledgments

I'd like to express my sincere appreciation to those who made my baptism into publishing so special: the booksellers, libraries, readers, reviewers, authors and, of course, my friends and family. Thank you hardly seems adequate.

To my mother and father, Pat and Jim McBride, for being my biggest fans and cheering every little success. To my sister, Molly; my aunts, Linda Meisel and Doris Mountjoy; my godmother, Kiki Tomson; and my dear friends Janice Edgin, Diane Gotfryd, Nan Johnson, Ginnie Bivona and O.J. Bryson for their unbelievable encouragement.

To Sgt. Bill Weibel for fact-checking *Overkill* and his guidance in answering my questions about police procedure. Any mistakes are my own —though I like to call it "literary license".

To Marilyn Davis with the Special School District in St. Louis and Marilee Ingoldsbee, former principal of the Neuwoehner School, for their help in understanding special needs children. Also thanks to Denise Stybr, school psychologist, for her expertise and advice.

To the TeaBuds, my fabulous Purple Sisters, whose support and friendship are boundless.

To Denise Swanson and Letha Albright, my Deadly Divas. What would I do without you?

To Charlaine Harris, friend and author extraordinaire, for always making me laugh.

To all the wonderful independent mystery booksellers, especially Helen Simpson of Big Sleep Books in St. Louis, Alice Ann Carpenter and John Leininger of Grave Matters in Cincinnati, and Kate Birkel of the Mystery Bookstore in Omaha, who took a chance on an unknown.

To the Overdue Book Club in Chesterfield for "adopting" me, and particularly Julie Belzer and Barb Topp for reading an early draft of this novel and sharing their opinions.

To Rory, Robin and Kevin at The BookSource in St. Louis for their enthusiasm.

For their generosity: Donna Andrews, Debbie Brod, Elyane Dezon-Jones, Jerrilyn Farmer, Julie Wray Herman, Cathy Gallagher, Kent Krueger, Martha Powers, Ann Prospero, Marty Smith and CJ Songer. You inspire me!

To Billie Laney, Cae Carter and the Springfield Girls. You're awesome!

To Donna Ross and Alexa Hull for such fun monthly critique group meetings. And to Michael Oestreich for proofing and for my new author photos.

To my friends at work, past and present—Jane Verble and the SLMC crowd and the gang at St. Louis Clayton Orthopedics—and to my Jazzercise buddies, Gina Hopkins, Meg Kupferer, Wendi Lucchesi, Linda Godsey and Penny Rhodes for always being there when I needed them!

To my comrades at DorothyL, MMA and EMWA for their lively discussions and shrewd insights regarding the crazy world of publishing.

Last but not least, to Doris Wenzel of Mayhaven Publishing for allowing me the opportunity to have the experience of a lifetime.

Chapter One

The ringing phone awoke her, jerking her out of a shallow sleep.

She bolted upright, eyes blinking at the dark as she groped for the phone on the bedside table.

"Maggie Ryan," she croaked and squinted at the glowing green of the alarm clock.

Five past four.

She groaned and leaned back against the wooden headboard. It was too damned early for anyone to call but the dispatcher.

"Okay, Susie, what's up? And don't tell me the chief's 12-year-old son took his car for another joyride."

But the voice that answered wasn't Susie's.

"Oh, God, honey, something awful's happened."

"Delores?" Maggie's mouth went dry, and a familiar knot tightened up in her belly. She drew her knees to her chest and wrapped an arm around them. "What's wrong with Momma now?"

"I'm sorry, baby." Delores sounded breathless. "She must've gone out of the house in her nightgown when I was sleeping. I didn't know a thing until the police came bangin' on the door. Thank the Lord I'd had enough sense to sew a tag with the address into her clothes..."

"Where are you?" Maggie cut her off.

"Parkland Hospital."

"Is she hurt?"

9

"She was hit by a car. The police said the fellow didn't see her till it was too late."

Maggie grimaced. "How bad is she?"

"They've got her in surgery now, and, honey"—the molasses smooth voice cracked— "I'm not sure she's gonna make it."

"It'll be all right," she said as Delores sobbed softly. It was her automatic response to any problems that concerned her mother, and there had been plenty of late: Momma disrobing in the Tom Thumb while grocery shopping with Delores, drinking from the shampoo bottle, swallowing the wrong pills so that Delores had to summon the paramedics, throwing away her gold watch or her underwear, slipping out from under Delores' nose during the day and ending up in the neighbor's pool, disappearing in the middle of the night and wandering into the street.

"I'll be there just as soon as I can," Maggie said in a rush and pushed back the covers, sliding her legs over the bed until her toes touched ground.

"Please hurry," Delores urged.

"I will."

She had been running all her life.

The drive from Litchfield into Dallas took about twenty-five minutes, the traffic far less at half past four in the morning than during any other time of day when it would've taken her twice as long to reach Parkland Memorial Hospital.

The place was hardly a stranger to Maggie. She'd come to know it well during her five years with the Dallas police. Victims of drive-bys and gang violence constantly rolled into the ER here on stretchers, though she'd often wondered how many of the kids they patched up and discharged ended up sending someone else to the ER or turned up at the Dallas County morgue with tags on their toes.

That was one of the reasons she'd left the DPD and joined the Litchfield force. Seated outside the Dallas city limits, Litchfield had only recorded one homicide in the past decade, and Maggie wanted to keep it that way. She'd encountered enough violence in her twenty-nine years to last a lifetime.

She took the Tollway south to the Wycliff exit then headed west to Harry Hines. Across from Parkland a flashing neon sign advertised a pay-for-parking lot. Even at this hour, it looked crowded. A nearby bus stop already swelled with waiting passengers. Beneath the glow of the street lights, papers from an overflowing trashbin blew about like misguided butterflies and littered the trimmed lawn.

She drove around the back of the towering complex of buildings to where a carport sheltered ambulances and blue letters spelled out, "Emergency." She didn't bother with the mid-rise parking garage, just tucked her Mazda against the low wall across the road and locked it tight before heading for the entrance ramp.

An automatic door swung open and then another until she was inside with patient check-in dead ahead. Her gaze darted about, touching upon countless white, brown and black faces, on overhead signs with instructions in English and Spanish, and on the dozens of curtained exam rooms with flimsy sherbet-hued curtains. From somewhere nearby, an infant let out a hellacious cry, and the hair on her arms bristled.

At the Information desk, a petite Hispanic woman glanced up, smiling. "Puedo ayudarle? Can I help you?"

"I'm looking for my mother," Maggie told her and retrieved the leather wallet with her badge. She flipped it open and briefly held it beneath the woman's nose. It usually made things move faster, though this woman didn't even flinch, reminding Maggie they were used to uniforms around here. "She was brought in maybe an hour ago."

"Name?" The woman turned to her computer.

"Rothman. Violet Ryan Rothman."

"Just a second." There was a quick click-clack of fingers on a keyboard. "She's up in surgery. Go straight down the hall, take the elevator to the second floor, and check with the desk there. They can point the way to the Surgical ICU waiting."

Maggie thanked her, then wound her way around the three ER waiting rooms and past a sign indicating "Labor and Delivery." She followed the squared pattern of gray and white tiles, rushing through the narrow halls.

Too impatient for the elevator, she found the stairs and took them up two by two, spotting Delores pacing about near the Information desk the instant she emerged on the second floor.

"Dee?" she called out.

The slim body turned, tired eyes falling hard upon her. Instantly, the slender arms reached out. "Oh, honey."

Maggie's heart lurched at the sight of the tear-stained cheeks. She quickly found herself enfolded in a smothering embrace.

She drew back to arm's length and gazed at the cocoa-brown face. Delores Oliver was every bit the retired school teacher, forever wrapped in a wool cardigan. This one was yellow and hung nearly to her knees; though she'd donned a denim skirt, the plaid of her nightgown still peeked out beneath the hem. She still smelled of roses as she had all those years ago when she'd come by to see Momma some days after school before *he* got home from work. "Oh, child, how you grow," she used to say, and she'd smile so warmly that Maggie had wanted to whisper, "Take me out of here, please. Take me home with you, Dee."

"I can't believe it. Just can't believe it," Delores murmured, and Maggie shook off the memory.

"Tell me what happened," she said, catching the trembling hands in her own and leading Delores toward the doors of Surgical Waiting. She maneuvered her inside and found them seats.

"It's all my fault," Delores moaned, the dark eyes behind the owlish glasses red-veined and weepy. "It's my duty to look out for her, and I let her down. I should've heard the front door, I should've been more attuned."

"You were sleeping, for heaven's sake," Maggie reassured in a soft but firm tone. "No one's been a better friend to Momma than you. No one." And when Momma had gotten sick, Delores had moved in with her, playing nursemaid and rejecting any offers of money for doing it.

"She'd been worse these past few weeks." Delores dug into the pocket of her cardigan, pulling out a wadded tissue in her clenched fist. She dabbed at her eyes as she spoke. "That's why I spent the night again. She could hardly remember who she was, much less who I am. And she'd been wetting herself, you know, which makes her angry."

Maggie's chest constricted. She should have been the one watching out for Momma, not Delores. She was the only family Momma had any more, but it wasn't that simple. It never had been. Not since her father had walked out on them when Maggie was five, and Momma had married a man who'd made them live a lie for eight years.

"This Alzheimer's, it's a bad way to go," Delores murmured. Maggie squeezed the brown fingers between her pale ones.

"There's no good way to go," she said, having viewed enough battered corpses to know there was nothing pleasant about dying.

"I want to pass in my sleep," Delores whispered. "I just want my heart to give out while I'm dreaming. That's the way God intended."

Maggie patted her hand and said nothing. She had no idea what God intended any more.

Though several other weary-looking men and women came into the room to wait for news of loved ones, it was an hour or more before a sturdy-looking fellow in scrubs stepped through the door.

All heads turned at his entrance.

"Violet Rothman's family?" he asked to the room in general. Beneath his chin hung his surgical mask. Over his sneakers, he wore plastic booties.

Delores scrambled to her feet, dislodging the clump of tissues from her lap to the floor.

"Oh, Lord, how is she?"

Maggie rose more slowly, arms crossed over her chest. "She's my mother," she stated as the surgeon approached them.

"I'm Dr. Benton." His face was wide and unlined with a smattering of freckles. He barely looked old enough to have a medical license.

"How is she?" Delores asked again, her hands worrying themselves into an ever-moving ball. "Vi's gonna be okay, isn't she?"

Benton pulled off his skullcap and fiddled with it, nearly mirroring

Delores' anxious hand-churning. His flattened hair gleamed beneath the overhead lights. "She had internal injuries. Her spleen was ruptured and her right lung was punctured by a pair of broken ribs."

"Did you fix her up, Doc?" Delores prodded, her voice so hopeful it pained Maggie to hear it. "Tell me she's gonna be okay?"

He avoided the question, shifting his eyes from Delores to Maggie. "She also had intracranial bleeding, and there's an awful lot of swelling. She's still unconscious. We've got her on a respirator." As if she didn't understand what that meant, he added, "She's not breathing on her own right now."

"She's in a coma?" Maggie asked him.

"Yes."

"And she might not come out of it?"

He blinked at her bluntness. "That's a possibility."

Delores moaned, "No, no, no."

"I'm sorry," Benton told them, but Maggie had already stopped listening.

Chapter Two

She went back to her condo, stripped off her jeans and sweatshirt, and stepped into the shower. Her eyes closed, she braced her hands against the tiles and let the water pelt her squarely in the face.

She was tired as hell. And she felt guilty.

Not because she hadn't been there with Momma when she'd wandered out of the house in the middle of the night. Not for what she hadn't done.

For what she wasn't feeling.

She wasn't a good daughter, not the kind Momma needed now. But then the same could be said in reverse.

Don't do this, Maggie, she warned herself.

She shut off the water and stepped from the shower. She towel-dried her hair, then dressed in her usual uniform of khakis, turtleneck, and blue blazer, slipping her stockinged feet into the pair of scuffed loafers that poked out from under the bed.

She went to the kitchen long enough to pour some Frosted Flakes and milk into a plastic bowl. She ate about half and dumped what was left down the drain, then was out the door.

The Litchfield police station was barely ten minutes from her place, a small one-bedroom in a well-maintained complex that bordered the Litchfield Country Club, not coincidentally called Country Club Acres. It was quiet and people kept to themselves, which was just the way she liked it.

She guided her RX7 from the condo, the engine shifting into a reassuring hum while the police band crackled on and off in a familiar lullaby.

She squinted through the early morning brightness, passing fenced-in pasture where horses grazed juxtaposed against spanking new subdivisions with pastel-painted houses built so close together the eaves nearly kissed.

A strip mall with a doughnut shop, shoe store, and one-hour photo swept past on her right; a small stucco office building squatted low on her left.

She rolled down her window allowing in a rush of air that felt cool for October. Indian summers were the norm in North Texas. This was as good as fall got here.

She leaned her head nearer the window, and the wind tugged at her hair, tossing it around her face. She inhaled deeply, breathing in the scent of freshly-mowed grass and the faint tang of manure.

She wrinkled her nose, but figured it sure as hell beat the Dallas freeways and rush hour traffic, moving ahead inch by inch, the air so gray with exhaust it looked as dirty as it smelled.

In another five minutes, she pulled into the parking lot at the Litchfield police station. The red brick edifice resembled a small school house with its white trim and frontyard flagpole, though the handful of blue and whites lined up outside quickly dispelled further comparisons.

The building was small but had more than enough room for a department with only four detectives on its roster and just four times that number of uniformed patrol officers. Litchfield barely had enough crime to support the size of the force it had now. They were not large enough for specialization, so they generalized. Whether it be crimes against property or persons, one detective or a pair of detectives followed an investigation from start to finish. They had to look outside for help if more was needed.

Maggie didn't miss working the Dallas death beat. The daily diet of blood and battered bodies had ridden roughshod on her psyche, and the need to prove herself and save the world had suddenly seemed less important than her sanity. She'd taken refuge with the Litchfield force in order to escape. To start over.

No, if there was one thing she didn't miss about the city, it was the body count.

Overkill

She parked around back and headed in, her nose leading her straight to the coffee machine. Hot cup in hand, she went to her desk and settled into her chair. She stared at the phone and sipped on the strong brew, nearly emptying the mug before she reached forward to pick up the receiver. She dialed Parkland Hospital and connected to the Surgical ICU nurses' station, only to be told there'd been no change in Momma's condition.

She was hanging up when John Phillips walked in. His leathery face was flushed and the strategically positioned hairs across his near-bald crown had been blown off-kilter by the wind. He ran a hand over his head, patting everything in place.

"You hit traffic?" she asked him.

"Hell, I'm right on time." He checked the battered Timex on his wrist, then glanced at her. "You look beat. What'd you do? Spend the night again?" He plucked a doughnut from the opened box near Mr. Coffee. "Everything okay?"

Maggie sat up a little straighter. "Nothing I can't handle."

"Nothing I can't handle," he mimicked with a shake of his head. "Anyone ever tell you you're a hard-ass?" He stuffed most of a doughnut into his mouth and picked up another. "You ever had a vacation in your life? Hell, I already know the answer. You probably think Club Med is where doctors work out."

She ignored the bait and leaned back, tapping a pen against her palm. "Speaking of working out, I thought you were supposed to be watching your cholesterol," she said, as he came toward her.

"My wife's watching my cholesterol," he mumbled with his mouth full. "Every few months she goes on a get-in-shape kick, even got the two girls into Jazzercise class. Christ Almighty." He pushed another piece of doughnut in. "Sometimes I think I married Richard Simmons."

Maggie leveled her gaze on his belly, which protruded enough to par- tially obscure the Texas-shaped buckle on his belt. "She just wants you to make it out of your forties, Phillips. But, if you ask me, she's got a big damn job ahead of her."

He snorted. "It's good to have some extra weight on when the weather turns cool. Keeps a person insulated."

"I might even buy that if we lived in Alaska. But since we're a day's drive from Mexico, I'd say you're reaching."

"Hell, I'd rather clog up my heart pipes with creme-filleds than eat another bran muffin."

"I'll have them put that on your tombstone."

Her partner pushed the last hunk of doughnut into his mouth then waved off her remark with a hand speckled with powdered sugar. "Skinny people." He grunted, licking off his fingertips as he angled around her desk en route to his. "They should have you hog-tied and force-feed you chicken fried steak till your blood turns to grease."

Maggie tried not to smile.

He was good for her, and she knew it.

She was lucky to get him as a partner. She trusted him as much as anyone, and he'd never once made any cracks about her gender. She'd had lousy luck on the Dallas P.D., getting paired time and again with macho types who'd decided two breasts did not a penis make.

Phillips had never subscribed to that notion, not as far as Maggie was aware. He took things at face value. If she could do the job, he had no beef with her. He also understood where she came from, having left a much larger Fort Worth P.D. to join the Litchfield force. He'd been as burned out by the constant grind of murders and rapes as she and had transplanted his family so his little girls could grow up in an environment still considered safe.

She hoped that neither of them would live to regret their decisions.

With a sigh, she pulled out some files from her bottom drawer, had barely opened up the first when a slender woman in regulation blue came barreling into the squad room. "There's been a shooting on a school bus at Fifth and Elm."

Maggie looked across the aisle at her partner.

Their chairs scraped the floor in unison.

"I'll drive," Phillips volunteered before they'd even hit the door.

Maggie caught the clock on their way out.

It was just 8:15.

Overkill

She hurried after him, getting into the Ford and leaning her head back against the worn vinyl seat. Only then did she draw in a slow breath.

"What a way t' start the day, huh?" her partner muttered as he turned the key in the ignition.

Chapter Three

She spotted the blue and whites blocking off the site as Phillips headed up Fifth toward the Elm Street intersection. There, he pulled over, bumping a tire against the curb. Even before they'd come to a complete stop, Maggie had her door open.

"Back, please...stay back," a cry carried over on the wind, above the noisy cackle of a blue jay and the hum of nervous voices.

Neat brick ranch houses with mowed lawns and trimmed shrubs ran up and down either side of Elm Street, and Fifth, running perpendicular, was not much different. It was a thoroughly middle class neighborhood where a lost cat was big news. Now it looked like some kind of suburban war zone. There were uniforms everywhere. Dispatch must've called in all available units.

Maggie hurried alongside Phillips toward the scene, her eyes quickly scanning the school bus cordoned off with yellow tape strung from signposts to trees to streetlamps. About a dozen on-lookers had already begun to gather behind the makeshift barricades. Cops detoured cars approaching from either direction.

Her badge hooked over her front jacket pocket, Maggie nodded at the nearest officer who was doing his best to keep the gawkers back. About twenty feet from the bus, a patrolman crouched beside the opened door of a squad car. She could make out at least one small figure in the front seat and a second in back.

Overkill

Another pair of officers hovered over a man in a blood-stained shirt and pants laid out on a blanket in the middle of the street.

From where she stood, Maggie couldn't tell if he were alive or dead.

Phillips held up a stretch of yellow tape, and she ducked underneath.

"What the fuck?" she heard him ask as they headed toward the downed man. Her shoulder bag banged against her hip, and she reached down to still it.

Jorge Rameriz rose to his feet as they neared. His dark features were grim, and there were brownish smudges on the pale blue of his shirt. He had on latex gloves which also bore blood smears.

"Hey, Detectives. This one's breathing at least." He nodded at the man on the ground. "Took two hits, and he's lost some blood. He's pretty shocky. Wish to hell the EMTs would get here."

A female officer pressed a towel against the victim's thigh. A second towel had been balled at his right upper torso. Maggie caught a glimpse of sallow skin, a doughy face, and sandy-colored hair on a pale chest where his shirt had been opened. She could see the shallow rise and fall of his belly and the spasms that sporadically shook his body. His eyes were closed, and she knew he'd answered all the questions he'd answer this morning. He was more than "pretty shocky" by the looks of him.

Rameriz pointed behind them. "We couldn't do nothing for the one on the bus, so we tried not to disturb the body."

"A student was killed?" Maggie asked, hoping she'd heard wrong.

"Yes, ma'am," Rameriz confirmed her worst fears, and a muscle at his jaw twitched.

"Shit," Phillips muttered.

Maggie turned and started walking.

The bus was parked beside the Elm Street curb, as if waiting at a stop. Black lines ran across its side, trapping between them the words, "Transportation Management." A smaller sign near the front read, "Litchfield Special School." She glanced up at the row of windows and saw the shattered glass, sunlight sparkling on the web of crystal cracks.

The back door—the emergency exit—had been popped open, though

Maggie could see little inside, just the backs of green seats and the stretch of aisle.

She stepped up over the curb and went around the oversized vehicle, moving carefully, taking everything in, noting the seams in the side outlining a door no doubt used for loading wheelchair-bound riders. She followed the sidewalk toward the front-most door, which was folded into a neat accordion pleat. Near the base of the steps, she paused, her gaze dropping.

Dark puddles and blood-smeared footprints stained the metal stairs and left a trail on the street, curb and sidewalk close to where she stood. The nearby grass appeared trampled, the pockets of exposed soil a befuddling mess of shoe prints. There were numbered cards and chalk circles marking where bullet casings lay, a few on the bus steps and a few more on the pavement, the brass dully gleaming.

A familiar smell, metallic and sweet, emanated from the opened door, and Maggie's chest constricted.

"Be careful, Detective."

A hand touched her from behind, and she jerked around to face a pony-tailed officer in blues with a frown on her face.

"My God, Charlotte. Tell me it's just a bad dream."

"Wish I could." Charlotte Ramsey paled. She put her hands on her holstered hips, but Maggie could see they were trembling. "Shooter on the Special School bus, would you believe."

"He got away?"

"Vanished like a rabbit in a hat."

Maggie felt a stab of pain behind her eyes. Things like this didn't go on in Litchfield. Maybe in Dallas or Fort Worth. But not here.

"Driver had barely started his usual route when a kid waved at him from the curb. It wasn't a scheduled stop, but he said he gets new ones on occasion, kids who don't know what's what, so he pulled over and opened up." Charlotte paused for a breath. "Gunman came up the steps and drew his piece before the driver knew what hit him. He was shot twice at close range. Right thigh and shoulder. He had enough of his wits to use his radio to call for help and get the two other kids off the bus."

"Were they hurt?" Maggie asked.

"Not a scratch on either girl. McMartin's got them in his car now. They're trying to contact the parents."

The small figures Maggie had seen in the squad car.

"They're twins," Ramsey continued. "Both have Down's syndrome. They're shaken up, but physically unharmed. Just cried and asked for their mother. There was only one other passenger."

"Who was he?" Phillips demanded.

"*We couldn't do nothing for the one on the bus...*" Rameriz's words ran through Maggie's brain, and she already knew she wouldn't like what she'd hear.

"It's a her," Ramsey said and shifted on her feet. "She wasn't as lucky as the others. By our count, the shooter took five shots at her. One hit the window, but she caught four in the head. Right in the face actually. I've never seen anything like it..." Ramsey paused to suck in a slow breath.

"She was sitting near the front?" Maggie prodded, her mouth dry. Her ribs felt tight around her heart. She had left the DPD because of cases like this. Killers who preyed on the weak. Indiscriminate acts of violence. Things nobody should ever have to see.

"Two seats behind the driver. Close enough for the shooter to make out the color of her eyes." Ramsey shifted on her feet. "She's still on the bus. We left her right were she was. There wasn't a reason not to. It was pretty obvious she was dead, though we did check for vitals. We found a house key on a piece of yarn around her neck, but I didn't see any jewelry or a purse. Just a lunch sack."

"Did you move anything?"

"No, nothing. We didn't want to disturb the evidence any more than it already was."

There were beads of sweat on Charlotte's brow despite the lingering morning chill. "We put a call into the county ME the same time we radioed dispatch. They should be here pretty soon."

"What about forensics?"

"I requested a tech, too."

Maggie nodded, knowing they'd need help on this one even before Charlotte had answered. Their lab wasn't nearly as well-equipped as the county's. It was fine for the basics, like fingerprinting a B&E, but not for something like this. Their station house had pentium-chip computers which were on-line with law enforcement agencies across the country: the National Crime Information Center, the National Center for Missing and Exploited Children, and the Automated Fingerprint Identification System, to name a few.

But in a place where crime was rare and homicides infrequent, they were ill-prepared to deal with the collection and analysis of evidence that could include DNA-typing and the need for half a dozen different specialists. Litchfield might spend a quarter of a million on a huge baseball complex for its Little Leaguers, but adding staff to the Girl Scout troop-sized police department wasn't in the budget. Not, she realized, until crimes like this became ordinary.

"The scene's an awful mess," Ramsey apologized. "The driver and two kids tracked through the blood when they got off, before we even arrived. And I had to board the bus myself to make sure about the girl. Sort of lost my Poptarts in there," she confessed with obvious embarrassment.

"It happens," Maggie told her, though Charlotte didn't seem reassured.

Phillips shook his head and looked away.

"Did you recover the weapon?" Maggie asked, the glint of a casing on the grass catching her eye.

"Not yet, but maybe we'll get lucky." Ramsey said, shrugging. "We've got the extra patrols in now to help search the neighborhood. He used a .45 caliber. Damn near emptied the thing. He left behind plenty of casings and slugs...in the bus driver's arm and leg, and"—she wet her lips—"in the deceased. Maybe ballistics can get a match on the FBI database."

"Maybe," Maggie agreed, though she sounded no more convinced than Ramsey. Hell, even a rookie knew these days what a long shot it was to match a bullet and its casing with one of the 500,000 images on the FBI's database. With over 200 million firearms out there, the odds of winning the lottery were better.

Overkill

"We'll need to check the nearby sewers, all right?" Maggie told her, trying to think of something, anything to make this situation seem less bleak. "He might've dumped the gun down an open grate. You'll want to run metal detectors through the bushes around here, too."

Charlotte's eyes filled with panic. She looked overwhelmed. "I can get right on it..."

"First things first, okay?" Maggie stopped her. "Tell me what we know about the shooter."

Ramsey fumbled in her breastpocket and withdrew a small notebook. She flipped through several pages before poking a finger at a sheet full of chicken scratches.

"Driver identified the suspect as a male, medium build, wearing a Rangers baseball cap pulled down low so that he couldn't tell about the hair color or cut. He said the guy was average-looking, and he had on a Dallas Cowboys jacket and blue jeans."

"Christ, was he white, black, green?" Phillips pressed. "That kind of thing narrows it down, you know," he snapped, turning Charlotte's already pale face bloodless, and Maggie glared at him.

"The driver said he could've been a light skinned black or maybe Hispanic," Charlotte stammered. "He wasn't real sure, and I can't blame him."

Phillips grunted, kicking a toe against the ground.

"Were there any other witnesses?" Maggie asked, keeping her tone level, despite the rise of noise around them, the buzzing voices and the distant sound of sirens.

"We talked to a couple of people who were helping out the driver and the kids when we arrived. They said they think they might've heard something a little before eight, but they figured it was backfire or the TV, so they didn't pay much attention at first." Charlotte thumbed through her notebook again. "We got their statements, but no one saw anything until after the fact."

"Anyone see the male suspect waiting for the bus at the curb? Or catch sight of his ride? If he's not from the neighborhood, then he had to have a way to get here and get out."

"No, ma'am, nothing like that."

"How'd you manage to track down the parents of the twin girls so quickly?"

Charlotte's brow wrinkled. "They had labels inside their collars."

"Thank the Lord I'd had enough sense to sew a tag with the address into her clothes...."

Maggie heard Delores' voice inside her head, and her belly clenched.

"Sandy and Sarah Potter," Charlotte read from her notes. "Driver picked them up first a couple blocks down. The dead girl's stop was next, and she always sat two seats behind him. Her name's Pauletta Thomas. He told us where she lives. He thinks she's sixteen, but she could be a little older."

Ramsey squinted at her scribbles again.

"According to the driver, she waited at the same stop for the past two years since she was enrolled at the Special School. She never missed a day, he said."

Until now, Maggie realized.

Phillips cursed under his breath and ran a hand over his thinning hair. "Christ," he kept muttering. "Christ Almighty, but this pisses me off."

Maggie knew how he must feel, what with him having two daughters of his own.

"Nice world we live in," he ground out, his leathery face turning an unhealthy shade of purple. "God help us when our kids aren't even safe on a goddamned school bus. A Special Ed bus, for crap's sake. He had 'em trapped, Ryan, you picturing that? It was like shooting monkeys in a barrel. It's amazing that just one of them bought it and not all four."

Maggie swallowed the taste of bile that rose to her throat and shifted her eyes back toward the opened bus door.

"This is crazy, you know that? What's the deal with school shootings these days? It's becoming an epidemic," Phillips grumbled.

"Only our shooter couldn't even wait until these kids got to school."

"You think it was some kinda gang initiation?" Phillips looked around them. "Or just a random thing? Some kind of satanic ritual maybe?"

"Halloween's not for weeks," she said, knowing where he was headed.

Overkill

"Some nutball probably got tired of playing *Doom* in the arcade and decided to see what it felt like to really kill someone," he declared in an angry monotone. "Seems to be happening a lot lately. Kids going gun crazy, like every school and street corner are the OK Corral and it's high noon."

"You think someone plotted to ambush a Special Ed bus just for kicks?"

"You got any better ideas?"

"No," Maggie admitted, hating the helplessness of not being able to answer the question. Hating that it had happened in a quiet neighborhood where people were supposed to be safe.

A blue jay squawked at her from a tree branch overhead, and she felt the hair on the back of her neck prickle.

"EMS," Phillips said, nudging her lightly, and she shook off the chill.

She heard the siren, drawing nearer.

Chapter Four

The EMS van rolled up the street, stopping at the line of yellow tape.

The noise of the siren shut off with a whoop but the orange and blue lights still flashed on the roof. The front doors popped open, and the EMTs hopped down and raced around to the rear of the van, emerging with a gurney which they quickly propped onto its wheels. Dumping their cases atop it, they ran it over to the injured bus driver, assessing his wounds, checking his vitals and hooking up an IV. Then, with the help of the officers, they lifted him onto the stretcher, wheeled him to the ambulance and shut him inside.

The sirens started up again as the van took off, heading for Methodist Hospital.

They were gone as quickly as they'd come, and Maggie released a slow breath as the ambulance drove out of view and the sirens faded from earshot.

If she'd been Catholic, she would've crossed herself, thankful the driver's condition wasn't likely fatal. That they had a witness was a miracle. That the shooter had left the twins untouched was even more unbelievable.

The van from the Dallas County Medical Examiner's office appeared next, without blazing lights or blaring siren. A blue sedan followed on its heels.

The patrol officers did their best to hold at bay the ever-growing crowd of neighbors in order to clear the way for the necessary vehicles to park near the scene.

Overkill

Maggie had yet to detect any media in the area, one advantage to being outside the city limits. But she knew it wouldn't last, not when the Dallas stations got wind of what had happened.

She watched as a gurney was removed from the rear of the ME's van. This one bore a body bag. They parked it alongside the bus.

She pressed her mouth into a thin line as she fought back the wave of emotions rising to the surface. Anger, frustration, sadness.

"That's your friend Mahoney, isn't it?" Phillips asked, nudging her with an elbow as a slender man with a headful of brown curls surfaced from the blue four-door and headed their way, a black case in hand. Behind him, a woman with cropped gray hair quickened her steps to keep up with him, her pace doubtless slowed by the large equipment box she carried.

"How about I check on the Potter girls, and you keep tabs on your old buddy from the morgue," her partner said, and Maggie gave a quick nod.

Despite the tragedy that had brought him out to Litchfield this morning, Brian Mahoney was grinning as he approached.

"Well, if it isn't Maggie Ryan," he began, a gentle teasing underscoring each word. "Of all the gin joints in the world, and you have to walk into mine."

"I think it's my gin joint, Mahoney. Or it would be if we weren't standing in the street."

"Right you are." He squared his shoulders, squinting through his oval-shaped glasses as he looked around him, the smile slipping away. "Thought you left the DPD so you wouldn't have to deal with murder and mayhem."

She cocked her head, finally meeting his eyes. A faint smile brushed her lips. "And I thought I got out so I wouldn't have to listen to any more of your bullshit."

"Ouch."

Mahoney was among about a dozen MEs on the payroll of Dallas County, and their paths had crossed numerous times during her years with the city. On the job and off.

He gave her a quick once-over. "You lost weight?"

She arched her eyebrows.

"Not that you weren't always thin," he stammered, cheeks pinkening, "but you look downright skinny. You still living on adrenaline and Sugar Smacks?"

"It's Frosted Flakes."

"Mea culpa," he quipped and ducked his head.

She opened her mouth to spit out a witty comeback, but they were interrupted.

The gray-haired woman caught up with them and set the huge evidence case down at her feet, extending her small hand in Maggie's direction. "Emma Slater," she said, deep-set crow's feet radiating from her eyes.

"Emma's one of the best evidence techs around," Mahoney said without skipping a beat.

Maggie nodded, hoping only that Emma would live up to her billing.

"Has the body been moved?" Mahoney asked, but his eyes were already on the school bus with its shattered window.

"Not to my knowledge," Maggie told him and filled him in on what Charlotte Ramsey had earlier reported as they headed over to the bus.

"You gonna stick around?" Mahoney said as they paused near the rear of the vehicle.

"How else can I keep an eye on you?"

"You hear that, Emma? We've got ourselves a chaperone."

Emma Slater answered with a grunt as she snapped open her black case and pulled on a pair of rubber gloves, booties and an apron reserved for messy crime scenes. Then she dug out a Polaroid, loaded it with fresh film, and, shooting photographs as she went, carefully made her way up the steps and onto the bus.

Maggie left her blazer and bag in the care of a uniform and slipped on the booties and gloves that Mahoney extracted from his own black bag.

"Scene like this makes me feel right at home, like I never left the city," he said as he pulled on a plastic apron like the one Emma had donned.

"I thought I had," Maggie murmured. "In my rearview mirror."

"It's like the creeping crud, isn't it? No matter where you go these days, it's right there beside you."

Overkill

"So I've noticed."

There was a momentary groan of metal hinges as Emma Slater carefully pushed wide the rear emergency exit.

"It'd be best if you came aboard this way," she told them, standing in the doorframe. "I've already got enough tracks running through the scene as it is, and someone puked up front near the driver's seat, like my job's not enjoyable enough, right? Oh, hey, Mahoney, bring my kit up, would you? And watch where you step."

Maggie helped Mahoney lift the bulky black box as well as his own case onto the back of the bus.

She climbed up after him, standing in the slim aisle between the two rows of seats. The smell of blood was stronger now, filling her nose, mixed with the cloying odor of vomit.

She swallowed hard, forcing herself to look forward at the place two seats behind the driver where Mahoney and Emma knelt.

She could see clearly, now, what before had only been a dark shadow against the shattered window.

The head lay slack against the seatback, abutting the glass. Reddish brown spatter clung to the cracked pane. Matted dark hair tied with a bow.

She took a few steps up the aisle, and her eyes honed in on the collar of the victim's blouse. If it had once been white, it wasn't now.

I've never seen anything like it....

Mahoney let out a whistle, and Maggie's skin prickled.

"Poor girl never had a chance," he said to Emma. "Large caliber. A .45?"

"Yep, and that's my final answer," Slater told him.

Mahoney looked back at Maggie. "You said the driver was hit twice?"

"Shoulder and thigh."

"And he's alive?"

"Yes."

"Was he robbed?"

If only it were that simple. "It doesn't appear robbery was a motive."

"So he gets on the bus, pops the driver twice, then massacres this girl, and he doesn't so much as steal her lunch money. Doesn't make sense, does it?"

Maggie moved slowly ahead, lightly touching the high backs she passed with gloved fingers.

Emma maneuvered her way toward the driver's seat, a tape measure in hand.

"Take a look for yourself," Mahoney said, motioning her closer. He had his mag-lite out and was peering at her with his forehead bunched up in thought. "Pretty blatant case of overkill if you ask me."

Maggie could hardly breathe with the stench of death swimming inside her head, and she tasted this morning's Frosted Flakes in the back of her throat.

She avoided the battered face of the victim and focused instead on the mottled Peter Pan collar neatly set outside the placket of a stained blue cardigan.

A nylon lunch bag sat beside a slack hand.

"*Her name's Pauletta Thomas...he thinks she's sixteen...never missed a day...*"

"She looks like target practice," Mahoney remarked, a tightness to his voice, and Maggie slowly lifted her eyes to the face and found only a grisly mask in its place.

"The driver takes two bullets and lives, and she gets hammered," Mahoney said softly, as if he were talking to himself and Maggie merely eavesdropping. "It doesn't make sense," he said again.

Maggie couldn't argue with him.

It made no sense at all.

Chapter Five

Two men carried the body out of the bus, the form cocooned in black.

Maggie stood on the sidewalk with Phillips, watching as the morgue attendants placed it on the stretcher then wheeled it over to the van.

"And she thought she was on her way to class," Phillips muttered. "Christ, but this is the last day my girls ride the bus."

Maggie tried not to think of the victim as she'd last seen her before Mahoney had paper-bagged the hands and head. But the smell of blood stuck to her clothes and skin.

She saw Emma Slater crossing the street toward the blue sedan, the crime tech kit clutched in her hand, the evidence she'd gathered, bagged and numbered headed for the county lab.

She'd managed to pull some latent prints off the bus railing, but Maggie had no delusions that those would lead anywhere. She tried to imagine how many dozens—if not hundreds—of hands had touched the metal day after day.

The ache behind her eyes intensified, and she squinted against the brightness of the morning.

Why? was all she could think at the moment.

Why target a school bus?

Why shoot the driver?

Why kill a Special Ed student?

What could possibly have been the motive?

"*Could be a gang initiation*," Phillips had said, and Maggie seriously weighed the suggestion, because it was as good as any other.

Was it an addict on a murderous rampage or a gun crazy teenager out to kill for kicks?

Or how about a semi-toting, gang-banging junkie with a psychotic hatred of Special Ed students?

The throbbing spread to her temples.

She let out a slow breath.

Mahoney walked up in his ambling gait. "You want me to call you when we've got her on the table?"

"When d'you think it'll be?" Phillps asked.

"I've got a couple drive-bys first and an MVA victim, then I'll get to your girl ASAP."

"Sure, Doc. I think I'd like to come watch you at work." Phillips nodded, extending his hand which Mahoney clasped. "Maggie says you're first rate."

"She does?" Mahoney's thick eyebrows lifted above the rim of his glasses, and a faint pink settled in his cheeks. "Shucks, Ryan, I didn't think you cared."

"The image of you cracking a skull with a power saw isn't something a girl forgets," Maggie said dryly, catching his oddly pleased expression, before she looked away.

"You coming, too?" The hopeful tone in his voice would've been hard to miss.

She almost hated telling him, "I think I'll pass, all right? I saw enough already to know what killed her. I don't think you'll find anything at autopsy that'll make much difference."

"Sure." Mahoney's face sagged with disappointment, but the morgue was the last place Maggie wanted to go. She had a hard enough time in hospitals. The antiseptic smells, the too-green lighting, the sick people. Or, in this case, the dead ones. Phillips was right. She knew Mahoney did his job well. But she'd always been an uncomfortable spectator.

Brian rubbed his hands together. "All right, then I'll give you a call,

Detective Phillips, so you can catch a front row seat."

"I'll see ya, Doc."

Maggie looked up, their eyes connecting for an instant, before he turned and walked away. The van from the morgue drove off first with the blue sedan close behind it.

She turned to find her partner watching her, curiosity bright in his eyes, but she was hardly in the mood for a personal interrogation.

He started to talk, but only got out a, "Hey, Ryan...," before she cut him off at the pass with a hurried, "You check on the girls before McMartin took them to the station to meet their parents?"

"Yes, ma'am."

"They okay?"

He toed the pavement. "I don't think they really understood what the hell happened."

"They have Down's syndrome, right? Isn't that what Ramsey said?"

"Yep."

"Is that what Pauletta Thomas had?"

He scratched his chin. "Beats me. Did she look like she did? They have pretty recognizable features."

"I couldn't tell from what was left of her."

She squinted at a spot at least a block away where a couple uniforms fished with magnets down open storm drain grates for the murder weapon. Another officer was going through a nearby yard with a metal detector. They were more apt to find Jimmy Hoffa than the gun used by their shooter.

"They locate the victim's parents?" she asked, turning back to her partner.

His leathered face crinkled, his frown deepening. "We sent an officer down to where the driver said the victim lived, but no one was home. Next-door neighbor had an emergency number for the mother at work. Lady said the Thomases are separated. Apparently, the father moved out. Candace Thomas is employed at Cybercytes off the Parkway in Plano."

Maggie nodded.

"You heard of it?"

35

"I read about it in the paper. They register web site domain names. Guy who started the company's already a billionaire, and the stock's gone through the roof."

Phillips shrugged. "My girls know a helluva lot more about technology than I do. Christ, I've still got an eight track."

Maggie patted his shoulder. "At least you'll never have to worry about servers or upgrades or cleaning out your cache."

"Hey, I always worry about someone cleaning out my cash."

"No, John, that's not what I meant," Maggie tried to tell him, but her response was lost in the air-beating whir of a helicopter, swooping out of the sky overhead, the logo of Dallas' Channel 8 painted on its white tail.

"Let's get out of here," Phillips shouted above the din.

Maggie's wristwatch showed half past ten. It was still morning, but it felt like a lifetime since Delores' phone call from Parkland.

"Wish I'd never gotten out of bed," she said, gazing out the window as they drove, gritting her teeth at the thought of having to tell a mother that her teenaged daughter was murdered on her school bus by a guy in a Cowboys jacket who'd disappeared into thin air.

Chapter Six

They rolled at the speed limit along the four-laned Plano Parkway, following the gray ribbon that meandered through Plano, Texas, another suburban extension of the ever-expanding Far North Dallas.

Maggie took notes as they drove, recording their time of arrival at the crime scene, the location and description, and the on-site examination of the body. She wrote rapidly, as it was easy enough to remember the details, so clearly were they burned into her brain.

The trampled grass. The blood-stained footprints on the sidewalk. The shell casings.

The once white collar atop the blue cardigan.

She finished up, then put away her pen and pad, staring out the window. But there was little in the way of scenery to draw her thoughts from the matter at hand.

Between the roads that turned off into neighborhoods or strip malls with mini-marts, there was brush and yellowed grass stretched out on either side. An occasional fenced-in plot with a cow or horse beyond the wire served to remind her that this place had once been pasture before the migration from Dallas had begun in the '70s when developers had decided the air was cleaner here, the streets safer, and the land more available and far cheaper outside the city limits.

She thought of that line from *Field of Dreams*: "If you build it, they will come."

And they had.

Maggie wondered if this was how Litchfield would look in another decade with miles of concrete roadway, clouds of exhaust, and car dealerships proliferating at every twist and turn; with a right and wrong side of the tracks and an ever-growing crime rate and drug problem to confirm that there was no thing closer to extinction than innocence.

"There she is," Phillips said.

Maggie shifted her gaze to the other side of the road, the car gently bumping as he eased into the left turn lane.

Beyond a chain-link fence and small, crowded parking lot, she saw a low steel and glass building with large red letters near the roofline spelling out, "Cybercytes."

There was nothing vaguely interesting about the building itself or the obligatory landscaping with rainbow-hued pansies and elfin trees ringed with dark mulch. It looked like any number of edifices that kept springing up from nothingness as new technology firms staked out their territory in and around Dallas. The region was turning into the Silicon Valley of North Texas.

Still, Maggie felt her pulse quicken as Phillips pulled the four-door Ford into an empty parking space.

She scanned the nearby cars, wondering which of them belonged to Candace Thomas. The woman had come to work this day just like any other. She had probably waved her daughter onto the school bus before driving away. Maybe she was already planning what to pick up for dinner on the way home, something Pauletta would like.

Only Pauletta wouldn't be there.

"You ready?"

Phillips watched her, his expression as grave as her own.

"Do I have a choice?"

She reached for the door handle, drawing her bag behind her as she freed herself from the car and headed toward the smoky glass doors that led into the building. Berber carpeting muffled their footsteps.

A security guard in blue uniform monitored a U-shaped desk in the lobby. He looked about twenty-one with Marine-short blond hair still damp from the shower. He wore a shiny silver badge over his left breast and was armed with only a black walkie-talkie. She figured he was more show than substance.

How much security did a domain name registry need? she wondered. It's not like there was a secret formula to be guarded under lock and key, like a software program or a smaller, faster computer chip...or even the ingredients to Coke or the special sauce on a Big Mac.

"Can I help y'all?" the guard asked as they approached, crossing his arms so that his muscled biceps bulged below his shirt sleeves.

"Hope you can, son," Phillips said and stepped up to the desk, dramatically withdrawing his leather wallet from his back pocket and flipping it wide to show his ID.

"You're cops?"

"The real thing." Phillips slowly replaced his wallet in his pocket.

The guard looked suddenly less rooster-like, his arms falling to his sides. Beneath his clean-shaven chin, his Adam's apple did a jig. "What can I do for you, officers?"

"That's detectives, son," Phillips corrected, and the guard quickly repeated, "Detectives, yes, sir," like a kid in basic training.

A sheen of sweat slickened his brow, and Maggie almost felt sorry for him and the way Phillips was trying to out-macho him.

"We're looking for a lady named Candace Thomas," her partner said and braced his hands on the desk, leaning forward, his voice lowered though there was no one else around. "We need to talk to her. In private."

"Candy Thomas? Mr. Gray's assistant?"

"Mr. Gray?"

"Dave Gray. He's the boss. Is she in trouble or something?"

"It's a private matter," was all Phillips would volunteer, and he glanced sideways at Maggie as he said it.

The guard picked up a slim black telephone and punched a few numbers into the keypad.

Maggie walked halfway around the U-shaped desk and saw a black and white video monitor, its picture slightly grainy but clear enough that she could make out the figures that moved about on-camera. Somebody's office, she guessed, spotting a man behind a desk. Seconds after, the screen changed, showing another room entirely, where a woman stood beside a copy machine.

Was that Candace Thomas? She found herself wondering, until the image again shifted, the woman disappearing only to be replaced by a room filled with a dozen square cubicles.

Maggie turned her head at the sudden slap of plastic on plastic as the guard hung up the phone.

"She'll be out shortly," he said to Phillips. "You can wait over there." He pointed across the way to a grouping of beige furniture. Generic floral prints hung on the walls above the mantel of a fake fireplace.

Maggie had only just lowered herself onto the arm of the nearest chair and picked up a much-thumbed through copy of *Byte* when she heard a voice ask uncertainly, "Detectives? Darnell said you wanted to see me."

Maggie dropped the magazine and scrambled to her feet.

"Candace Thomas?"

"Candy, please."

She was dressed in a navy blue suit with a wide-collared blue blouse that was shiny and about the same shade as the dead girl's sweater.

She was blond, which Maggie would have expected of someone called Candy. It had that stripper connotation. But this woman was petite, her shoulders slim, her features dainty, though her skin was slightly worn around the eyes and mouth. There was, though, a vaguely hard edge to her, in her eyes, in the set of her jaw, which was in contrast to her otherwise delicate appearance. Momma would've said she looked like she'd "been around the block enough times to wear out the soles of her shoes," though Maggie realized raising a child with a disability could not have been easy. She wondered if that had anything to do with her marriage dissipating.

"I'm Detective Ryan," she introduced herself and, as Phillips came up beside her, "My partner, John Phillips."

Mrs. Thomas clutched her hands together. "I don't know why you'd

40

need to see me, unless it has to do with the restraining order."

Maggie exchanged glances with her partner.

"Restraining order?"

"The one that was served against my husband."

Maggie shook her head.

"If this isn't about Brad—what? Did I forget to pay a parking ticket?"

Phillips cleared his throat. "No, ma'am. It's not about a parking ticket or a restraining order."

Her gaze darted from Maggie to Phillips, then back again. "I don't understand why you're here then, unless"—her eyes went wide as awareness sunk in—"Oh, my God," she said in a breathless, staccato-quick tone. "It's Pauletta, isn't it?"

"Is there somewhere more private we could talk?" Maggie asked, taking a step toward her.

"Where is she?" The woman's voice rose. Her hands fanned the air. "Where's Pauletta? Is it her heart? Is she at the hospital? It must be bad if you came out here. Dear God, tell me she's okay? Tell me!"

The guard was watching them now, one hand on the walkie-talkie at his hip as if ready to summon the cavalry.

Maggie kept her tone low. "Please, Mrs. Thomas. Could we discuss this somewhere other than the lobby?"

The woman clutched her hands at her breasts, visibly shaken, her face a mixture of fear and confusion.

Maggie tried again gently. "Is there an empty office we could use?"

"Ma'am?" Phillips walked over to the woman, touching her arm, and Mrs. Thomas looked up at him, as if coming awake.

"We could go...there's the conference room." Her voice broke. She was already fighting back tears.

"You want to show us the way?"

She smoothed her hands on the front of her skirt. They were shaking. Then she turned on her heel and crossed the lobby.

Phillips' eyes briefly met Maggie's, and she saw in them how much he hated this. There was a restrained fury in his face, in the pinch of muscle at his jawline, in the hard set of his mouth. It was their job and, as the saying went, somebody had to do it. But it never got easier.

She walked behind him as they trailed Candace Thomas, passing through a set of smoky doors into a reception area where a big-haired blonde attacked busy phone lines and several others worked at computer stations.

No one seemed to take much notice of them. They bypassed several more offices before veering left at a hallway and finally entering a glass-walled room with venetian blinds lowered all the way around for privacy. An octagonal-shaped table and a dozen black leather chairs filled the space.

Phillips held out the first chair for Mrs. Thomas while Maggie closed the door behind them and leaned against it for a moment.

"You okay, ma'am?" Phillips asked the woman. "You need a glass of water or something?"

Mrs. Thomas shook her head. "I just need to know...I need you to tell me if Pauletta...is she okay?"

"We'll tell you what we know, I promise," Phillips assured her and settled into a chair, turning it so that he faced her.

Maggie peeled herself away from the door and took a few steps toward them.

She could see Candace Thomas' hands in her lap, so tightly clasped that her fingers were white at the knuckles.

Maggie wiped her palms on the front of her slacks. "Could you describe what your daughter was wearing this morning when she left the house?"

Mrs. Thomas blinked. "Blue jeans, with a white blouse and a blue cardigan."

"Did she have anything with her?"

"Anything with her?"

"Personal belongings," Maggie clarified. "Anything identifiable, like a piece of jewelry."

The woman wrinkled her brow. "She wore a house key around her neck on a string. And she had her lunch bag."

"Is it nylon?"

Overkill

"Yes."

Maggie looked over at her partner. Phillips ran a hand over his head, his face sagging. Candy Thomas had confirmed what they already knew.

Maggie turned back to Mrs. Thomas. Her palms still felt slick. Her turtleneck stuck to her skin beneath the wool of her blazer. "I'm sorry, ma'am. Truly sorry."

Candy's eyes were pale and clear as they abruptly connected with Maggie's.

"Oh, God. She's dead, isn't she?"

Maggie answered honestly. "Yes."

"Are you sure it's her? Are you certain?" the frightened voice rose in pitch. Candy Thomas came halfway out of her seat. "Maybe I should go see her...maybe there's been a mistake."

"Mrs. Thomas, there's no mistake." Maggie hated to say the words, wished she could tell her otherwise. But there was no way around it. "The bus driver identified your daughter. We also found her name written inside her lunch bag, and she was wearing the clothing you described."

Candy vehemently shook her head. "No, no, you must be wrong. I watched her walk out to the bus myself. She waved at me from the steps before I pulled my car out of the driveway."

Maggie didn't know what else to tell her but to say again, "I'm sorry."

"You're wrong, you're wrong," the woman moaned, drawing a hand to her mouth, bending forward as if she might be sick. "She's not dead...can't be dead...Pauletta...my sweet Pauletta."

Phillips reached forward and put a hand on her shoulder.

"How?" she asked suddenly, twisting in her seat to look up again at Maggie. "How did it happen? Was it her heart? Did it give out on her?"

"No, ma'am."

Candy appeared clearly puzzled. "Was the bus in an accident?"

Maggie pursed her lips. There was no way to sugar coat what had happened, so she just said it: "She was shot, on the bus, several blocks from her stop."

"Shot on the bus?" Mrs. Thomas appeared completely stunned by the statement. "How could that happen? I don't understand?"

"Neither do we, ma'am," Phillips said. "That's why we need your help."

"But who would shoot Pauletta?" she cried out. Her tearful gaze begged Maggie for answers. "Who in God's name could have done something so hideous? Who would want to hurt my sweet angel and take her away from me?"

Phillips sent Maggie a look she well recognized.

This was her ballgame.

Maybe it was chauvinistic, but he always backed off when things got emotional, when he thought the situation seemed to call for a feminine touch. Tearful women made him retreat like a turtle to its shell. Which Maggie had always thought was ironic, considering he was actually the more expressive of the two. She tended to keep things to herself, to put her own feelings under lock and key. Maybe it was exactly that control he sought.

"Why would anyone want to harm her? Why would anyone want Pauletta dead?" Mrs. Thomas was crying, tears slipping down her face, smearing the makeup around her eyes, though she didn't seem to care. She simply let them fall, staining the blue silk of her blouse. "Pauletta...she was as kind as could be...had never hurt anyone in her life."

"We don't know, ma'am." Maggie wished she had something more, something definite to tell her, but she had no clue why Pauletta was dead. It was as senseless an act as she'd seen. What threat could a mentally disabled teenager have been to anyone? Why had someone wanted to obliterate a girl like Pauletta Thomas? Because that's what they'd done. If Phillips was right and it was a gang initiation, a morbid rite of passage, then it would mean the barbarians weren't just at Litchfield's gate, they had entered uninvited.

"Pauletta's body was taken to the Dallas County morgue for autopsy," Maggie quietly told the grieving mother, though not even a gentle tone of voice could make the statement less final. "You'll need to go down to make a visual ID. Then we'll let you know when her examination is complete, so you can go ahead with funeral arrangements."

"Visual ID? Autopsy? Oh, God." Mrs. Thomas let out a whimper and hugged herself, rocking back and forth.

"We could talk later, if you're not up to it now," Maggie said, part of her wanting to leave this woman in peace, and the other half needing to stay, to try to find some bit of information that could help to catch a killer. "Mrs. Thomas, would you like us to go?"

The quivering chin jerked up. "No, I want to finish this now. I want to do it so you can find whoever did such a thing."

Maggie crouched down, balancing her forearms on her thighs, at eye level with Candace Thomas. "Pauletta was how old, exactly?" she eased into her questioning, asking something simple to answer.

"She would have been seventeen next month."

"And she'd been attending the Litchfield Special School for how long?"

"Two years." The reply came without hesitation. "We moved to Litchfield just so she could attend the Special School. The student to teacher ratio was so much better, and the facilities newer. We didn't know what else to do for her. There are no special programs for Williams' kids, none we could afford anyway."

"Williams'?" Maggie had no idea what that meant.

Mrs. Thomas nodded, wiping moisture from her cheeks with trembling fingers. "She was diagnosed with Williams' syndrome several years ago."

"I've never heard of it." Maggie glanced at her partner who shrugged, obviously no better informed than she.

Candy's voice quivered as she told them, "Not many people have. It can only be accurately diagnosed through a *FISH* test."

"A *FISH* test?" Maggie asked, looking over at Phillips, who shrugged back.

"A blood test. It checks for elastin deletion in the blood," Candy Thomas said through her tears. "It's the one way to be sure. Before that, we went a long time without knowing what was wrong."

The talking seemed to keep the tears from coming so fast, so Maggie didn't interrupt her. "Pauletta wasn't well as a baby. She cried, almost all the time, the first three years. And she had all sorts of physical problems. Her calcium level was too high, she didn't want to take the formula, and the pediatrician seemed to regard us suspiciously because of her failure to thrive."

"So Williams' is a physical disability?" Maggie said, but Candy shook her head.

"There are both physical and mental deficiencies related to having the syndrome. And, God, we've gone through the gamut." She paused, biting her lip, seeming to gather her thoughts, composing herself, though her voice trembled as she continued. "Pauletta suffered from a heart abnormality, a narrowing of the aorta that required several surgeries to patch."

Maggie realized why the woman had at first assumed her daughter had suffered a heart attack.

"She had incredibly high blood pressure, more like an old man than a little girl, usually around 270/120. She was on medication for that as well as chronic diarrhea, urinary problems, ear infections, but she was mine. My sweet little girl. I would've done whatever it took to keep her going."

"Did your husband feel the same way?'

Brad was always complaining about the medical costs. We were always fighting with the insurance company, trying to get them to cover expenses they said were out of pocket. Brad didn't have much interaction with Pauletta. Not unless he had to. He had such a temper, was so impatient with her. I was always afraid he might hurt her. I tried never to leave him alone with her."

Maggie noticed Phillip's jaw tighten.

"Pauletta didn't speak until she was three. Not 'mama' or 'dada' or anything." Candy raised her head, nodding absently. "But when she did start talking, she never stopped. She picked up words at an unbelievable rate, though the way she used them didn't always make sense. We enrolled her in preschool, but she was behind the other kids. Her teacher suggested genetic testing."

"Is that when they diagnosed her?" Maggie asked.

Candy brushed at her damp eyes and sniffed. "They could only tell us she was 'developmentally delayed.' They put her in special education and kept doing more testing. It was quite clear something wasn't right. They said she was somewhat retarded, but she seemed so bright in some ways. I remember her talking about dinosaurs once. Tyranosaurus, brontosaurus, all sorts of sauruses. I'd never even heard of some of them.

"But there were things she couldn't do that didn't make sense. She couldn't tie her own shoes or cut paperdolls. All kinds of sounds distracted her. And she simply didn't grasp math, not even the basics. She could never tell time or make change. I worried for her...for her future, wondered what I might've done during the pregnancy to harm her. A glass of wine too many? Having my hair colored? God knows. I blamed myself."

She stared at her lap again, tears skidding down her face. "But she surprised me with her personality. It seemed to make up for everything she was missing. She was fearless. She'd go up to complete strangers and hug them. I had to watch her closely when we went out. I was the one who was afraid."

She sighed, drawing in a shaky breath, the color returning to her cheeks. "She looked different from the other kids. That's why Williams' kids are referred to as 'pixie people.' They have triangular-shaped faces, beautiful wide-spaced eyes and pointed chins. Pauletta looked like a little elf. A magical little elf." Her voice caught, and she pressed her her hands to her mouth.

Maggie caught Phillips' eye. She read the frustration in his gaze. Raising kids had to be hard enough these days without dealing with doctors, social workers, school psychologists and tests ad nauseum, only to realize your child wasn't 'normal' and never would be no matter how much you loved her.

Candy's soft voice picked up again. "She was nearly ten when she was diagnosed. We'd never heard of Williams before. We thought putting a name to her problems would solve everything. They told us that Williams' kids test like retarded children, talk like gifted children, behave like disturbed children and function like a learning disabled child."

"Must've been hard on you."

"Public schools generally don't serve Williams' kids well. We arranged for her to attend a privately-run facility in Dallas, a day school, but the expense..." She shook her head. "It was too much to bear. She was getting older, harder to care for. Because of that, I wasn't working. Brad's salary couldn't begin to stretch as far as we needed it to go."

"Did Pauletta have difficulty getting along with other kids?"

"No, never," Candy replied in a rush. "She was an angel. She thought of others before herself, always. She constantly asked how I was. 'You look tiresome, Mommy,' she'd say." The flicker of memory brightened Candy's eyes before defeat set in again. "There were some tough times. My husband and I seemed to disagree about everything. Pauletta used to hear us and cry." She bit down on her lip.

"She sounds like a special child," Maggie remarked.

"Oh, she is." Mrs. Thomas lifted her chin, her eyes glistening, beseeching. "Are you sure it was her on the bus?"

Maggie's throat constricted so tightly she couldn't breathe much less answer.

Thankfully, Phillips spoke up. "Yes, ma'am. We're sure."

Mrs. Thomas made a noisy hiccough, as if fighting to catch her breath. Then she turned to Maggie.

"Have you told Brad yet?" she asked.

"No," Maggie conjured up a hoarse whisper, admitting, "We came to you first."

Candy visibly tensed. "Brad and I...we're polar opposites. He used to say that he was fire and I was ice." Her shoulders stiffened. "He didn't want children, but he seemed pleased when I got pregnant with Pauletta. He was hoping for a boy to play ball with. Instead, I gave him a girl, and a child with problems we couldn't solve."

"You and Mr. Thomas have separated?"

"Yes."

"When?"

Candy pressed her fingers to her quivering lips. She closed her eyes a moment, drawing in a deep breath and exhaling slowly. "It's been about

three months. He seemed to understand at first, even to agree that we needed some time apart, as much for Pauletta's sake as for our own. But, lately..." She paused, wetting her lips, looking even more uncomfortable.
"Lately, he'd been calling at all hours, coming by in the middle of the night
and ringing the bell, banging on the door. I had the locks changed when he
moved out, and he didn't like that. Didn't like the fact that I...that Pauletta
and I were doing fine without him. We were better off, I'd say."

Maggie stood up, smoothing her hands on her wrinkled pants. "Is that
why you filed a restraining order, Mrs. Thomas? Because your husband was
harassing you? Sounds like he wasn't happy about the separation."

"A friend of mine...he knew what was going on and had me see his
lawyer. They thought it would be a good idea to protect Pauletta and me."

Her face tightened with each word, and Maggie thought she saw fear
in her eyes.

"Brad didn't like the fact that Pauletta would be dependent upon us for
the rest of her life. He suggested a group home. I realize it's about the only
way she could be close to independent." Her voice dropped, and her gaze
fell as well, hiding her expression. "But I just couldn't do that." She shook
her head. "I couldn't send away my only child."

So she sent her husband away instead, Maggie thought, suddenly eager
to talk to Brad Thomas.

"Mrs. Thomas, where can we find your husband?" Maggie asked.

The face that returned her gaze looked battered. Mascara smudged
shadows beneath wet lashes and her mouth now wore chewed away lipstick. The once pristine blue silk blouse was as blotchy as her skin. "You're
going to see him?"

"He's her father," Maggie said.

"Right, her father." Candy repeated. "He has an apartment at 1600
Cherry. He's in building A. The number's 210."

"Is he at work?"

"He was a lineman for Southwestern Bell, but he was laid off about the
time we split up."

A double whammy, Maggie mused as she retrieved her notebook and jotted down Brad Thomas' address.

"*What the hell's going on here?*"

Maggie raised her eyes to the angry voice and found an angry face to match staring at her from the doorway. She hadn't heard anyone come in. She'd been so focused on Candace Thomas.

The man closed the door behind him, shutting it hard enough so that the mini-blinds rattled.

He was about Maggie's height—5′6″—and slim, his pants neatly creased, belted at his waist, shiny leather loafers peeking out beneath sharp cuffs. He wore a paisley-print tie and neat button-down collar. His hair was sandy-colored and thinning. Round wire-framed glasses seemed to magnify dark eyes that challenged Maggie and Phillips with every glare.

"I'll say it again, what's going on?"

"We're detectives from the Litchfield Police Department...," Maggie tried to explain, but he cut her off with a brusque, "I don't give a damn who you are." He looked straight at Candace. "Are you okay? What the hell did they say to make you so upset?"

"Excuse me, sir," Maggie shot back, shoulders squared, and Phillips slid off his perch on the table to stand beside her as if to give her strength in numbers. "But we're in the middle of..."

"Whatever you've done, it's quite enough. I can see that much."

"It's all right, Dave." Mrs. Thomas rose from her chair as he approached. "It's not what you think," she said, reaching out to him. He took her hand between his own and held it possessively.

"Is this about Brad?" he quietly asked Candy, but not so quietly that Maggie couldn't hear him. "What's the son of a bitch done this time?"

Candy shook her head, and her eyes welled with tears. "It's about Pauletta."

"Bad news?"

"The worst."

The purplish flush in his face faded, and he let go of her hand to catch her by the shoulders. "Tell me, Candy. You know I'd do anything for you."

"Pauletta's dead," she sobbed, her tears falling anew, only this time she couldn't control them. Her shoulders shook, and he enfolded her in his arms, glaring at Maggie as he stroked her blond head.

"Is there anything else you think we ought to know about your daughter, Mrs. Thomas," Maggie asked, not flinching beneath his hard stare.

But Candy Thomas didn't answer. Instead, the man announced, "I think you'd better go." It was clearly an order and not a request.

Maggie saw Phillips nod and head toward the door. She hesitated long enough to dig her card out and jot her pager number on the back. She left it on the table.

"We'll be in touch, Mrs. Thomas."

But she wasn't sure that Candy even heard her. The woman's face was still buried in the guy's armpit.

Maggie followed Phillips out, pulling the door closed with a click.

Phillips had his hands in his pockets as they retraced their footsteps through the maze of secretaries and receptionists, out into the lobby and past the young security guard who stood with one hand on his walkie-talkie, his eyes following them as they left the building.

Neither said a word to the other until they'd reached the parking lot.

Maggie leaned against the Ford and looked at her partner across its faded roof. She squinted through the hazy morning sunlight that now threatened the treetops.

"So that was Dave Gray," she said, and he paused as he opened the driver's side door.

"The guy the rent-a-cop said was the boss?" he asked, setting his forearms on the car's roof, his keys in one fist.

Despite herself, Maggie smiled. "She did call him Dave, and he acted like he owned the place."

"If he does own the place"—Phillips rubbed his jaw— "that would explain his attitude."

"You think they're an item?"

Her partner's answering smile was tight. "From the way he consoled her, I doubt either of them's sleeping alone. And I'd bet my life he's the 'friend' whose lawyer helped her file the restraining order against her hubby."

Maggie looked back at the Cybercytes building. "I wonder how Mr. Thomas feels about that. His wife seeing another man when they're still legally married."

"She's obviously afraid of him."

"You think?"

"Why else would she get a restraining order?"

"I wonder if she had something to be scared of," Maggie said as she got into the car and shut the door, belting herself in. And, if Candy Thomas felt threatened by her husband, could Pauletta have too?

Chapter Seven

They drove in silence from Plano back to Litchfield. Phillips stared ahead at the road, a look of pained concentration on his face, and Maggie knew not to try to draw him into conversation.

She was glad for the momentary quiet. She needed to think, to try to understand what had happened this morning and digest it.

She put what pieces they had together.

Candy Thomas had watched her teenaged daughter climb onto the bus, had waited until she was safely on board before she'd driven off for work sometime before eight o'clock. The driver had made a second stop, picking up the twins with Down's syndrome, and then he'd gone about a block further when he'd been flagged down by a male youth wearing a baseball cap and Cowboys jacket.

The driver had opened the door, and the young man had stepped up into the bus, drawing a .45 and firing twice at the driver and then targeting Pauletta, aiming five rounds at her head.

Within a minute or two, it was over. The assailant had fled, and the still-conscious driver had managed to radio a bus company dispatcher for help.

Maggie frowned.

Why Pauletta?

Why not the Potter girls, too?

With a sigh, she leaned back against the headrest and stared out the window, trying to focus on the passing cars, the clumps of trees, the bill-boards. But the steady roll of the tires beneath made her sleepy, and she sighed, closing her eyes.

A vision of Momma came to mind, of the frail form beneath the white hospital sheets, the fluff of white hair, her faded features nearly disguised by tape binding tubes to her nose and mouth. IV poles stood like reed-thin metal mannequins at bedside, dripping medicines and nourishment into her body. Wires sprouted from her chest and limbs, hooking her up to the blipping and blinking monitors keeping track of every heartbeat. She could still hear the steady groan of the machine that forced her mother to breathe. Groan, whoosh. Groan, whoosh. Soft as a whisper.

"She had intracranial bleeding...she's still unconscious...on a respira-tor..."

A seventy year old woman near death at Parkland Hospital.

A young woman with a disability called Williams' syndrome lying on a table in the county morgue awaiting an autopsy.

Maggie rubbed at her eyes, exhausted by the day's events.

It had been a lousy morning by any standards.

"I don't like it."

"What?" She looked sideways at Phillips.

His big hands tightened their grip on the wheel. "I don't like this whole setup."

Maggie pulled the visor down, trying to cut off the glare of sunlight. They had turned off the Parkway and were back in Litchfield. In another few minutes, they'd reach Cherry Street and the apartment complex where Brad Thomas lived.

She stretched her back, stifling a yawn, and tried to blink away her fatigue. "I know," she told him. "I don't like it either. Damn it, but I wish we had the gun. At least we'd have a chance of tracing it."

"That's not what I meant."

She shifted her hips beneath the seatbelt to face him. "I'm listening."

His bearish face puckered up, his deep brow wrinkled. "I'm getting a bad taste in my mouth, Ryan. This whole domestic situation with the

Overkill

Thomases. They hadn't been getting along, and it sounds like the root of the problem was their daughter."

"Go on."

"It's classic domestic warfare." He brushed a hand in the air, picking up where he'd left off. "They fought about expenses, where to school her, who would care for her, whether to send her away or keep her at home until it drove a wedge between them. The wife falls into her boss' arms, and the husband ends up alone, getting canned from his job on top of everything."

Maggie knew just where he was heading. "You think he would've taken out his own kid just to get back at his wife? That's pretty brutal."

He slowed at a stop sign. "The world's a brutal place, Ryan. I wouldn't put anything past anyone these days. There's no rhyme or reason to killing anymore. Used to be people had motives for mowing somebody down. Jealousy. Money. Revenge. The sort of stuff you can put your finger on. Guess those were the good old days, huh?" He shook his head. "Hell, now we're all walking targets in a great big video game."

Maggie wanted to disagree.

But she couldn't.

Cherry Street was on the south side of town where the buildings were older and the residences were lower rent and nothing like the shiny glass-walled buildings or half-million dollar Dallas palaces that were constantly sprouting up to the north and west. The houses they passed were tiny with peeled paint and patched roofs; but, for the most part, the yards were kept up and the sidewalks swept. An occasional car with a decidedly '70s make sat on concrete blocks in a driveway and bikes and deflated rubber balls littered square lawns behind chain-link fences.

"Here we are. Sixteen hundred," Phillips uttered, and Maggie's chest tightened, her heartbeat accelerating.

Phillips pulled off Cherry into the parking lot of the Blossom Hills Apartments, though there were no hills much less blossoms of any sort. Just an overflowing dumpster that had attracted a flock of large black crows and a smattering of older cars with flaking paint and rusted bumpers.

"Sort of a come-down from his old neighborhood," Phillips remarked as he pointed his Ford toward the nearest building of tan brick which had a large red "A" painted under its roofline.

"The scarlet letter," Maggie said with a half-smile, though Phillips merely rumpled his brow. "You know, Hester Prynne? Arthur Dimmesdale?" She hesitated at his silence. "You ever read Nathaniel Hawthorne?" she asked, but her partner only squinted.

"That the guy who wrote about the whale?"

Maggie shook her head. "Never mind."

With most of the renters probably at work, there were plenty of available spaces, and Phillips pulled into one beside a pale blue Nissan pickup with a dozen dents.

Maggie reached a hand inside her bag and touched her .38, reassured by its presence, though she'd had little reason to carry it since her move to Litchfield. Being unarmed on the DPD would've been suicide, but not here. Not yet.

She preceded her partner up the concrete stairs to the second story landing. Behind her, Phillips huffed and puffed, his footsteps thudding, the metal railing rattling beneath his grip.

"You should think about buying one of those stair climbing machines," she told him as she waited for him to reach the top.

He paused when he got there, catching his breath, muttering back at her, "We have one."

"But do you use it?"

"Yeah, smart ass, I use it," he told her, raising a hand to smooth the thin strands of hair over his bald pate. "I hang my coat on it sometimes."

"You're hopeless," she said.

He flashed her a wicked smile.

Then she looked over her shoulder and saw it.

The door numbered 210.

She felt a prickle at the back of her neck and tried to shrug off her sense of unease.

Phillips nudged her. "Let's get this over with."

She stepped up to the door and rapped solidly with her knuckles.

Overkill

A shadow crossed the peephole, then the door came slowly open. A slender man in worn jeans appeared, his long face peppered with stubble, salt-and-pepper hair ruffled as if he'd awakened from a nap. He looked different than she'd imagined. Vulnerable. And not at all like a guy who'd have his daughter killed to get back at his wife.

His hazel eyes narrowed. "Do I know you?"

"I'm Detective Ryan." Maggie handed him her card, and he took it from her, peering at it with presbyopic intensity before stuffing into his pocket.

She inclined her head. "My partner, Detective Phillips."

"Am I in trouble?" he asked, shifting uneasily, and Maggie noted his bare feet, pale beneath the ragged hem of blue denim.

"We just need a few minutes, Mr. Thomas," Maggie said, watching his eyes nervously shift back and forth from her to Phillips.

"This about my wife?"

"It's about your daughter, Pauletta, actually. Some bad news, I'm afraid."

His Adam's apple bobbed and then he nodded, pulling the door wide and stepping aside.

Maggie went in, Phillips right behind her. She could hear his noisy breaths and his heavy tread upon the floor.

She looked around her at the small, dark room with the shades drawn on the windows. Only a dim lamp yielded light from near a chair in the far corner. Everything seemed a shade of gray, sapped of color.

Then she heard the door slap shut, and Thomas muttered, "Sorry for the mess."

He snapped on the overhead fixture, and the gray room took on pigments of orange, brown and yellow. Maggie noticed the folded sections of newspaper that littered the ground beside a stained velour recliner.

She breathed in and felt a tickle in her throat. It smelled musty and closed off. Like the windows were never opened, the fresh air kept out. There was the lingering odor of maleness, of sweat. The heat was turned up, and it was warm enough to be uncomfortable.

Thomas came around in front of them, sticking his hands in his back pockets, rocking on his heels. "It's not much, I know, but it's all I've got. I keep thinking...well, I hope it won't be for long." He smiled nervously, and Maggie felt the urge to smile back. He looked so needy.

He sidestepped them, going over to the couch and repositioning seat cushions. Then he gathered up the scattered newspapers and dropped them behind the chair, out of sight. He motioned for them to sit down, and Maggie glanced uncertainly at Phillips before taking a seat on the sofa. "*You really think this man had the balls to harm his daughter?*" she wanted to ask him, wondering if he could see the doubt in her eyes.

But Phillips remained unmoved, standing with his arms crossed, his face a hard mask.

Brad Thomas settled on the recliner, perching at its very edge, hands rubbing together as if to warm them. "You said this was about Paulie."

He shifted his gaze to somewhere across the room, and Maggie did likewise, spotting a framed photograph hung on the wall—the only visible personal stamp that Brad Thomas had put on this place. She could make out the face well enough from where she sat to know that it had to be Pauletta. Dark hair with a fringe of bangs around a triangular face which crinkled up into an impossibly large grin.

"Paulie's a good kid," Thomas commented, his voice drawing Maggie's focus back to him. "She's mentally disabled, you know," he said matter-of-factly. "So she's different than average kids. She didn't go through that rebellious crap that most teenagers do. She's like a puppy, always happy to see you. Not a bad bone in her body. I can't imagine what sort of trouble she could get into that'd warrant the police showing up on my doorstep." His hands ceased their motion, and his forehead wrinkled beneath the tousled hair.

"Unless...unless." His long face contorted, and he let out a snort. "Oh, I get it. Candy's cooked up something else to try'n make me disappear, is that it? Like some custody thing? What's she want to do now? Serve me with papers to make me stay away from my own kid?"

His voice rose, the edge to it sharp, so that Maggie could feel his bitterness jabbing her like a finger in the ribs.

"It's just the kind of crap he'd put her up to. He got her an unlisted number first, but I've still got friends at Bell. So now she has that Caller-ID and call-blocker crap so she can avoid talkin' to me." He ran his hands through his messy hair, laughing bitterly. "Anything to cut my heart out, right? Like she hasn't hurt me enough already."

A trickle of perspiration slid down Maggie's spine.

Brad Thomas came out of the chair so that the recliner rocked back and forth at his sudden release. "Is it a custody issue? Is that it?" He put his hands on his hips, his face red with anger. One foot tapped the faded carpeting. "Did Gray's lawyers dream up some scheme to keep me from seeing my daughter?"

Phillips cleared his throat. "We're not here to serve any papers, Mr. Thomas. We're here to notify you of a tragedy. Pauletta died this morning."

There was no softness in Phillips' words, none of the gentleness he'd used earlier with this man's wife. Just a directness that sounded harsh to Maggie's ears. Accusing.

"What?" Thomas stopped his restless movements. His gaze flickered from Phillips to Maggie. He stared at her, his mouth slightly parted in disbelief. "Paulie's dead?"

The color seeped from his face, seeming to disappear below the collar of his plaid flannel shirt. His shoulders sagged. His bravado of moments before quickly melted away. "I don't understand? Did her blood pressure pop or something? Was there an accident?"

"It wasn't an accident." Maggie spoke up before he could surmise further. "I'm sorry, Mr. Thomas, but your daughter was killed this morning on her way to school."

"But...that doesn't make sense." He sank back down into the recliner, his fingers curling against the bend of his bones, clutching tightly. His wide eyes struggled with his confusion. His voice rose. "What are you saying then? That someone murdered Paulie? While she was on the bus going to school?"

Maggie felt like a rat for the second time that day. Her mouth was dry, her tongue unwieldy, as if it had doubled in size, making it hard to speak.

She ran her hands over her thighs. "A gunman entered her bus this morning about two blocks beyond Pauletta's stop. He shot the bus driver. He's in surgery at Methodist. Your daughter was not so lucky. She was dead at the scene."

"No." He came to his feet, face flushed, hands clenched. "No, it's not true. You're lying. This is some trick that Candy and her boyfriend cooked up to mess with my head."

"It's no trick, Mr. Thomas," Phillips told him in a tone that made Maggie flinch. "Your wife was informed of the incident just prior to our coming here."

"Candy knows?" he asked, turning to Maggie. "She knows already?"

She nodded. "We spoke to her at Cybercytes."

Thomas' face darkened. "And I'll bet he was there, wasn't he? Holding her hand, telling her he'd take care of everything?"

"Dave Gray?" Maggie asked him, though she was sure that's exactly who Brad was talking about.

"God damn him," Thomas hissed through clenched teeth, pushing a fist into his palm. "God damn him for being a lying, two-faced son-of-a-bitch. He wanted Paulie sent away to live in some group home so he could have Candy all to himself." He glanced up at Maggie and said with unveiled bitterness, "Well, now she's gone all right. Guess he finally got what he wanted, didn't he?"

He wanted Paulie sent away? Maggie shot a glance at Phillips. "You didn't think Pauletta should leave home?"

All color suddenly drained from his face. "Who told you that? Candy?" He waved his hands frantically. "Hey, I'll admit that Paulie and I weren't always tight. I had to work overtime to try to pay the bills. The kid had so many problems, and Candy was with her every minute anyway. She was better with the kid. Paulie needed her, not me."

He sucked in a shaky breath, then pointed a finger straight at Maggie as he finished, "But she was my kid just the same, all right? No way in hell would I have suggested shipping her off. It was Gray, that's who. He checked out someplace in Minnesota. Candy let that slip a few weeks back. She didn't tell you?" He made a noise of disgust. "The bitch." He covered his face with his hands, whispering into them so that Maggie could barely hear, "The fucking bitch."

"Mr. Thomas?" His shoulders shook, shuddering like a man in seizure.

She rose from the couch and went toward him, reaching out. "Mr. Thomas, are you okay? Can we call someone for you?"

Abruptly, he was still.

"Just leave me alone, all right?" His voice was an odd, detached monotone.

He turned away from her, walking toward the far wall. He stood there, hands gripped at his sides, not saying a word.

Phillips caught Maggie's eye. She reached for her bag settled near her feet.

A howl broke the silence, ripping across the room and prickling the hair on Maggie's arms, setting her eardrums on fire.

"NOooo!"

Thomas drew back his fist and slammed it into the wall, cracking paint and plaster.

Then he crumbled to the floor, cradling his fist in his belly, shaking his head from side to side. "Damn you, Candy," he cried over and over again. "It's your fault, goddammit...your fault."

Maggie rushed to him, kneeling beside him. She touched his shoulder. His hand was bloodied at the knuckles, white with the plaster dust that spotted his clothes and hair like baby powder.

She looked up helplessly at Phillips. He shrugged and raised his eyebrows.

"We should take you to the hospital," she said to Brad Thomas, trying to hold her voice even. "You might need x-rays..."

"No!" Brad shook his head violently. "Just leave me alone," he said, turning his face away, skin flushed, jaw stiff. "Just get the hell out. I don't feel much like company."

"Mr. Thomas, please," Maggie said and reached for his arm, but he shook off her touch.

"Get the fuck out of here!"

Maggie felt his hot breath on her face.

"Ryan," Phillips said her name in a way that was as telling as a shout.

"Okay," she breathed the word, her heart banging against her ribs. "Okay."

She stood up, backing away.

Phillips held the door wide, but she paused at the threshold.

Her eyes went to the balled figured on the floor, at the lean shoulders that shook, up at the broken plaster.

"I'm truly sorry," she said, though she wasn't sure he heard her.

"C'mon." Phillips nudged her gently from behind, and she stepped into daylight.

Chapter Eight

"Do you really believe Brad Thomas could've arranged for his daughter's murder?"

She posed the question to her partner just as soon as they were in the car. "Okay, he's got a temper like a rabid dog, and he's truly pissed at his wife and at Dave Gray, I'll give you that. But I think he was being honest with us. Makes me wonder who's telling the truth."

Phillips rested his arms on the steering wheel and glanced up at the closed door to apartment 210. "Christ, I don't know what to think," he said and stabbed the key into the ignition, starting up the old Ford.

Maggie belted herself in, hooking a hand around the black nylon strip that crossed her shoulder. "He was surprised, Phillips. His shock was genuine as far as I could tell. He's furious at Candy, at Dave Gray, not at Pauletta."

"Anger's a real good motivator," he shot back, and Maggie knew that he'd disliked Brad Thomas before he'd even set eyes on him.

As unchauvinistic as he was on the job, Maggie knew Phillips wasn't as progressive where everyday life was concerned. His internal code of conduct still caused him to open doors for females, to stand when a woman entered a room, to hold out a chair for anyone with boobs. Basically, to protect the womenfolk, especially a petite blond like Candy Thomas.

His voice was a grumble, "You and I both know that someone so riled by an ex can do pretty vicious things to kick 'em where it hurts. Take that jerk-ass who set his son on fire. Or how about all the murder-suicides where an estranged husband's taken out his own kids, his ex-wife, the in-laws... hell, the whole fucking family?"

"Candy's not his ex yet," she reminded him.

"She's as good as one, and he seems to blame her for all the shit that's happened to him since she kicked him out."

"But enough to have his own daughter killed? Don't you think that's extreme?"

Phillips shrugged, his eyes on the road ahead of them. "Maybe he only wanted her injured. You know, so they could cry over her hospital bed together."

Maggie glanced out the window at the nearly cloudless sky and saw the bloodied face of Pauletta Thomas floating upon the pristine blue. "If the point was to wound her, then why is she so very dead? The guy hit her with four rounds, for Pete's sake."

His fingers rattled on the steering wheel. "Maybe the plan went bad. Maybe the asswipe he paid to shoot up the school bus got carried away in the heat of the moment."

"Maybe." Maggie's head felt foggy with all the "what if"-ing. This wasn't getting them anywhere. She felt no closer to finding out who killed Pauletta Thomas than she had at the scene.

"As far as I can see, there's only two things that make sense," Phillips went on, though Maggie turned away from him and stared out the window, only half-listening. "If our father of the year wasn't involved and if the shooter wasn't paid to carry out a hit, then it was either a gang initiation or some Columbine High wannabe. Only a banger or a nutball would climb on a Special Ed bus, plug the driver a couple times, and then make mashed potatoes out of an innocent girl just for the hell of it."

"Or, if it was an addict," Phillips continued, digging in, his voice picking up a bit, "a guy so wired he didn't know what he was doing, then it fits, too." He gave the steering wheel a couple taps. "Plano's got that problem with heroin. Maybe one of those Generation X junkies stole Pop's gun and came into Litchfield looking for thrills."

Overkill

Maggie shook her head. "Heroin's putting those kids in comas, Phillips. A junkie in a coma can't kill anyone."

"You got any better ideas?"

"Not a one."

They rode the rest of the way back to Litchfield in silence.

It wasn't until they were barely a block from the station that the quiet was shattered.

"Fuck."

Phillips hit the brakes, and Maggie lurched forward against her seatbelt, bracing her palms against the dash.

She started to curse at him, but then she looked ahead and realized what had upset him enough to nearly give her whiplash.

The station was overrun with vans from Dallas TV and radio stations, some with satellite dishes perched on their roofs like alien spacecraft.

She groaned as the pounding at her temples started up again. It would be chaos inside at the front desk, and both of them knew it. The last time they'd had a case that had attracted this much attention from outside Litchfield had involved a four-year-old child who'd been abducted. She was just as unhappy to see them this time around.

"They get off on this, don't they?" Phillips said under his breath.

"Maybe they don't have a choice," she found herself saying. "It's their job, right?"

He turned to her, and his mouth pulled into a tight grin. "You're full of it, Ryan. I know you don't like 'em any more than I do."

"We have to work with them, whether we like it or not," she said, although she was no more trusting of the relationship than he was. "They can help us when they want to. They can take a minute to run a composite sketch that gets us more tips than spending days canvassing neighborhoods."

Phillips flicked a hand in the direction of the station and the cars that clogged the parking lot. "They're not in it to help us, Ryan. They're in it for the entertainment value. Otherwise, you wouldn't have Charlie Manson back on TV every year. And, if not him, they spend an hour glamorizing some other serial killer. Even Barbara Walters gets in on it. And I used to think she had class."

Maggie rolled down her window. "You're steaming up the car with all this hot air."

Phillips grunted. "Hell, if I ran over a reporter, I don't think I'd even flinch."

"C'mon, John."

"Bet I'd even get a citation."

She cuffed his shoulder, but he shook his finger at her.

"You and I both worked big cities, Ryan, and you know it's the truth. They're like piranhas who smell flesh and attack in a feeding frenzy."

She squirmed in her seat, unhooking the seatbelt so she could breathe more easily. Her eyes surveyed the bold logos on the sides of the half dozen media vans, watching the people who moved around them, in and out of the station's front door. Men with video cameras hiked up on their shoulders. Women who posed before the cameras with mikes in hand wearing skirts and high heels with jackets in overbright hues. She wondered if they'd already hit the crime scene, photographing the blood-stained footprints that remained on the sidewalk, interviewing neighbors and spreading panic.

Maggie blinked hard as sunlight glinted off the windshield. She hated to imagine what they'd tell the public, filling them with fear about a gunman on the loose, a killer who'd blown away a disabled young woman on a school bus. A maniac who could be in their neighborhoods, after their kids next.

The trouble was, she couldn't say that they were wrong, not for certain.

"Just go around back," she urged her partner, not wanting to face a microphone. She had nothing to tell them anyway, not when the investigation was barely hours old. Let someone feed them the usual line for awhile. They hadn't officially released Pauletta's name yet and wouldn't until the time was right.

With a grunt, Phillips pulled on the wheel, avoiding the logjam at the front of the parking lot and slipping into a space at the rear of the station.

Maggie climbed out of the car, snatched up her purse and closed the door. She turned to find she was not alone. A reporter and his cameraman pinned her against the Ford. The black ball of a microphone grazed her nose.

"Hey, officer, can you give us anything on the school bus killing," the mike-wielding reporter asked, slightly winded, his wide-jawed features tanned with pancake makeup. The cameraman scrambled behind him, adjusting the equipment on his shoulder. "Have you ID'd a suspect?"

Maggie pushed the mike away. "I have no comment at this time."

"We heard a kid was shot at point-blank range."

"Geez! Can't you guys even wait till the body's cold?" Phillips snapped, slamming the car door and rounding the Ford toward Maggie.

"Just tell us if you've found the gun. Word is it's a .45."

Maggie's face flushed. "That's not public information yet." She tried to sidestep them, but it was like doing a tango with two clumsy partners who kept squishing her toes.

"The lady said she was finished," Phillips barked and stepped between the men and Maggie, catching her arm and quickly ushering her toward the back door. He was still scowling even as he pulled the door closed in their faces.

She heard the lock click into place and realized how fast her heart was pounding.

"And I thought I was pushy." She raised an unsteady finger to brush the hair from her eyes.

Phillips touched her shoulder. "You okay?"

She nodded.

"Piranhas." He said, although he might as well have said, "I told you so."

Maggie tipped her head right and left, tweaking the tightened muscles in her neck. "The murder rate in Dallas must be slow."

"And thing's are only gonna get worse," Phillips warned her as they passed the booking room and headed for the cramped detective's bay.

George Leonard and Harold Washington had beat them there. In fact, every detective on the Litchfield P.D. was present and accounted for.

Maggie almost resented their intrusion on a case she already thought of as hers and Phillips; but, she knew that on something as high profile as this, the entire force pooled resources in order to close the case quickly. This wasn't vandalism or a missing dog or a stolen lawn ornament. Litchfield wasn't used to murder, didn't want it here. So, when it happened, it was everybody's problem, everyone's worst fear.

The mayor's public relations guru had recently come up with a new slogan for the burg—Litchfield, Texas, A Slice of Heaven on Earth—so she knew they were probably shitting bricks at City Hall over the schoolbus shooting and threatening the chief with a public butt kicking if his department didn't clean up this giant mess before it got to smelling any worse.

A slice of heaven on earth, Maggie mused.

She couldn't imagine anyone's idea of heaven as a place where a disabled young woman could get killed on her way to school.

"I'll call Methodist and see if there's any news on the bus driver," Phillips said over his shoulder. Maggie followed him to his desk.

She checked her fingers for hangnails until he finished talking and plunked down the receiver.

"What's up?"

"Nurse says the bus driver's still in surgery and might be for another few hours, but so far so good." His hands were in his pockets, jangling coins and keys. "That'll give us time to get over to the Special School and talk to Pauletta's teachers. You game?"

It beat sitting on her ass making phone calls and fighting off the press the rest of the morning.

Chapter Nine

Despite its name, the Litchfield Special School looked rather ordinary: flat roofed and one-storied brick encompassed by concrete.

Maggie was surprised to find no reporters hovering about the premises. Give them time, she thought. The swarm from the station would make its way across town soon enough, like African bees with a scent for human flesh.

Phillips drove around the building twice, through the parking area and past the playground before he ran across an empty space to his liking. Every few months, it seemed, he got more particular about "finding a good spot." Maggie had to bite her tongue from telling him it wouldn't hurt him to park as far away as possible and walk. She'd just be wasting her breath.

She got out and stretched, taking a moment to survey their surroundings. Wide sidewalks and ramps led to and from the building, making the place clearly wheelchair accessible. As they neared the entrance, she saw the warning signs about the power doors, one of which popped wide as they neared it.

Inside, the hallway swept both left and right. Painted on the cinderblock wall ahead were the words, "Welcome to Litchfield School. Home of the Eagles."

A maintenance worker in gray coveralls appeared from around the corner and he smiled at them, leaning atop the wide-based dust mop he was pushing over the floors. The patch below his shoulder stitched out

"Delbert" in red. "Can I help you folks?"

"We're here to see Dr. Candor," Phillips said. "She's expecting us."

The man nodded. "To your left and keep walkin'. You can't miss it."

"Thanks."

Their footsteps, tapping on the speckled tiles, echoed down the hall, their rhythm not quite in sync. Maggie inhaled the smell of lemon cleaning solution, body odor and peanut butter. Reminded her of the locker room at the station.

The walls were painted bright yellow with blue stripes interrupted by hand-written lists of "My Favorite Things," "What's Great About Me," and "This Month's Character Trait," which was integrity. Posters of puppies and kittens were tacked along the walls. Construction paper signs lettered in Magic Marker advertised a candy sale and cut-outs on a large bulletin board touted "The Three R's: Respect, Rectitude, and Responsbility."

Phillips must've been scoping the walls, too. He muttered, "Rectitude? What the hell is that? Makes me think of my proctologist."

Maggie stifled a smile. "It means honesty."

"Then why don't they just say that?"

"Because then it'd be two R's and an H."

"Christ Almighty."

A child in jeans and a winter jacket wandered out from a rest room, staring at them with bespectacled eyes as he passed. His hair stuck straight up. He uttered a soft, "Hi," and Phillips gave him a hearty "Morning, son," in return.

They passed doors labeled "Health Rooms" and closed classrooms, though Maggie could see the students through small windows. She paused at the gymnasium doors, peering through wire-meshed panes at a circle of wheelchair bound children lifting their arms in exercise as a woman in pink sweatpants clapped her hands.

Several girls emerged from a door just ahead, one slender and black, the other with dishevelled dishwater hair and thick glasses. Both clutched books and carried bags with large name tags attached to the straps. The two stared at Maggie and her partner as if they were sideshow freaks.

Overkill

"Here we are," Phillips said, though it would've been hard to miss the sign denoting the "Principal's Office."

The window-framed door was wide open.

Three brown wooden chairs lined up to the wall on the left. Ahead loomed a countertop filled with assorted forms and flyers. Beyond that, an unoccupied desk complete with computer and a dying plant sat empty. A phone with multiple lines blinked red and beeped.

To Maggie's immediate right were dozens of labeled mail slots.

There was also a half-closed door through which she could hear someone sobbing.

"Please, try to hold yourself together, Sally, for the children's sake," a firm voice urged.

Maggie hesitated outside the Principal's office, glancing at the nameplate above the door: Gertrude Candor, Ph.D. Taped to the molding was a piece of lined notepaper with a smiling face and the words, "Best Principal Ever."

She peered around the jamb to find a solidly-built gray-haired woman patting the shoulder of a sobbing female half her girth and half her age.

She knocked soundly on the doorframe, and both heads turned.

"Dr. Gertrude Candor? We're from the Litchfield Police," she said. The elder of the pair raised her hand, ushering them in.

"I spoke with a man earlier," she said. "Detective Phillips." She cocked her head, giving her the appearance of a well-fed pigeon.

"I'm Detective Phillips, ma'am," John responded, coming around her. He jerked a thumb at Maggie. "My partner, Detective Ryan."

Dr. Candor's dark face appeared haggard, nearly as rumpled as her suit. She didn't look so much like a school principal as someone's grandmother, though the many photographs and certificates adorning the walls reminded Maggie she was that, at least in a figurative sense.

"Sally, dear, why don't you tend the phone so it doesn't ring right off the hook," she instructed, and the younger woman dabbed at her tear-smeared cheeks with a tissue, sniffed and excused herself, brushing blindly past Maggie as she exited the office.

"Sally's our school secretary," Dr. Candor explained, giving a self-conscious tug to her lapels before crossing behind a cherrywood desk and sitting down. "She's distraught about Pauletta, of course. We haven't shared the news with all the teachers yet nor with the students. But we'll have to tell them soon, before they hear it elsewhere."

She beckoned them to sit, then folded her hands one atop the other, though Maggie could see they shook despite her calm facade. "The bus driver was shot, too, you said. Do you know how he's doing?"

Phillips cleared his throat. "Yes, ma'am. He was hit in the right leg and shoulder, but he's alive."

"Thank goodness for that," Candor said, though the tension in her face did not lessen.

"Do you know him well?" Maggie asked.

"I make it a point to familiarize myself with everyone who works with us," she said with more than a little starch in her voice. "His name is Ronald Biggins. He has a wife and a little boy and a baby on the way."

"We haven't had the opportunity to talk with him yet," Maggie admitted. "He's still in surgery."

"I see." The principal sighed. "I can only tell you that Mr. Biggins is employed by the company through which we lease the buses. Transportation Management. They're based in Addison. We contracted with them a few years ago after we had a bad experience with a bus driver who worked for another service."

"The name of that service?" Maggie pressed.

Dr. Candor touched a hand to her coiffed gray hair. "Reeder Leasing, it was called. They went out of business about a month ago, I heard." She lowered her voice. "Too many accidents and too many positive urine tests. Not the kind of folks you'd want in charge of precious cargo like children, eh, Detective Phillips?"

Her partner wriggled in his seat. "Definitely not, ma'am."

"But what's done is done, and, thankfully, we never had anyone injured," Candor added with a dismissive wave of her hand.

Maggie retrieved her notepad and pen, quickly jotting down the name of Reeder Leasing.

"We've had no troubles with Transportation Management. Until now, that is. Mr. Biggins takes good care of the children. He goes out of his way for them. To think he might have been killed, too. And for what reason?" Candor's eyes sought Maggie's, beseeching. "It makes no sense, shooting at an unarmed bus driver and a defenseless young woman. At least the twins were spared."

They were spared bullets, Maggie silently agreed, but not the anguish of witnessing a murder. She only hoped they could soon forget what they'd been through.

Dr. Candor's gaze dropped to her hands. "I don't know how we'll tell the children. How do you explain senseless violence? Thank heaven we have our social worker on hand to counsel them, and Dr. Abley, of course. He's our visiting psychologist. He comes several times a month and has done wonders for some of our worst behavioral cases."

She frowned, shaking her head. "It's just horrible, isn't it? I wouldn't have believed it was true if I hadn't talked to you personally, Detective Phillips."

Phillips sat stiffly in his chair, hands primly on his knees. Maggie pictured him as a kid, called into the principal's office, sitting much the same way, willing himself not to move. "I will not chew gum in class," she envisioned him writing 100 times on the chalkboard as punishment.

She caught herself, realizing how dated her images were.

Getting punished for chewing gum in class. Throwing spitballs, talking out of turn, pulling a pigtail.

That was truly the age of innocence.

Today's school problems leaned more toward sexual harrassment, assault, blowing up toilets with bombs made from an Internet recipe, or packing heat in a book bag.

Dr. Candor sighed. "We've had children pass away, you know, so we do have a plan in place for gathering the students together and explaining what happened. Serious physical and mental problems are part of what we live with around here. But, murder?" She looked stricken. "Pauletta came to us two years ago when her parents moved to Litchfield. From what her mother told me, she wasn't properly diagnosed until she was 10. Williams' syndrome is tricky. There are such contradictions."

Maggie waited, sure there was more to come.

"Williams' syndrome isn't so well-known as Down's, autism or ADD," she explained. "Its diagnosis is fairly new, comparatively speaking. Many educators don't even realize what it is." Her dark eyes fixed on Maggie. "Do you know much about it, Detective?"

Maggie glanced at Phillips and cleared her throat. "Only what Mrs. Thomas told us about Pauletta. She had health problems that required medication and monitoring, and mental problems that kept her from functioning independently."

"That's right." Dr. Candor nodded, and Maggie felt as if she'd passed some kind of test. "In the last decade, more literature on the condition has become available. Before, there wasn't much to go on. We do know people with Williams are missing some 20 genes. They have difficulty with the simplest of tasks, brushing their teeth, tying their shoes, crossing the street. But they can be amazingly articulate, despite a penchant for confusing the meaning of words. They can appear very bright and eager, but their brains have a missing connection."

"We're told Pauletta had no fears about approaching strangers, even hugging them," Maggie recalled, leaning forward in her chair.

"It's called the cocktail party personality," she said. "And, yes, it does make Williams' children more vulnerable to various types of exploitation. They tend to be extremely sociable. People assume they're just outgoing. They don't immediately see the disability. What they do see is a friendly child with a face like a pixie. Unfortunately, these children don't comprehend the fact that such gregarious behavior could place them in danger."

She rose from her seat with a creak of leather and squeal of chair, pressing her hands to her breasts as she walked toward the wall, slowly reaching out to remove one of the pictures that hung there. She cradled it for a moment. Then she came forward, almost reluctantly releasing the framed photograph to Phillips.

Overkill

He glanced at it solemnly before passing it to Maggie.

She held it by the edges of its black wood frame as if afraid to get her fingerprints upon the glass. Afraid to touch the face that so silently stared up at her. It was already far too real.

The fringe of dark hair. The turned up nose and greenish eyes. The pointed chin and wide smile.

It was the same picture she'd seen in Brad Thomas' apartment.

"This is Pauletta's most recent school photo. You may keep it," Dr. Candor informed her, though Maggie hadn't asked. "I'm sure you could use it."

"Thank you." Maggie held it firmly in her lap.

"You mentioned speaking to Mrs. Thomas," Candor continued. "Have you talked with both parents then?"

Maggie told her, "Yes."

Gertrude Candor's eyebrows pinched inward. "So you know their situation?"

"That they're separated? Yes." And had enough animosity between them to start a bonfire without striking a match.

"Pauletta had been seeing our visiting clinical psychologist, Dr. Abley, whenever he was available. Her mother agreed it was a good idea. Did she mention this to you?"

Phillips cleared his throat.

"Ah, no," Maggie answered, her surprise causing her voice to catch. "But then Mrs. Thomas appeared pretty overwhelmed when we spoke to her."

Dr. Candor sniffed. "I see."

Seeing an opening, Maggie pushed. "Had her situation at home caused any problems for her at school?"

Dr. Candor didn't answer right away, and Maggie wondered why she was weighing her words so carefully this time around.

"Pauletta was a delightful young woman. We had begun to mainstream her into a few freshman level classes at the high school just this year. She seemed to be enjoying herself."

"She attended classes at the high school?"

"Yes, for several hours every afternoon, though you must understand she wasn't expected to hold her own academically. It was purely for social-ization purposes."

Maggie found this quite interesting. "How'd she get there?"

Dr. Candor didn't even blink. "She walked. It's just across the field behind us."

"Was she supervised?"

The cords in Candor's neck tightened. "Her teacher accompanied her, of course. It made the transition easier for all concerned." The principal raised an eyebrow. "You can't think someone from the high school killed Pauletta?"

Maggie shrugged. "We haven't ruled anything out, which is why we're here. We need some insight from those who knew her best."

"Surely you can't suspect anyone from the LSS to have been involved?" Her dark eyes probed Maggie's. A flush ruddied her dark skin, and she squared her padded shoulders like a peacock spreading its tail feathers for protection.

"What about students with severe behavioral problems, violent kids," Maggie remarked. "Perhaps there was someone in particular who had trou-ble with Pauletta, an instance where Pauletta was physically threatened?"

Dr. Candor remained calm. "I've had students attack teachers and classmates, you're right about that, Detective Ryan, but never one who has killed another human being. I cannot imagine where one of our kids would get a gun much less have the foresight to plot a murder."

"Point taken," Maggie said, feeling apologetic, wishing for once that Phillips wasn't sitting there so silently beside her, letting her take the flack for questions that had to be asked. "We're just trying to find an answer that makes sense."

"Well, I don't think you'll find it here."

"I hope you're right."

Dr. Candor stood, hands clasped and brow cinched. "I assume you'd like to meet her teacher, Mr. Prentice?"

Overkill

"I would." Maggie rose to her feet. "You coming, John?"

Phillips patted the arm of his chair. "If you ladies don't mind, I think I'll hang back and talk a bit with Sally."

Dr. Candor turned on him. "Sally's in quite a fragile state, Detective. She's still young enough not to have dealt with death so often as you or I."

"I'll go easy on her, ma'am," Phillips assured her with a slow smile, and the principal gave a grudging nod of assent.

"Detective Ryan? Please, follow me."

Maggie slipped her purse over her shoulder, hanging onto Pauletta's picture.

Dr. Candor's stride was as sturdy as her build, and Maggie found she had to pick up her pace to keep up with the older woman.

As they left the administration office, doors burst open along the hallway. The click of their heels on the floor was suddenly overwhelmed by a rush of voices.

Streams of children appeared, a blend of heights, colors and disabilities. Maggie noticed a few teenage girls with red and purple streaks in their hair, and a broad-shouldered young man with a pierced eyebrow.

An older woman in sensible oxfords and white ponytail tried to round up one group.

"To the gym," she kept saying. "This way, Louise and Baxter."

Dr. Candor smiled. "Anita, you seem short a few today."

The teacher turned toward them, ponytail flapping. "It's the flu," she said over her shoulder.

"Ah, yes," Candor murmured. "Seems to be a lot of that going around. We've had several teachers off lately, and we're short-handed enough as it is."

A girl, nearly as tall as Maggie, ran up to Dr. Candor and grabbed her hand.

"'lo, Doc," the child said. Dr. Candor stroked the head of blond hair in such a comforting way, Maggie knew the woman was clearly fond of her charges.

"'lo," the girl said, turning to Maggie. She pointed toward the framed photograph. "Tha's Pauletta. You know her?"

"I'm just getting to know her," Maggie replied, twisting the truth ever so slightly, grateful when Dr. Candor stepped in.

"Now, Emily, go on with your class. They're waiting for you up the hallway."

"'kay, Doc," she uttered and hurried off to join the group, apparently unconcerned that her question had gone unanswered.

"Thank you, Detective," Dr. Candor said bluntly, "for not telling her about Pauletta."

Maggie fiddled with her bag, managing to stuff the picture inside, not wanting to inspire further curiosity.

"How many kids attend the LSS?" she asked.

"About a hundred, but the number keeps growing as more families move out this way," Candor told her. "Most of our kids are 12 to 21. We group them by age and cognitive levels as best we can. Those in our Gold Program are our high achievers. Then there are others with such severe disabilities that they must be in Total Care."

"Is your objective to mainstream higher functioning students into regular public school classes?"

"Our goal is to get them to function in the community. We have no delusions about these children going on to college. Our classes focus on social skills, language, and routine chores, even general home maintenance, some basic plumbing and carpentry. Several of our older kids have found jobs outside the school, and we're so proud of them. Others work here, at the cafeteria, for example."

"Did Pauletta work outside the school?"

"Of course not. She couldn't add two and two, Detective. She was frighteningly unprepared for the real world. Not all of our students will be capable of independence. For many, success is simply getting through each day."

"I understand." Maggie felt as if she'd been reprimanded.

She followed Dr. Candor around a corner and up another hallway into a brightly lit room where a slender man was bending over a boy seated at a table, an opened book the obvious focus of their attention.

Maggie counted 11 desks. Seven were occupied. Maggie had been told some were absent with the flu, but she knew one would remain empty.

"Mr. Prentice?" Dr. Candor spoke out to get his attention.

He straightened, one hand on a young boy's shoulder.

Maggie guessed he was about her own age, in his late twenties or early thirties. His straw-colored hair was cut jaw-length and neatly tucked behind his ears. His features were fine, but irregular. He looked, she thought, like a musician, not a teacher. Thin, slightly melancholic. Something about his eyes, the shyness of his smile, made him appealing. When he spoke, his voice was honey smooth with just the slightest drawl blurring the edges.

"Dr. Candor, what brings you to my classroom?" he asked, but his gaze went to Maggie.

"Matthew Prentice, this is Detective Ryan from the Litchfield police." The principal inclined her head toward Maggie.

Prentice had begun to extend his hand, then hesitated. "Police?" He frowned.

"We're investigating the death of Pauletta Thomas," she said in a hushed tone.

"Oh, God." His already-pale face turned ashen. "Pauletta."

Dr. Candor leaned nearer Maggie. "I informed Matthew as soon as Detective Phillips called. I wanted him to know why Pauletta would not be here today. I didn't want to risk him calling Mrs. Thomas to inquire about her absence."

"Has anyone else wondered where she is?" Maggie asked, keeping her voice low.

His eyes clouded. "Yes, of course. Our classes are small, as you've probably noticed, and the kids look out for each other. It's really going to hit them hard when they find out the truth."

"We're planning an assembly for this afternoon," Dr. Candor noted, looking at Prentice.

"Do you mind if I ask a few questions, Mr. Prentice?" Maggie interrupted.

"Of me?" Prentice seemed surprised.

The teacher looked to Dr. Candor, who nodded. "Tell her what you can, Matthew. It's nearly time for your kids to go to exercise, isn't it? I'll take them to the gym and you can pick them up when you're through." She turned to Maggie. "Detective Ryan, do let me know if I can be of further assistance."

Maggie smiled. "I will. Thank you, Dr. Candor."

With the efficiency of a drill sergeant, Candor clapped her hands and gathered up the students. The exodus from the room was a noisy mix of voices and the shuffle of feet.

When the door was shut firmly behind them, Maggie faced Matthew Prentice.

He brushed a strand of hair from his face. "I don't know how much help I can be to you, Detective. I can't think of anyone who would want to harm Pauletta Thomas. Everyone who knew her loved her."

She was an angel.

It was like the chorus of a familiar song, Maggie mused, one she'd heard over and over again this morning. And yet Pauletta Thomas would not go home tonight, would never awaken to see another morning. Someone had certainly wanted to harm her in the worst way.

"How long have you been Pauletta's teacher?"

"Two years."

"Since her family moved to Litchfield and she enrolled in the Special School?"

"Yes. I work with 12 to 16-year-olds, and Pauletta fell into that range."

"So you knew her well?"

"I make that effort with all my students."

Prentice crossed the room toward one of the high-set windows. He stopped and stared out through the glass.

"Students with disabilities have a difficult time communicating, Detective," he said. "That's the hardest part for them. But if you can understand a child by what you see in her eyes or her expression, then it can make all the difference in the world. But Pauletta was special. She could communicate very well, and she certainly liked to talk. There were moments when I found myself forgetting why she was here. Then I'd remark about something abstract. Why birds fly south or why the Earth is round. And she'd stare at me as if I were speaking Swahili."

"Trying to understand this Williams' syndrome is a little like Swahili to me," Maggie remarked, wanting to take the edge off, make him relax a bit more.

He almost smiled. "Even the scientists can't fully comprehend the condition. It's not surprising it's confusing to the rest of us."

"Did you work one-on-one with Pauletta?"

"Each child has an Individual Education Plan, so, yes, there's a certain amount of attention given to each student. They don't all progress at the same rate. Some don't progress at all."

"Sounds tough," she said.

"In more ways than one. There's a tremendous amount of paperwork involved beyond teaching in the classroom."

Maggie half-smiled, thinking of the number of reports she'd had to fill out every day of her working life. "I do know something about paperwork."

He pressed his palm flat against the pane of glass. From where Maggie stood, it looked as if he were touching the sky. "It's strange to think I'll never see her again. I know it sounds trite, but she was like sunshine. She had the most brilliant smile."

Maggie swallowed hard. "Were any students in your class ever violent, Mr. Prentice? Dr. Candor mentioned there being some incidents at school, but she didn't say if any involved Pauletta."

He took a slow look around the room, his gaze stopping on a small grayish cubicle in the corner. "We have a time out booth for when a kid loses control, but we rarely use it." He faced her. "The last time we had to call a Team Red was months ago."

"A team red?"

"Like a hospital Code Blue, only this alerts staff to a student who's gone ballistic."

Maggie made a mental note. "Did this last Team Red incident happen in your classroom?"

"No, Detective, it didn't."

He checked his watch, but Maggie ignored his body language. "So tell me about Pauletta mainstreaming at the high school. Dr. Candor said you went with her each afternoon."

"I had to keep tabs on her work there, make sure it's modified to her ability level and meets her IEP. I used to teach remedial English classes in Dallas public schools before I came here, so the curriculum is old hat."

"Did she ever mention anything to you about being afraid of someone? Another student who'd threatened her? If not here, then at the high school, perhaps?"

His eyes widened. "You think whoever killed her had threatened her first? I thought it was a random thing?"

"We're trying to sort that out."

He shook his head, his dark blond hair falling loose across his brow. "No way was she being harrassed at LSS. I know the kids. They were like her family. And I was with her most every minute at the high school. No one would've had the chance to get near her without my noticing."

"Did she ever tell you she was frightened of anyone? A family member? A neighbor?"

He pushed his hair behind his ear. "Not that I recall."

"Was she dating anyone?"

"Dating?" He pursed his lips and turned away, again staring out the window. "I'm not the one to ask. Her mother would know better. She was a normal young woman in some ways. Curious, even flirtatious, sometimes." He turned to Maggie. "Just because someone has a mental or physical disability doesn't mean they don't feel the same emotions we do."

Lust? Longing? Love? Maggie wanted to ask him, but said instead, "Was there anything about Pauletta that led you to believe she may have had a boyfriend?"

"I don't honestly know how to answer that." He glanced at his watch again. "Look, Detective, I'm not the best source for information on Pauletta's love life, if she even had one. My God, with all the sexual images kids are exposed to today, I'm sure she wondered about the same things any female her age would."

"Of course." Maggie didn't push the point. "Did she seem herself lately? Was there any indication that something was wrong? Had she acted out? Did she seem unwilling to leave the school, or uncomfortable being in class all of a sudden?"

Prentice turned toward her. His eyes narrowed. "Are you fishing for my opinion on her home life?"

"Yes."

"Her parents had split a couple months ago. She was no doubt feeling insecure. But scared?" he repeated with a shake of his head. "You'd have to ask Dr. Abley about that. She was seeing him twice a month when he visited LSS."

"Dr. Candor mentioned that. We'll be speaking with him soon, I'm sure."

"There is one thing," Prentice volunteered. "She did talk about her mother's 'man friend' once. That's what she called him. She seemed agitated, which wasn't like her, and I asked if he made her feel uneasy. But I could tell she didn't fully understand what that meant, so I can't offer you anything more substantial. That's the problem with Williams'. The words are all there, but the meaning often isn't."

Candy's "man friend" had to be Dave Gray, Maggie decided, thinking she didn't much like the guy herself. Maybe Pauletta didn't either.

"Don't get me wrong. Pauletta loved her mother. They seemed pretty close as far as I could tell, at least before the Thomases split. I haven't seen as much of her in the past three months as I used to. But she's truly made an impression on her daughter," Prentice quickly added. "When we talked about jobs people have, Pauletta talked about being a mommy."

Maggie had to plead ignorant. "Would that have been possible with her disability?"

His face tightened. "Yes. Williams' people can have babies, but there's a fifty-fifty chance of passing on the syndrome if one parent has it, and the odds increase if both do. But Pauletta certainly could bear children."

"Are you a parent, Mr. Prentice?"

He shook his head. "Right now, I'm married to the school and these kids are like my own. I don't play favorites, but Pauletta sort of stood out. We play classical music sometimes, and once in awhile Pauletta would pick out a piece on the piano. She was gifted that way. Musically, I mean. She liked Chopin and Von Suppe, but would wrinkle her nose at Beethoven." He teared up and looked away. "I'm sorry."

"Hey, it's okay."

Maggie gave him a minute to pull himself together. She took in the room around her, the bright yellow walls and ten gallon fish tank. Cut-out coins hovered above the blackboard as did pictures of clocks with their hands on different times and red and yellow street signs. There were several computers on a table and even on an upright piano with a songbook opened to its center. She imagined Pauletta's fingers stroking the keys.

"Most of our students are decent kids, Detective." Matthew Prentice found the voice to reassure her. "We have a few who can get out of control, but we can handle them. It's not their fault. Dr. Candor calls our job prioritizing crises. Our first goal is to keep them safe. I would have known if Pauletta was scared of anyone."

From what she'd seen and heard so far, Maggie was inclined to agree.

The students who attended this school weren't menaces to society. They didn't wear colors and do drive-bys at night when they had nothing better to do. These were people who couldn't understand numbers, who couldn't read and comprehend, who oftentimes couldn't tie their own shoes, or focus their attention to finish a sentence.

"Do you have any leads so far?"

"It's still early," she said, because it was the simple truth.

"Well, if you want my opinion, you're wasting your time here at LSS. You'd do better to look elsewhere. There's a sick person running loose who's armed and cold-blooded enough to have murdered an innocent girl. But he's not here." He tapped his watch. "So, if you don't mind, I've got to pick up my kids."

He walked out, leaving her alone in the room.

Overkill

Maggie closed her eyes and exhaled. She slowly opened them and looked around her, trying to see it as Pauletta would—a place where she'd been loved—a place where she'd felt safe.

Prentice was right. She didn't sense fear or hate in this place. Quite the opposite.

Maggie went to the table to retrieve her bag. Sliding out Pauletta's photograph, she stared at the girl's face as she struggled to understand.

Okay, so lately her home life had been the pits. She'd had an unemployed and angry father who may or may not have wanted her sent away and a confused and bitter mother with a controlling boyfriend. She'd been counseled by the visiting psychologist at his twice-a-month visits to try to come to grips with the disintegration of her family. She was loved by her teachers and fellow students. She was called kind, talkative, caring, and curious—an angel.

Maggie touched the glass above Pauletta's frozen smile. "Who did this to you?" she whispered.

"Ryan?"

She jumped at the voice and spun around to see Phillips standing in the doorway.

"You through here?"

"Yeah." She pushed the frame back into her bag and grabbed the leather straps.

"What'd you get out of the teacher?" he asked as they headed up the hallway.

She recounted what Prentice had told her, ditto Dr. Candor's comments.

They exited the school into the midday sunshine, and Phillips stopped her with a touch on her arm.

"Well, I got a little something out of Sally."

"Such as?"

He patted his breast pocket where he kept a tiny notebook. "The address of one Francis Abley, M.D. Although he's at a seminar in Austin until tomorrow."

"Good."

"And I got the address for the bus company."

"Transportation Management?" She could still see its name on the side of the school bus.

He frowned. "I wonder about this high school thing. Who she might've met."

Maggie sighed, having wondered the same thing herself until Prentice had pooh-poohed the idea. "Her teacher was with her at the high school every afternoon. He said she was rarely out of his sight."

"Bet that bummed her out. Having the old guy hanging over her shoulder."

Maggie grinned. "Matthew Prentice can't be much older than I am."

"And that's not old to a teenager? You too young to remember that saying about not trusting anyone over thirty?"

She had to bite her tongue. "I think I've heard that one, yes."

Phillips ran a hand over the few hairs on his head. "You want to go over to the bus company now?"

Her stomach growled again. "Lunch first?" she suggested, opening up the passenger door.

"Sounds good. I'll even spring for it."

"Whoa, John." Maggie groaned. "Not McDonald's again."

"I gotta get those bean bags for my kids. They still don't have the pink one. Or is it the green one? Hell, parents are beating each other up over those things."

"You're kidding, right?"

"Hey, they're practically priceless."

"So's my stomach," Maggie muttered, sliding into the car and slamming the door.

Chapter Ten

A Channel 11 news van whizzed past them as they drove off the school grounds.

Phillips shook his head at the sight. "God help them," he muttered.

"Poor Sally," Maggie muttered.

"Poor Sally?" He grunted. "God help the vultures when they come up against Candor. You can bet she won't take shit from them."

"Wouldn't you like to be a fly on the wall," Maggie remarked, seeing the pleased expression on his face. He was no doubt hoping Candor would kick them out on their asses.

Now wouldn't that be worth tuning in to the six o'clock news? she mused and turned toward the window so he wouldn't catch her grin.

The sun was high and bright against the sky with only scattered wisps of clouds to break up the powder blue ceiling. It was like most other fall days in North Texas, the weather taking on an almost depressing monotony of mild temperatures and sunshine.

Maggie liked the rain, which they didn't get much this far north of the Gulf. Summers seemed to go on forever, almost bypassing fall altogether, and there was little winter to speak of. If it wasn't for the big storms that rolled through every so often, pelting them with wind and fat wet drops and hail, there would just be the low-hanging, never-ending blue that seemed to hover at the treetops, so close you could write in the sky with your fingertip.

Such clear, sunny days made her feel strangely exposed, like everyone could see every pore in her skin and pick out every blemish. Like there was nowhere to hide.

Nowhere to hide.

"*You blamed yourself?*"

"*Yes.*"

"*You figured you deserved it?*"

Maggie squirmed beneath her seatbelt. Terry Fitzhugh was a friend. She was merely trying to help by getting her to talk about the past. She was the only one who knew the whole truth and nothing but. That she was a psychotherapist who daily counseled abused children in Dallas County made her an expert on the subject. Still, Terry's insistence that she remember in order to forget was difficult for her. It felt like ripping off scabs.

"*You just wanted to be protected.*"

Wasn't that what every child wanted? Expected?

Pauletta Thomas had been no safer than she despite having what seemed like the world looking out for her.

"Mind if I make a quick detour?" Phillips said, breaking through her thoughts, and Maggie shrugged, her voice caught somewhere deep. She hadn't even realized where they were until then, where he was taking them.

Her belly growled, reminding her she'd had nothing to eat since half a bowl of Frosted Flakes that morning.

She put a hand over her stomach, feeling it flutter for another reason altogether.

Phillips had made a "quick detour" right back to the crime scene.

"I just wanted a fresh picture in my mind," he said as they headed up Fifth Street. The Elm intersection lay dead ahead.

"Before lunch?" She winced.

"Easier to take than after."

Been there, done that, she wanted to tell him. She didn't need to be reminded of what she'd seen hours earlier at this very site.

She chewed her lip. Her eyes were drawn outside the window, regardless.

She shouldn't have worried.

Overkill

There was little left of the crime scene except for an area still encompassed in yellow tape wrapped from tree to tree, its yellow tail fluttering in the breeze. From her shotgun view, she could make out the dark smears on the sidewalk and the trampled grass at the curb. The school bus was gone, hauled away to the impound lot, and the rest of the area had already been meticulously processed.

The reporters had doubtless come and gone, staying just long enough to tape a quick "live" shot and to interview neighbors who likely hadn't even known the victim. There were always plenty of Warhol's 15 minuters around, each with a lifelong hankering to get on television. Then they'd zip back to Big D to cover a bank robbery or drug bust or—on a very good day—the arraignment of a Dallas Cowboys player charged with DWI or rape.

Up ahead, a marked car was parked on the street, though there was no sign of officers. They were probably still trolling the area for the gun and talking to residents who doubtless had heard and seen nothing. Suburban dwellers tended to let their guard down. They convinced themselves that strange noises were squirrels on the roof or firecrackers or backfire. Bad stuff didn't happen to them, so they didn't look for it.

"He could have walked from another house in the area," Phillips said, squinting as he surveyed the street.

She tried another scenario. "What if he tailed the bus from Addison or from somewhere in between?"

"So he had a car?"

"That'd be my guess."

"He parked it where? In the back alley?"

"Could be," she agreed. The alleys ran behind the rows of houses, parallel to the streets. This suburban device effectively kept trash bins invisible and hid cluttered garages. "He could've just parked on the street."

There were a number of vehicles curbed on either side of Elm now. Who would've noticed one more?

"He could've had help, someone driving him."

"Maybe," she said but wasn't convinced.

"Okay, I've seen enough," her partner decided, his face tight.

"Ditto."

Maggie turned her head as the old Ford rolled forward on Elm until she could see only the wind-whipped ribbon of police tape out of the corner of her eye.

Maybe they'd find the gun, she told herself, or at least find someone who recalled something that could help them. A strange car, a license plate. Although she wouldn't hold her breath for that either.

Most people could remember what they wore at their senior prom fifty years before, but they couldn't recount what they'd had for dinner last evening. No wonder they made terrible witnesses.

She eyed the stream of neat one-story houses they passed, one not unlike the next, and she wondered about the families living inside.

Were they happy? Did they feel safe?

She shifted in her seat.

Her own childhood had been anything but safe or happy. Her father had left before her first day of kindergarten, and she'd blamed herself for that. Momma had given her no other reason. She was "an accident," so Momma'd told her, one that had not pleased her father. So, bam, he'd walked and, bam, Momma'd remarried. Then it had started up. She'd wished herself dead at first, then she'd wished him dead, and finally Momma for not protecting her and for pretending that everything was picture perfect when, in truth, it was anything but. Maggie hadn't understood then, as she did now, that her mother had put more stock in having a man around than in what that man was doing to her daughter.

A chill came over her, and she shivered, fighting to push her dark thoughts away.

It was like a birthmark that went too deep below her skin to ever be excised. And it had made her who she was, hadn't it? It had driven her harder to turn her life into something useful. She wanted desperately to put things right for someone else in ways that no one had for her. Or, at the very least, to give them back some dignity.

She reached down where her bag sat between her feet, touching the hard corner of the frame that held Pauletta's photograph.

Let me help you, Pauletta.

The car moved slowly ahead a few blocks to the house where Pauletta had lived. Despite the similarity of the facades on either side, it was easy enough to pick out. "Thomas" was clearly lettered in white on the black mailbox at the curb.

For a second, she thought Phillips might pull over, but he didn't. He merely braked for a moment, giving her the chance for a long look, before cruising ahead.

Maggie spotted a blue Taurus in the driveway and wondered if it belonged to Candace. She'd seen so many like it in the Cybercytes parking lot. She wondered, too, if Dave Gray had come home with her or if she was in there by herself, grieving alone, making funeral arrangements for her daughter? Had she even talked to her husband?

She thought of Brad Thomas slamming his fist into the wall of his apartment and felt a stab of pity for them both. It was too bad they couldn't mourn their daughter together, share their loss.

But she doubted if all the king's horses and all the king's men could put Candy and Brad back together again.

"Her mother had a new 'man friend'...she seemed agitated...I asked her if he made her feel uneasy..."

"God damn him...the lying, two-faced son-of-a-bitch...he wanted Paulie sent away to school so he could have Candy all to himself...well, now she's gone, all right...guess he finally got what he wanted..."

Maggie frowned as the words of Matthew Prentice and Brad Thomas resurfaced.

What did they really know about Dave Gray? What was his relationship to Candy? To Pauletta?

"If you want my opinion, you're wasting your time here at LSS...there's a sick person out there who's armed and cold-blooded enough to have murdered an innocent girl. But he's not here...."

Maggie figured Prentice was right. She didn't see how a kid from the Litchfield School with an IQ below 70 could've plotted a murder.

Which led her back to Pauletta's home life, certainly a complete mess. Maybe messier than someone could bear.

Was it possible that Gray had wanted Pauletta out of the way enough to have her killed?

"There she blows."

Maggie put aside her questions and glanced up through the gritty windshield.

The golden arches loomed ahead, and Phillips guided the car toward them like a Patriot missile locked on a target. He pulled around to the drivethru where he ordered them two Happy Meals so he could get the bean bag toys that came inside.

Then he slipped into an empty space in the lot and cut the engine. Tongue poking out the side of his mouth, he pried open the boxes and dug into them, expelling a curse when he withdrew two yellow bean bags.

He tossed them into the back seat.

"Not such a happy meal after all," Maggie remarked, and he frowned as he handed her a lukewarm box.

She set it in her lap, unwrapping the dry burger and biting into it. The taste was at least a step above the tuna from the vending machine at the station.

"How can kids eat this crap?" Phillips grumbled with his mouth full.

"Over a zillion served," she said and reached back into her box, hoping she had some Tums left in her purse.

Chapter Eleven

The offices of Transportation Management were located in the town of Addison, another leg extending from the body of the spider that was Dallas. Beltline Road was the main thoroughfare, a busy street often called "Restaurant Row" for all the eateries that lined the corridor. Italian next to seafood next to Korean next to an American grill and so on westward toward Carrollton.

Maggie longingly eyed a few as they passed, still tasting the Happy Meal from McDonald's, now a lump in her stomach. They should put a sign in front of the golden arches similar to those at amusement park rides: No one over this high can eat here.

Kids had iron guts.

They turned onto Quorum where a host of apartments were in mid-construction. It seemed like new structures went up every week some-where on the fringes of the city. As long as there was land—even an old parking lot—the investors and contractors would figure out something that needed building.

Not far from the tiny Addison airport stood the low-lying brick com-plex that housed Transportation Management. It was a far cry from the modern steel and glass of Cybercytes in Plano.

She spotted a fenced-in area around the side where a number of yel-low-orange buses and assorted trucks stood shoulder to shoulder, the after-noon sun glinting off the windows.

Maggie rubbed a finger over her front teeth. Nothing like something green lodged in the pearly-whites to blow the intimidation factor. She wished she had a stick of gum to smother her onion breath, but had to make due with the cherry Tums she'd excavated from the bottom of her purse.

She chewed two down as they walked toward the glass door marked with the "TM" logo.

Inside, the place reminded her of the dentist's office Momma had dragged her to when she was a kid. Brown shag carpeting with a rectangle faded from the sun. The chairs had molded plastic bucket seats and orange vinyl cushions that had probably been hip when Nixon was president.

Somebody needed to make an urgent call to the Salvation Army.

"They must put all their profit back into the company," Phillips hissed in her ear.

She whispered back, "Bet the owner drives a Ferrari and has a summer house in the Vineyard."

"Is that near Grapevine?"

She nudged him toward the old metal desk where the receptionist toiled. Even her heavy makeup couldn't mask the irritation in her face. The phone rang every time she put it down, and she kept punching the buttons with impossibly long nails, answering each time, "Transportation Management, can you hold, please... Transportation Management, can you hold?"

She had yet to look up at either of them.

Maggie cleared her throat and removed her ID, flipping it open so that her badge was in point-blank range of the woman's nose.

Phillips did the same.

The receptionist held up a finger tipped with two-inches of shocking pink as she let loose another, "Can you hold, please?" Then she punched a button, turned her head, and yelled toward the back room, "For God's sake, Rhonda, would you help with the frigging phones?"

Finally, her black-outlined eyes focused on Maggie and Phillips, and she gave them a tight-lipped pink smile. Her powder blue eye shadow was as frozen in time as the plastic furnishings.

Overkill

"I'm Dede," she said with a solid twang to each word, her introduction aimed at Phillips. "How can I help you, Chief?"

"It's Detective, ma'am," Phillips corrected. He tugged at his belt with its brass buckle and sucked his gut in. "You can tell your boss we need to talk to him about the shooting on one of your buses this morning at Fifth and Elm in Litchfield. The driver was Ronald Biggins."

"Oh, yeah, the shooting. Can't believe something like that happened," she said, her painted lips frowning. "First the crazies shoot up high schools, now they're terrorizing school buses." She primped at the dyed red pouf of her hair. "Is nothing sacred?" she sighed.

"Your boss?" Phillips reminded her.

"Wish I could help you, Detective, but you can't talk to him now. Freddie's not here. He went over to the insurance company to talk to our agent and fill out a crapload of paperwork. It's just me and Rhonda this afternoon, and all's we're doing is mannin' the friggin' phones."

Although Rhonda was the only one doing the manning at the moment while this middle-aged Juliet batted false lashes at Phillips.

"Maybe you can help me then, ma'am." Phillips managed a smile he didn't often use; one that crinkled the corners of his eyes, setting off faintly coffee-stained teeth against skin browned from too many Sundays on the golf course.

Phillips was getting into this, Maggie realized, noting the lift to his shoulders, the cocky tilt of his head. A wink from Dede, and suddenly he wasn't partially bald, forty-four, twenty pounds overweight, and very married with two bean bag collecting daughters.

She resisted the urge to pinch his arm and bring him back to reality. Instead, she moved away from the desk and feigned interest in the maps of Dallas tacked on the walls and the advertising posters for Transportation Management featuring big rigs and orange buses.

"I'll bet you know lots about the business, Dede. Almost as much as Freddie." Phillips laid it on as thick as Dede's pancake.

But the woman seemed to take the bait like a starved pike. "I pretty much run the office, so, yeah, I'd say I know what's what."

"Does Transportation Management contract with many schools in the area?"

"Sure, plenty. I mean, we're not the biggest operation by far, but we do all right. We've got most of the city schools hooked up, and we just added a couple in Lewisville and The Colony."

"Bet you picked up some jobs when Reeder went belly-up. Maybe what was left of their business."

"So you heard about that?"

"Uh-huh."

Dede tittered. "Freddie used to call 'em Reefer Leasing. You would've thought the 'Legalize Pot' bumper stickers would've tipped off the cops before all the accidents and tox reports did 'em in. Oh, God, did I say that? I'm just kidding."

"You're a funny lady."

"You think so?"

Maggie fought off the urge to gag and hid behind a year-old copy of *Guns and Ammo*.

"You figure someone at Reeder resented TM for taking over their contracts?"

"Are you saying that someone from Reeder got on Ronnie's bus with a gun and shot at him and the girl because we stole their business?"

"Maybe an employee from Reeder blames TM for losing his job." Phillips braced his palms on the desk and leaned toward the receptionist.

She twirled a cotton candied strand of red around her finger. For a moment, her made-up face puckered with worry. "I never thought of that," she murmured.

"Or maybe someone had a grudge against Ronald Biggins."

"Ronnie?" Dede scoffed, the drawl in her voice underscoring her skepticism. "You ever seen Ronnie, Detective?"

"Briefly," Phillips said, and Maggie recalled the pale-faced man with bloodied shoulder and thigh, lying on the street near the bus.

"Ronnie's got a three-year-old son and his wife's about to pop out number two. Besides, I'd know if he'd been into anything illegal."

Overkill

"How's that?"

Maggie put down the magazine, not bothering at this point to act as if she weren't listening.

"I ran the check on him myself before Freddie hired him around three years ago. Not even a traffic ticket. Besides, he's a real religious guy. He was always tryin' to get me to come to Bible study at his house. Can you imagine that? Me at Bible study." She giggled.

"Mind if I see his personnel file?"

Dede's grin widened. "Only if that's a subpoena in your pocket."

Maggie fought down the urge to laugh.

Phillips cleared his throat. "You ever heard of Dave Gray?"

"Don't think so."

"How about Brad Thomas?"

"Nope."

Phillips pulled a card from inside his shirt. "Tell your boss we dropped in," he said and mumbled a thank you. Then he walked out, leaving Dede holding the card in her pink-tipped hand.

When they were safely in the car, Maggie couldn't resist. "Is that a subpoena in your pocket or are ya just glad to see me?" she mimicked with Dede's thick drawl.

"Shut up," he said and started the engine, but even he was grinning.

Chapter Twelve

Things were no quieter at the station. Reporters from the Dallas media still hung around the lot, jabbing mikes in the faces of anyone coming or going. Inside, the switchboard was so overwhelmed with calls that they'd had to summon extra help to cover the phone lines.

The mayor had wanted manpower, and so it seemed every officer on the payroll had clocked in. Now they had plenty of chefs in the kitchen.

What they needed was a suspect.

As things stood, they didn't even know who to look for. Trying to get a composite had been impossible. Sandy and Sarah Potter couldn't give them a description and would never be able to pick the gunman out of a lineup.

Everything depended on the bus driver remembering the face of the man who'd shot him.

Maggie had phoned Litchfield Methodist Hospital several times already. Biggins had come out of surgery but was in serious condition and unable to answer any questions. Try again in the morning, they told her. If he remained stable and was moved from ICU, then she could talk to him.

He was their only chance to get this guy, their only eyewitness to Pauletta's murder.

They needed him to work with their computer artist, give them something to go on. When she had a face on paper, she'd gladly hand that sucker over to the hungry media. Hell, she couldn't wait to see it plastered across every paper and TV screen in the county. Word had gone out that their man had worn a Cowboys jacket and Rangers cap. She'd even caught wind of a radio station in the city offering the shooter an autographed Stars jersey if he turned himself in.

Jesus.

Maggie rubbed her eyes, then took a long swig on a warm can of Coke. She'd been up since a little past four a.m., and her adrenaline had hit low tide. She was wearing down and waiting for the caffeine to kick in.

She picked up a pencil riddled with her own teethmarks and tapped the eraser against the papers on her desk.

Delores had called from Parkland, letting her know she was heading home for awhile, to eat and clean up, before she'd resume her vigil in ICU for a chance of a few minutes with Momma every hour. Momma's condition was apparently unimproved, and Delores had wanted to know if Maggie planned to make it over to the hospital.

Parkland was the last place on earth Maggie wanted to go that night.

What could she do for Momma anyway? Hold her hand? Talk to her and pretend she could hear?

No, she didn't have the time to think of Momma now. Maybe later. Maybe tomorrow after she'd talked with Ronald Biggins, when they had a composite of their suspect and knew more than they did today; after they had the results of Mahoney's autopsy on Pauletta Thomas.

"Hey."

She glanced up to see Phillips standing over her desk. He had on his jacket, buttoned snugly over his belly, a sure sign that he was heading out.

"You gonna sleep here?" he asked as he always did, and she gave him her usual answer.

"Think I'll stick around for a little while more and get some of this paperwork done."

"You're not gonna close this one before the sun rises," he said gently. "So let it go for a few hours."

"Who says I won't?" She gave him the slow smile she knew he was waiting for. To reassure him she was all right.

"I mean it, Ryan." He crossed his arms, concern on his face. "You get your ass out of here before too long, you hear me? You need some sleep or else you'll be able to pack for a week in those bags under your eyes."

"Jesus, John." She threw her pencil at him.

It missed by a hair.

He lifted a hand over his shoulder as he left the squad room, and Maggie fixed her eyes back on the report in front of her. She'd used her handwritten notes to type up a detailed description of the scene, of the victim as they'd found her, of the individuals they'd interviewed, everything about Pauletta Thomas' murder except who had killed her.

"Help me, Pauletta," she said under her breath, shutting out the other noises around her, the voices and faces that might otherwise distract her. She pushed up the soft sleeves of her turtleneck and rubbed her arms, letting out a slow breath and closing her eyes, focusing hard, trying to see what she couldn't see.

Usually, she had a good feel for a case, a strong sense of what it was all about. Maybe she didn't have a name of the prime suspect, but she knew the kind of perp who'd done it.

So where were her instincts on this one?

There were so many questions, so much she didn't understand. The most important being this: If Pauletta Thomas was as loveable as everyone claimed, then why was she dead?

Was she just an innocent bystander, as Phillips had suggested initially, the random target of gang violence? Or had Pauletta gotten tangled in another scenario entirely, one similarly out of her control? Was she the sacrifical lamb in the feud between a bitter husband and wife, or merely a hapless special-ed student caught in the crossfire of a vengeful employee whose company had been driven out of business?

Could any one be possible? And, if so, which?

Maggie opened her eyes, too tired to decide. She drew the Coke to her lips, taking a slow sip and mulled over everything again.

Maybe Phillips' theory about Reeder Leasing wasn't such a stretch after all.

What if Transportation Management had actually played a part in the collapse of Reeder? What if they'd wanted to lose the competition and had pointed a finger when no one was paying attention to the "accidents" that Reeder's drivers kept having? What if someone at TM had tipped off the Department of Transportation about drug use by Reeder employees?

Could revenge had been the motive in the shooting on the Litchfield Special School bus? Would an angry ex-Reeder driver have actually maimed Ronald Biggins and murdered a student just to get back at the rival company that had stolen his job?

She wasn't sure she bought it, but it was plausible enough. Stranger things had happened. People killed each other everyday over situations that seemed meaningless. "He cut me off on the highway" was becoming as common an explanation for murder as "she tried to leave me" or "his dog crapped on my grass."

Phillips was right about it being a different time, a different world than it used to be, even since she'd come out of the police academy. Little Rock, Paducah and Littleton were perfect examples. There were more and more people out there who lacked a conscience, and they were getting younger and younger everyday.

Christ, a man had smothered his own baby to get back at his wife for missing his father's funeral. Worse still, he'd planned the murder even before the child had been conceived.

Her extension buzzed, and she jumped at the noise, knocking over what remained of her soda. A puddle of fizzing brown oozed onto her desk, wetting the papers in its path.

Shit, shit, shit.

She grabbed for tissues, blotting her desk as she snatched up the phone only to hear her partner's voice on the other end.

"Ryan?"

"Yeah?"

"Go home," he said and hung up.

Chapter Thirteen

Belted into her Mazda, tucked safe and snug inside the frame of plastic and metal, Maggie felt herself unwind for the first time that day.

Alone at last.

No need for small talk or pretense, no worrying over fears or explanations. She was grateful for a moment of peace. She could sort through the clutter in her mind.

She switched the police band to low and turned on the radio to a classical station. She recognized the music as Mozart, one of his piano concertos, though she didn't know which. It didn't matter. The sweet notes sent a tingle up her spine, even made her smile.

Driving in the dark—her headlamps slicing through the pitch, the halos of the street lights glowing above her and the steady thump of the tires below—she felt separated from the world, cocooned in her own shell.

Something from Thoreau's Walden came to mind, a bit of college lit that had stuck with her: *I never found the companion that was so companionable as solitude. We are for the most part more lonely when we go abroad among men than when we stay in our chambers. A man thinking or working is always alone, let him be where he will.*

I get you, Henry David.

Solitude was something she understood all too well.

What she didn't understand were people who seemed afraid of themselves, so much that they couldn't stand to be without another human being for even an hour without climbing the walls. There was nothing so terrifying to her as dependence. It made people do things they ordinarily wouldn't do, blinded them to what they should rightly see.

Like Momma.

Ironically, she'd taught Maggie the value of independence by her own example of bondage.

You have a fear of commitment, Maggie Ryan.

Oh, really?

Wonder how that happened.

Let her be where she will.

The only times Maggie felt truly at peace were those when she could lock the door to the outside and shut herself in, withdrawing to her own safe corner.

She'd once told Terry that "disconnection" was her middle name.

It was true. Sometimes.

When it wasn't comfortable for her to be Margaret Louise Ryan.

"Maggie Lou...where's my pretty Maggie Lou?"

A long ago voice whispered, tugging at her memory, strange and familiar at once.

Who had called her that?

Not Momma.

And not *him*.

She frowned as she watched the road, her heart beating faster, her foot heavier on the gas.

It was hard for her to go so far back, impossible still to fill in all the gaps. There were birthdays and Christmases of which she had no recollection. Picnics and dance recitals Momma used to recount, before she'd begun to lose her own memories one by one. What a pair they made now: the child who didn't want to remember and the parent who couldn't.

It was best to keep some parts shut off, she'd decided. Best not to dredge up everything. What she could recall was bad enough.

She sighed and concentrated on the road ahead.

Country Club Acres.

The wooden sign jutted up from the ground like a limbless sculpture, its carved letters lit up by a spot.

She slowed into the turn, entering the condo grounds with its manmade lake, a new fountain in the center. The decorative lights were turned on as the weather was clear, and the water glittered gold and silver as it arced high into the air and gracefully fell back to earth.

Even if it was a tad pretentious, Maggie found it a nice touch.

The parking slots in front of her building were nearly full. It was late and most nine to fivers had been home for hours. They'd eaten dinner, read the paper, surfed the Net, and tucked the kiddies into bed.

Maggie eased the Mazda into an available space well down from her unit, locking it up only because of the radio equipment. Amidst the sea of spanking new Beamers and Explorers, not to mention a Mercedes or two, her ten-year-old import wasn't worth its weight in scrap metal to a car thief.

The porch was dark. The light had burned out days ago and she hadn't gotten around to replacing it herself or calling the condo office to do it, so she fumbled with her key in the pitch dark, finally letting herself inside. She nearly slipped on the mail that littered the floor beneath the door slot and kicked it into a pile with her loafered foot before bending to scoop it up.

She dumped the usual bills and junk mail onto the hall table along with her keys.

Switching on the lights as she went, she shuffled toward the bedroom where she dropped her purse onto the bed, withdrawing her .38 and setting it on her nightstand. She peeled her beeper off her belt and put it down next to the weapon.

Then she toed off her loafers and slipped out of her blazer. She used the bathroom, washing up when she was through, taking a long look at herself in the mirror and noting that Phillips was right about the bags under her eyes. She could pack for a week's vacation in each.

Maybe she'd finally get a good night's sleep, enough to erase them.

Yeah, right. When had she ever had a good night's sleep?

It was like Big Foot. There were people who swore it existed, but Maggie didn't believe them.

Overkill

She frowned and squinted hard at her reflection, at the unruly waves around her face, dark as strong coffee. Her olive-toned skin gleamed beneath the fluorescent lights; her eyes intense. There was nothing of Momma in her features. She always figured she must take after her father, though she couldn't recall his face and Momma had disposed of any photographs. She could only vaguely remember a rumbling laugh and gentle touch.

Was she like him? she wondered. Did he think about her? Did he wonder how she was? Or was Momma right that he didn't care?

Her ribs squeezed her heart like a clenched fist.

Maggie Lou....

Daddy?

She let out a slow breath, flipped off the bathroom lights and left the room.

She turned on the TV on her way to the kitchen. Her condo was little more than a thousand square feet with high ceilings, lots of cherry shelves filled with books and framed Monet prints hung on dark green walls. She loved the place despite its small confines. Like her old Mazda, it belonged to her. Okay, technically it belonged to the bank, but with every mortgage payment it became a little more her own, though it would take her thirty years to pay it off. Still, she liked the idea of being a homeowner. It sounded so permanent. Somehow that eased the frightened flutter of her soul.

It wasn't far from the living area to the galley kitchen, and she could plainly hear the beginning of the nightly news as she stood at the refrigerator, deciding what leftover takeout hadn't yet developed E. coli or salmonella. She wondered if eating something moldy counteracted consuming bacteria. Like getting a preventive shot of Penicillin.

She cringed at the sight of a half-green hunk of cheese, tossing it into the waste basket.

So much for the antibiotic booster.

She ended up microwaving a partial serving of pasta from the Spaghetti Warehouse, taken home in a tree hugger's nightmare of a styrofoam box after her lunch with Terry. That and a glass of milk would do fine after her meal at McDonald's which had made her stomach less than happy no matter what the box said.

Settling on the sand-colored sofa, she balanced the bowl of spaghetti on her lap and the glass of milk between her knees. No placemats, no napkins. Emily Post wouldn't have been too impressed with the presentation of her meal, nor would Momma.

Mabel, Mabel, if you're able, get your elbows off the table.

Momma had been a stickler for table manners. Serve to the left, pass to your right, don't eat with your mouth full, cloth napkin—not paper—and always in the lap, never tucked under the chin.

For all the good those manners had done her, when she usually ate on the run or at the station with food bought from a vending machine.

On the end table, her answering machine with Caller ID flickered red, but Maggie figured most of the messages were from Delores about Momma, or maybe Terry checking up on her. She wasn't in the mood for them yet. She'd listen later.

She relaxed into the soft cushions, shoveling the noodle-wrapped fork into her mouth. Not half bad, she thought, wriggling her toes against her cotton socks, feeling the tension slowly seep out of her neck and shoulders. She slurped messily, unmindful of the splatters of tomato sauce dribbled across her white turtleneck.

She took a slow chug of milk from the jelly jar glass and let out an "ah," wiping the back of her hand across her mouth.

Hell, Maggie, it doesn't take much to please you, does it? she was thinking when she heard the words that stopped her cold.

"...in nearby Litchfield, the normally quiet atmosphere was shattered this morning when a young woman was brutally murdered on her school bus..."

Maggie's chin shot up.

The Dallas anchorwoman with her helmut of blond hair solemnly recited the news about the shooting of Pauletta Thomas while a videotape of the scene ran beside her talking head.

"...the bus driver identified as Ronald Biggins was struck twice, once in the shoulder and once in the leg. The spokesman for Litchfield Methodist Hospital said he was in serious but stable condition after at least six hours in surgery..."

There was a shot of the school bus in the impound lot, then the yellow crime scene tape stretching from tree to tree on Elm Street, and, of course, a close-up of the blood-stained sidewalk.

It was everything she had imagined and worse.

"...for more on this situation, let's go to our on-the-beat report, Danita Hollis, who's live at the home of the victim's mother, Candace Thomas, and her employer, Internet mogul, David Gray. Danita?"

Maggie set her bowl and glass down on the coffee table with a clatter. *Jesus Christ.*

There he was. Dave Gray, the CEO of Cybercytes, seated on a busy floral print sofa beside a mournful Candace Thomas, a framed photograph of Pauletta strategically placed on the coffee table in front of them. Gray's hand rested on Candy's knee as her nervous fingers worked a ball of tissues in her lap.

There was no flush of anger in his face, none of the belligerence he'd demonstrated when Maggie had encountered him earlier, just the calm and concerned countenance of a buttoned-up businessman supporting his Girl Friday in her time of need.

She tasted bile in her mouth, and it had nothing to do with the day-old spaghetti.

Why had Candace Thomas allowed a reporter and cameraman into her house the very evening of her daughter's murder?

What the hell was going on?

Maggie stared at the TV in utter disbelief, barely registering the words either of them spoke, though Dave Gray did most of the talking while Candy sat glassy-eyed, a wax version of the woman Maggie had met this morning.

Her heart thudded loudly in her head. She could hardly hear. She grabbed the remote, turning the volume way up.

Gray leaned forward, eyes directed at the camera. "Pauletta Thomas was an innocent girl, this woman's only child, and deserved to live a long life. Instead, she was slaughtered on her school bus like a hunted animal."

Candace sobbed demurely, and he paused as he reached for her hand, gripping it atop his thigh. His mouth tightened, muscle twitching at his mandible.

Then he continued in an appropriately grave voice, "I'm offering a $100,000 reward for anyone who can provide information to the police that will bring Pauletta's killer to justice."

The screen flashed the number of the Litchfield Police Department, leaving it there long enough for everyone within satellite distance to jot down.

Oh, shit.

Maggie dropped the remote to the floor.

This was nuts.

Her phone rang, but she almost didn't realize it until she'd switched off the TV. Her pulse raced so fast she was dry-mouthed when she answered it.

"Did you fucking see what I just saw?"

It was Phillips.

"What the fuck did he mean by putting that poor woman on television and offering a fucking $100,000 reward that's going to get every crackpot within a hundred miles tying up P.D. resources? Who the fuck does he think he is, pissing on our grass?"

"A rich SOB who wants to buy a suspect with his money," Maggie jabbed.

"I wish we could bust his ass for interfering with our investigation."

"I don't think putting up big bucks to rat out a killer is subject to arrest, John."

"I wonder if the chief knew about this?"

"If he didn't, he does now."

"He's doing this for his ego, Ryan, and for no other reason."

She couldn't disagree with him there.

"Something about that guy yanks my short hairs."

Ditto.

Overkill

"You know our phones are gonna be ringing off the hook at the station, and I'll be damned if I'm gonna waste my time fielding calls when there's real goddamned work to be done."

Maggie hated that Dave Gray would make it harder for them, not easier. Hated that he hadn't talked to them before he'd gone and done something so grandiose less than 24 hours into the investigation.

But they couldn't do anything about it now. It was a put up or shut up situation.

"Maybe it'll loosen someone's lips," she suggested, trying to make herself believe it. "Maybe that much money will get us a name, maybe it'll lead us to the gun, so we can lock up whoever did this."

"Christ, I can't believe you even said that."

"Face it, John, the almighty dollar has a lot of clout these days, more than conscience or the law."

"I'm not gonna agree with you even if I do, because I don't approve of what he did."

"Not much we can do about it."

His steam seemed to run out, and Phillips sighed. "Think I'll have a beer and go to bed."

Maggie could imagine his beet-red face, could bet his blood pressure was through the roof. His wife wasn't the only one worried about his health. She didn't want him having a heart attack over Dave Gray's efforts to get himself and Cybercytes on the ten o'clock news.

"Why don't you try a cup of cocoa with those little marshmallows?" she advised, wondering if beer before bed was a good idea. He'd probably be up all night with heartburn and a full bladder.

He snorted. "Maybe I would if I were eight." But some of the bitterness had eased from his voice.

"Hell, you eat Happy Meals."

"Just for the bean bags, Ryan. Wait'll you have kids someday. You'll be amazed at what you'll do for them."

"That's a long way off," she told him, not wanting to go this route. It was too late, and she was too bushed. "I'll see you in the morning, all right?"

"Yeah, yeah," he murmured. "Just hope I don't sleepwalk over to Dave Gray's and strangle him with my bare hands. Except that sleep walking defense doesn't hold much water with jurors, does it? And I'd hate to make my wife a prison widow because of that asswipe."

"Good night, John," she told him and put the receiver back in its cradle.

Maggie rubbed the taut cords at the back of her neck.

Her eyes fell on the blinking light of the answering machine, and she reluctantly poked the play button with a fingertip, watching the names and numbers that rolled out on the built-in Caller ID.

"Maggie? It's Delores." The voice with its slow drawl was unmistakably weary. "I saw the TV in the waiting room and figured you'd be too busy to get to the hospital this evening, but I wish you'd call me when you could. I don't know what's gonna happen to Vi. The doctor said the EEG shows brain activity, but she's not waking up. There's still a chance, of course, and I've been prayin' like mad about it, but if she doesn't"—she sucked in a breath— "honey, we've got some talking to do, some decisions to make. I can't do this without you."

Maggie's chest tightened.

Beep.

"Mags? It's Terry. You okay? I wanted to see if you'd come for dinner tonight, but I heard about the bus shooting. My God, makes me scared to think about Andrew growing up. You call if you need me."

Beep.

"Hey, Ryan. It's Brian Mahoney. Just wanted to tell you I'll probably get to your girl tomorrow afternoon. By the way, her mother came down with some dickhead and made an ID today. Let your partner know, all right? Maybe you'll change your mind and come with him."

Click.

Maggie stood there, sock-footed and spaghetti-stained, unable to move for a moment, her equilibrium already off-kilter.

Momma wasn't waking up, might not ever regain consciousness. But if she did, she couldn't live alone any longer, not even with Delores there nearly 24 hours a day. Where would she go? "We have some talking to do, some decisions to make. I can't do this without you."

Not now, Maggie silently answered. Not now.

Pauletta would be autopsied tomorrow. Did she want to be there? Shouldn't she be there?

God, she was tired.

She drew her hands to her face and rubbed her eyes, catching her fingers in her curls, tugging at her scalp.

She didn't bother taking her half-eaten spaghetti to the kitchen. Instead, she switched off the lamps in the living room and headed straight for bed.

Not bothering with pajamas, she simply tugged off her khakis and the turtleneck, tossing them onto the floor, and crawled into bed. Pulling the sheet and down comforter up to her head, she buried her face in the pillow, willing her mind to go blank, trying to forget the bloody mess she'd seen on the school bus, the smell of it.

She curled into a tight ball, listening to her heartbeat as it echoed in her ears; slowly, it came down, and her breathing turned deep and even.

It seemed like she'd only just slipped off into a fog of gray when her beeper went off, the shrillness of it making her bolt upright.

She hit the lamp with her knuckles before she could switch it on, and she blinked blindly against the light as she tried to read the number on her pager.

It wasn't familiar.

She snatched up the phone and dialed, waiting for the first "hello," only half-awake and ready to ream the hell out of whoever it was. She hoped to God it had to do with the Pauletta Thomas case and, even then, it had better be urgent.

"Who is this?" she demanded when the phone on the other end was picked up mid-ring.

"Detective Ryan?"

"Yes."

"Thank God," a woman's voice sobbed.

"Who is this?" she repeated.

She heard a big gulp of breath. "It's Candy Thomas. Pauletta's mother. You gave me your card, and your pager number was on it. Could you get over here fast, Detective, please?"

"What's going on?"

"He's here...he's outside, and he's got a gun."

Maggie held the phone with two hands. "Who's outside, Mrs. Thomas?"

"I didn't set the alarm...I'd forgotten after all that's gone on..."

"Who?" Maggie ground out again.

"It's Brad," she said in a rush.

"Are you alone?"

Her answer was a scream and then the line went dead.

Chapter Fourteen

Maggie radioed for backup as she hightailed it to the Thomas house.

Domestic situations were a bitch, and she certainly didn't want to enter this one solo. She was in no mood to catch a bullet meant for a wife who'd been comforted on television by a man who wasn't her husband. This whole thing with the Thomases made her sick. Pauletta had been through enough. Couldn't they let her rest in peace?

She shook her head as she drove, wishing she could put an end to all the violence.

There were few cars out at this hour, giving her a clear shot across town. In five minutes flat, she approached the ranch house on Elm from the Fifth Street intersection.

It was the third time she'd been there in less than 24 hours.

The house was lit up from stem to stern, the windows bright behind gauzy drapes. A nearby street lamp feebly illuminated a corner of the front lawn, leaving the rest in shadow.

Maggie angled her car against the curb and cut the engine and her headlights. She let her eyes adjust to the dark and scanned the area for movement, but there was no indication that Brad Thomas was lurking in the bushes.

She recalled Candy's scream and assumed he was inside already.

Her every nerve tingled. She was tempted to go ahead without her backup, but her common sense ruled that out. She knew they'd be here in

113

another minute or two. She told herself that the Brad Thomas she'd met earlier wasn't capable of killing Candy.

She could still remember him on the floor of his apartment, a hole in the wall, plaster dust on his fist.

Now he'd broken into his own house in the dead of night to...to what? Threaten Candy? Slap her around a little?

Maggie sighed, frowning and angry.

She banged her palms against the steering wheel, cursing this whole freaking mess.

It was at times like this she almost wished she'd gone to secretarial school like Momma had wanted. At least then she'd know how to make decent coffee and type faster than a henpeck, and she wouldn't have to get out of bed in the middle of the night for any reason except to pee.

Pushing the car door open, she felt the cold night on her face, and a shot of adrenaline surged through her blood stream, erasing her fatigue.

She shut the door with a quiet click and stood on the sidewalk for a minute. She had her shoulder holster on beneath her jacket and removed her weapon. The metal cool against her skin, she held onto the .38, fitted snugly in her hand. She cocked her head, just listening. Despite her wool blazer, goosepimples rose on her skin.

A dog barked balefully from a nearby backyard and another answered in an unrehearsed duet.

She thought she heard the growing rumble of a car.

When she finally spotted the blue and white approaching, she breathed a sigh of relief. Its warning lights flashed, but its siren was silent. Tires crunched on the pavement as it came up behind her own car and stopped.

She nodded as the two uniforms came toward her, hands on their holstered hips.

"Detective Ryan?" one said, a short, black-haired man she recognized as Ernesto Arguiles. His partner was slender and pale. Duncan was his name. Both were reassuringly muscled and armed with station issue 9 mm Berettas.

"I'm assuming her estranged husband's in there with her," Maggie told

Overkill

them. "According to Mrs. Thomas, he's got a gun, and he's in violation of a restraining order. God knows what frame of mind he's in after his daughter's death this morning."

"Understood," Arguiles said. "So you want us to take the front, Detective?"

"She's all yours." Maggie hoped Brad Thomas wouldn't be stupid enough to shoot at police officers, though they had on the required Kevlar body armour beneath their blues. Her chest protection consisted only of a cotton sports bra which barely offered adequate support during a workout. By all means, gentleman, take the front, she wanted to say, but instead asked, "Just give me about thirty seconds to get around back, okay?"

"Sure, Detective."

They drew their weapons and started across the grass toward the front stoop.

Maggie took off on her own, heading for the shadowed line of bushes that ran around the corner of the house. She unlatched a low wooden fence and made her way into the rear yard.

She picked out the silhoutte of patio furniture on the deck: a single umbrella'd table and four chairs.

She crept up the planked steps, her heart beating a drum roll against her ribs.

The windows were covered with filmy shades that filtered the light and prevented her from seeing in. Still, she could discern muffled shouts.

Her shoe crunched down on something, and her gaze dropped to the ground to see a few shards of glass glinting upon the wood.

She lifted her head to spot a broken pane in the French door which stood slightly ajar. A smear of brown streaked the wood. Had Brad cut himself breaking in?

She nudged it wide, careful of the glass that littered the floor of a tiny utility room.

Light shone from a door further up, and she followed it forward, hearing the voices more clearly now. The slurred yells of Brad Thomas and Candy's pitiful wails. Maggie froze at the sudden cacophony of china smashing.

She crept ahead on the carpeted path, moving soundlessly, hugging the wall with her back, her .38 up against her shoulder, her pulse reverberating in her head.

Where the hell were Arguiles and Duncan? She figured their thirty seconds were up.

A bead of sweat slid between her breasts, tickling her skin.

"...it's all a show for him, isn't it?" Brad ground out, such pain in his voice Maggie felt a twinge of pity. "He wanted her gone, and now she is. Don't you see the connection, you stupid bitch? Don't you understan' what he's capable of? He'd do anythin' to get what he wanted, and now he's got it."

"He wouldn't do that, Brad, he wouldn't," Candy replied between noisy sobs.

"Of course you'd defen' him. He's got a boatload of money, and that's all you ever wanted, isn't it? So both of you've got your wish. I'm outta the way, and Paulie's outta the way, so you can be together and screw to your heart's content."

"Stop it!" Candy howled.

Maggie steadied herself before ducking her head around the jamb to see Brad Thomas standing in the center of the kitchen. His profile was to her, his brown hair matted with sweat. He was red-faced, eyes wild. Pots and pans were scattered around him as were pieces of glass and china.

He kicked at a saucepan, sending it flying, and let loose a string of profanity. Then he lifted his arm from his side and pointed a semiautomatic at Candy, who looked small and disheveled as she cowered against the oak-paneled cabinets. She whimpered and begged him to stop.

The hand that held the weapon was bruised and bloodied, and blood stained his shirt.

"I should kill you," he said, shaking the gun at his wife, and Maggie was sure he was drunk. "I should jus' shoot you now, you fucking whore. How long has it been goin' on with him, huh? How long were you banging your boss before you kicked me out?"

"I'm sorry...I'm sorry," Candy sobbed and covered her face, her whole body trembling. "Please, Brad, I'll do whatever you want."

"It's too late for that," he hissed at her. "It's too late for you t' try to make up for wha' you've done to me."

Maggie sucked in a deep breath.

Then she swung around the open door and held her .38 steady, her sights on Brad.

"Put your weapon down," she said.

His head jerked in her direction, his eyes registering her presence, but he didn't drop the gun. He kept it pointed at Candy's head.

"Detective Ryan, Litchfield P.D. Remember me, Mr. Thomas? We met this morning at your apartment. I understand you're upset, sir," she said, adding through gritted teeth, "but I must ask you to lower your weapon now."

She saw the glisten of tears on his unshaven cheeks but still he held onto the gun, even turning away from her to face his wife.

"Leave us alone, Detective," he said in a slow, quivering voice. "This is between Candy an' me. It's got nothing to do with you."

"You're violating a court-imposed restraining order, Mr. Thomas, and you're holding a woman hostage at gunpoint, so I'd say it does concern me. Just so you know, there are two armed officers at the front door, so this is no game you're playing. Put the gun down," Maggie again instructed, sweat slickening her palms. She tightened her grip on her weapon.

He looked confused, hesitant, and something inside her said to keep talking. "I can tell you've had too much to drink, and you're not thinking straight. You've lost your daughter, and you're grieving. Don't make this any worse than it is."

"Listen to her, Brad," Candy cried.

"Shut up! Just shut up!" His skin reddened, his voice rising to shouts, his rage shuddering through his body, shaking his shoulders and the hand that held the weapon. He braced his arm with the other, trying to keep it leveled at his wife. "She was sleeping with him before she kicked me out, weren't you, Candy?"

"No," she moaned and shook her head. "No, Brad, that's not true. It wasn't like that. Dave was a friend."

Maggie could see where this was going and didn't like it one bit. "Brad, put the gun down."

But he wasn't listening. "She deserves to die," he insisted as Candy whimpered. "It's all her fault, don't you see? She's the reason Paulie's dead." He spat the words, "Her boyfriend wanted me and Paulie out of the way, and that's what's happened. It's the truth, isn't it? Admit it, Candy!" he shouted at her, moving closer to his wife so that the barrel pressed against her hair. "Say it!"

A burst of splitting wood rent the air with the decibel of a fireworks explosion, distracting Brad for just an instant.

But it was enough.

Maggie lunged at him, hitting him hard with her shoulder and knocking him off-balance.

He fell sideways, feet slipping out from under him, arms flinging upward helplessly. His head struck the edge of the formica countertop with a distinct thump, then his body folded to the floor like a ragdoll. Dislodged from his grip, his gun flipped in the air before coming down for a landing. It skidded across the linoleum, skittered to a stop against the refrigerator grill and promptly discharged.

Candy screamed.

Maggie quickly ducked beside the slumped figure of Brad Thomas. Hell, it was his bullet. Let it hit him.

Before she'd had a chance to blink, the two uniforms rushed in like the cavalry, semis drawn, and Maggie shouted for them to hold their fire.

Candy started yelling all over again.

"Our boy's down," Maggie shouted.

"You okay, Detective?" Arguiles asked, dark eyes darting around the kitchen, at the pots, pans and overturned wastebaskets. He holstered his Beretta. "We heard a shot."

"Gun went off when he dropped it," Maggie nodded toward Brad, "I think he's out cold."

"We've got an ambulance on the way."

Overkill

"Good."

She returned her .38 to her holster and knelt beside Brad to touch the side of his neck. She felt his pulse beneath her fingertips, maybe a little rapid, but steady. She then drew up his eyelids to check his pupils. They did not appear dilated.

His skin was the color of ash, the grizzle on his cheeks and chin not much darker. The man seemed to have aged a dozen years since she first saw him that morning, and he smelled like he'd taken a bath in Budweiser.

"You son of a bitch," Candy shrieked as Officer Duncan helped her to her feet. She was crying and hiccuping, a mess of tangled blond hair, tears and snot. She kicked at Brad's leg with a stockinged foot, and Duncan caught her arm, pulling her apart. "I want you to throw the bastard in jail, you hear me?"

"We hear you, ma'am," Arguiles told her.

Loud and clear, Maggie thought.

"He was trespassing, and he damned well knew it. He broke into my house for God's sake," she railed as if they still didn't get the message. "He held me hostage in my own kitchen."

"I'll be glad to take your statement, ma'am," Officer Duncan told her, herding her toward the door. "If you'll just come in the other room."

Sirens blossomed in the distance.

She had never been so glad to hear the sound.

"This his weapon, I assume?" Officer Arguiles said, crunching through the broken bits of china and glass in his regulation shoes. He held the gun via a pen caught through the trigger. "Colt .45. Awful big piece for such a little guy."

"You should see where he lives now," Maggie said. "It's a far cry from this neighborhood."

"Wasn't a .45 used in the bus shooting?" Arguiles pressed, and Maggie stood, brushing her hands on her pants.

"You'd better bag and tag it. We'll have to send it to the ballistics. Check the registration first and see if Brad Thomas had it legally."

"He's the girl's father, yeah?"

Maggie nodded.

"Is he a suspect?"

"Everyone's a suspect, Arguiles."

His brown eyes mirrored her dispirit. "I'll take care of it, ma'am."

"Thanks."

She stood aside as the paramedics entered the kitchen, briefly explaining the situation. Brad Thomas was moaning as they booted aside the debris to make room for their medical paraphernalia and got down to examining him.

She listened as they reported a pulse and BP, saw Brad open his eyes and start to thrash around. She hoped he'd have a headache the size of Mount Rushmore.

Then she walked out.

Another patrol car had arrived, and several of the uniforms were talking with an agitated Candy Thomas in one of the brightly lit front rooms. Maggie glimpsed the flowered sofa where Candy had primly perched beside Dave Gray during their television interview. The framed photograph of Pauletta still sat on the coffee table, and Maggie felt queasy all over again.

She had to get out of here.

She stopped only to speak to Officer Arguiles, who'd accompany Brad Thomas to the hospital and make sure he checked out clean before he read him his rights and took him in for booking. She'd file her own report in the morning.

Despite the hour, there were more than just late night dog walkers on the front lawn, and Maggie strode past them without meeting their stares.

She was nearly to her Mazda when she saw the red Porsche squeal around the corner of Elm onto Fifth, jerking to a stop behind one of the blue and whites, nearly blocking in the ambulance.

A man got out, pushing through the thin line of curiosity seekers, moving swiftly toward the house with shoulders squared. Napoleon charging into battle.

Surprise, surprise, Maggie mused with a shake of her head. Dave Gray had ridden to Candy's rescue again.

Overkill

For an instant, she almost went after him to give him a piece of her mind, to tell him to stop interfering with their investigation and to let them do their job without him pulling out his wallet.

She clenched her teeth and got into her car.

Oddly enough, she felt sorry for Brad Thomas, not his wife. Unlike Phillips, she didn't think he was guilty of anything except bad luck. He'd lost his job, his marriage and his daughter.

Do not pass Go. Do not collect $200. Go straight to jail.

Poor bastard.

She started up the engine, glancing into the rearview before pulling away. Her eyes were bloodshot, ringed with gray. Every nerve that had tingled earlier with adrenaline was now numb.

She could hardly wait to see what was in store for her tomorrow.

Chapter Fifteen

She cried out in the dark, tears staining her cheeks as she struggled to surface, fingers clawing at the sheets tangled around her.

Gasping for air, she stared into the darkness, fear flooding her veins, setting her heart to racing until she caught her breath and remembered where she was.

A fine shaft of sunlight slanted through the crack between her bedroom curtains, helping her eyes adjust to the dim. She swept her gaze around the room from corner to corner, absorbing the silence around her.

It's okay, Maggie, she told herself. *You're safe.*

Her pulse slowed, thudding evenly at her temples, and she groaned and leaned back into the pillow, flinging an arm across her eyes.

What dream—or nightmare—had scared her so suddenly awake this time?

She tried to search her mind for answers, but, the harder she looked, the less she could recall. It was probably just the same-old, same-old. The memories that surfaced most when her eyes were closed. They seemed to haunt her when she was under stress. When she was on a tough case. When she felt most vulnerable.

The nightmares had never been so vivid or personal when she was on the Dallas P.D. She had squashed her childhood pain so deep inside her that, for years, she'd completely denied its existence. She'd buried herself in her job, forgotten all else except what she faced on the streets day to day. She'd stayed away from Momma as much as she could, stayed away from that house. Just working until there was little else of her left any more. Then she'd had moved away. Away from Momma, away from the city, her all-consuming job.

And then the nightmares had begun.

The investigation of a missing Litchfield girl had triggered memories she'd refused to face. The terror she had bottled up for so long unsettled her still. Telling Terry had helped to ease her guilt. She didn't blame herself now. But it would never be easy.

How was she supposed to forget being made to feel weak? Victimized? Betrayed by the man that Momma had married? There were times when she could smell him, feel his breath on her hair, even though he was dead and buried.

"*You're a hard ass*," she could hear Phillips saying, and she wanted to shout back, "No, I'm not. I'm scared."

But he probably wouldn't believe her.

She flipped onto her side, pressing her face into the pillow, not ready to get up yet.

Go back to sleep, she told herself, willing her brain to turn off, to stop thinking.

She had gone to bed without removing her clothing, too tired to undress, dropping onto her comforter and pulling the corner up over her knees. She could feel the slight pinch of her cotton slacks bunched up around her legs. Her right sock had come off during the night, and she wiggled her bare toes. Beneath the soft cotton turtleneck, her sports bra pinched her breasts, the elastic band risen too high.

She wondered if it wasn't better not to feel sometimes. Like Momma in her coma. Was she unmindful of all the tubes and needles going in and out of her body? Was there just a sense of peace and no pain? Or did she feel the scratchy seams of the hospital gown biting into her skin? Were the sheets pulled too tight? Did she want to complain but couldn't in her helpless state?

The phone shrilled on the nightstand, and Maggie grimaced at the noise, pulling the pillow to her ears, wanting to ignore it. Wanting to just stay in bed all day in her dirty clothes with the drapes drawn, pretending she wasn't here.

If she were a banker or a dentist, she'd just call in sick. Appointments could be rescheduled, right? A cavity could always wait another day.

But she knew she wouldn't do that. She'd let down Pauletta if she did. And then who would look out for her?

She reached for the receiver on the fourth ring, just before her machine would pick up.

"Ryan," she got out, her voice full of gravel.

"Heard you had some excitement last night."

She slowly drew herself upright, pushing her hair from her eyes. "Yeah, you missed a good comedy of errors, John. It wasn't a pretty sight."

"You could've called me..."

"Then we'd both be sleep-deprived today, and one of us has to see straight. Might as well be you, since you're the designated driver." Her tongue tasted fuzzy. She ran it over her teeth. "Maybe you're right about a little ethanol before bed."

"You don't drink."

"I could start."

Phillips laughed. "Hell, I didn't even get to suck on a Sam Adams before I turned in. The wife wouldn't let me. She made me a glass of warm milk with honey."

"And I thought you were a grown-up."

"*She's* the grown-up."

"You said it, not me." Maggie squinted at her wrist watch. It was nearly eight o'clock. She'd overslept. "Are you at the station?"

"Actually, I'm about to take off. The phones are going nuts, just like we figured. People're trying to turn in their own grandmas, for Christ's sake, just to get a crack at the hundred thou Gray is offering."

Maggie's stomach curdled. "How's Brad Thomas this morning?"

"His bond hearing's at eleven. Heard he's got a P.D."

A public defender.

Overkill

Maggie bit on her lower lip. Poor guy wouldn't make bail unless Dave Gray paid it or his wife decided to drop the charges. She hoped the judge would let him out to attend his daughter's funeral.

"Look, I'm getting in my car right now to come pick you up. Thought we'd head over to the hospital and have a little two-on-one with the bus driver. I called ahead, and the doc said he'd give us a minute or two. Biggins has been moved from ICU into a private room. He's doing well considering the alternative."

Maggie felt a surge of relief rush through her veins. Ronald Biggins was the key to this whole mess, the only one who could help them identify the gunman.

"We need someone trained in FACES," she said in a rush, her brain already beginning to whirl with everything they had to do. "We've got to get a composite."

"Done."

Maggie breathed easier, feeling better about the idea of having a composite of the shooter by the end of the morning.

"How much time've I got?"

"I'll be there in ten if I drive slow," he said, his car phone crackling. "So get your ass out of bed and get dressed. And, Ryan?"

"What?"

"Lose the blue blazer, all right? If I see that thing one more time this week, I think I'll have to burn it."

"And you wonder why I'm not married when I've got you to nag me."

"Smart ass," he said and hung up.

———

Litchfield Methodist Hospital was the Ritz compared to Parkland Hospital in Dallas. Built a handful of years before, the building covered a dozen acres on the edge of town, offering convenience in healthcare to residents who'd previously had to drive into Dallas or Plano.

Methodist was a marvel of modern architecture with lots of skylights above a five-storied central atrium where the sun could shine down upon patients able to stroll or roll from their rooms. Clusters of plants and flowers abounded and reminded Maggie more of a shopping mall than a hospital. There was even a popcorn vendor with a red and yellow pushcart, and the smell of the buttery stuff filled the air, nearly smothering the vague odor of disinfectant and illness altogether. Large animal sculptures prowled the atrium area, and a few children climbed atop them under the watchful eyes of their mothers. A fountain gurgled in the midst of it all, shiny coins glinting from below the water like sunken treasure. So many wishes and prayers.

Maggie breathed in the scent of chlorine. It brought to mind suddenly the rare summer days spent at the public swimming pool where she'd learned how to swim. When she'd gotten good, she'd toss a quarter to the bottom and dive to fetch it. *Hold your breath just a little longer*, she had told herself, seeing the coin glimmer at the bottom. *Just hold your breath.*

"Maggie?"

Phillips wiggled his fingers at her from near the bank of elevators. She headed over and, as they waited for one to come down, he told her, "The doc said Biggins might not remember much, that he could have some blank spots because of posttraumatic stress."

"All he has to remember is the gunman," she said. "You said we'd have a FACES guy here?"

"Patrick was trained in the software, Ryan, and he'll be here, so don't worry."

The elevator doors pinged open, and an attendant in white pushed out an old man in a wheelchair.

Phillips held a hand on the door until they had passed, making sure it wouldn't close on them. Then he waved Maggie in ahead of him.

"Press two," he told her, apparently knowing just where they were going.

She hit the button, then leaned back against the side rail.

The rear wall was mirrored, and Maggie caught her reflection as she turned her head. Messy brown curls, no makeup except a quick pass with mauve lipstick. She tugged at the bottom of the soft leather jacket she'd worn, a dark blue turtleneck beneath it.

"Glad you gave the blazer a rest," Phillips said, and she glanced aside to see him watching her.

She took in his plaid shirt and tan sports coat, belly pushing hard at the buttons around his middle and softening slightly over the belt with the Lone Star State buckle he'd been wearing since she'd known him.

"I doubt Blackwell would put either of us on his best-dressed list," she told him.

His brow crinkled. "Blackwell? Isn't he a magician?"

"My God, John." She gave him a look.

"What?"

The bell pinged, and the doors slid open.

A circular desk lay ahead, and they walked toward it.

The floors were a peach-colored tile, the walls a shade darker. Softly blurred watercolors of flowers and birds hung here and there, and even the lighting seemed subdued. Maggie almost felt as if she should whisper.

"Can I help you?"

Phillips pulled out his ID and showed it to the nurse in peach scrubs who impatiently greeted them. Her name tag read, "Connie Grass, LPN." Her red hair was blunt cut with a razor's edge as sharp as her tone.

"We're here to see Ronald Biggins," he said, and the woman sighed in an irritated fashion and punched a number into the telephone. She spoke briefly, then hung up.

"Dr. Kelly says no more than ten minutes."

"We'll try," Phillips promised, "but if our composite guy is a little late, we might need a few more..."

"Ten," she crisply reiterated.

"Yes, ma'am."

Maggie wanted to kick them both.

Signs posted around them showed arrows forking off in two directions.

The nurse led them toward the direction of the Surgical Recovery Wing.

They passed an elderly woman wandering around in backless gown and slippers, pulling an IV along with her, a male attendant at her elbow.

Maggie got flashes of Momma in the bed at Parkland, intubated and ventilated. She quickly shook them off.

"How's he doing really?" she asked the nurse as they walked.

"The bullet in his thigh came close to his femoral artery. About a half inch more, and the outcome might've been different," Connie said without missing a step. "He lost a lot of blood regardless, and we had to transfuse, so we've had to watch him closely for the last 24 hours. We've taken him off telemetry, and he seems to be doing remarkably well after what he's been through."

She stopped at the third door on the right. It was wide open.

"A moment, please?" Nurse Connie instructed with a pointed finger and went inside ahead of them. Maggie watched her pass the empty bed and push back a curtain hanging from a track on the ceiling. She then approached Biggins' railed bed and fiddled with the IV bags that dripped downward from metal poles, finally bending over her patient to check his pulse.

Phillips paced, making each second that passed more pronounced.

"I think a moment's up," Maggie muttered and walked into the room. She spotted the outline of feet and legs beneath the white sheets and was again reminded of Momma at Parkland's ICU. Only Biggins lacked the ominous machinery around him that crowded Momma's cubicle. It was a good sign anyway, and she could only hope his memory was equally uncluttered.

"You push the call button if you need anything, Mr. Biggins, you understand?" Nurse Connie said loudly enough for all to hear as she adjusted the bed and plumped a pillow behind her patient. Then she stepped aside to fiddle with the IV in his arm, and Maggie saw him more clearly.

His shoulder was thickly bandaged so the strips criss-crossed his chest. She caught a glimpse of a bandaged thigh as Connie flipped back the white sheet to assess the dressing.

Maggie moved ahead toward the foot of the bed, earning her a sideways glare from the nurse who snapped, "Ten minutes," as if they needed reminding, before she sauntered by Phillips and out the door.

"Patrick better get his ass here soon or Nurse Connie's gonna have the rent-a-cops after us," Phillips said dryly, coming up behind her.

Maggie hardly heard him.

Her eyes were on Ronald Biggins, on the wide face with skin so translucent she could see the blue lines of the veins at his temples. With his eyes closed, he appeared so young, his pink lips parted, wide nose slightly pug at the tip. He still had the appearance of baby fat at his chin and cheeks, and she wondered about his age. She knew he was old enough to be married with a three-year-old son and a second child in production.

She rounded the side of the bed and leaned a bit on the railing. "Mr. Biggins?" she said gently, and pale lashes fluttered on his cheeks. "How're you feeling?"

His eyes seemed slightly unfocused at first, then fixed deliberately on her. They were a striking sky blue. "I guess I'm gonna live," he said, and Maggie smiled sympathetically.

"So I hear."

"I don't remember seeing you before."

"I'm not surprised. You were in shock when we arrived on the scene. I'm Detective Ryan," she told him. "And this is my partner, John Phillips."

Biggins' gaze didn't waver from her face.

"We need to talk to you about the shooting if you're up to it."

"I guess so."

"Good. Someone'll be here shortly with a laptop so you can put together a composite of the gunman. Just tell me if we start to wear you out, okay?"

The nod of his head was barely perceptible, but Maggie heard his whispered, "Sure."

Phillips walked around his other side, standing beside the metal bed rail with his arms crossed.

Maggie started off with, "Do you remember what happened yesterday morning?"

He squished his eyes closed and grimaced. "Yes, I think so."

"You told the first officers on the scene that a light-skinned black or Hispanic male flagged down your bus not long after you'd picked up Pauletta Thomas at her regular stop."

"Yes."

"And you opened the door to him?"

"Yes." He blinked hard, as if clearing his head, his lips pursed for a moment. "He looked like a student," he said in a near-whisper. "Like any teenager. I don't know them all by sight, just my regulars. I thought maybe he was new...that he was confused and was in the wrong place. It happens with LSS kids." His voice sounded raw, breathy. "I might've thought twice about stopping back in the city, but not here. Oh, God, it was my decision, my mistake." His nostrils pinched. "I take full responsibility."

"Do you normally make unscheduled stops?"

"No." His eyes widened. "Well, almost never. It's against policy, but"—he wet his lips with the tip of his pink tongue—"like I said, with the Special School kids, you have to make allowances. I'd never had a problem before. But if I'd known...if I'd imagined anything like this could happen...dear Lord in heaven, forgive me."

Maggie glanced up and over at Phillips. He had a fist tucked under his chin and was shaking his head. She half-expected him to say, "It's a damned shame what this world has come to," or something to that effect, but knew that's what he was thinking.

"It could've been so different," Biggins said, choking on each word. "If I just hadn't been so careless, it wouldn't have happened, would it?"

No, Maggie wanted to tell him, but could see the horrible guilt in his face and knew he didn't need her to say so.

What if Biggins hadn't stopped for the kid? What if he'd just driven past to the next scheduled stop? Maybe Pauletta Thomas would still be alive and Biggins himself wouldn't be in the hospital wrapped up like an unfinished mummy.

Then again, maybe the shooter just would've found another bus, another victim.

As if taking her silence as an accusation, Biggins sobbed, confessing in a gasp, "It's all my fault...I'm so sorry." His eyes clouded and his mouth began to tremble.

Maggie reached for his hand and gripped it tightly. "You did what you could, Mr. Biggins, under the circumstances. You radioed for help. You saved your own life and the other two girls were spared. You couldn't save Pauletta."

Tears slipped from his eyes, rolling down sideways to plop onto the sterile white pillowcase.

"I'm gonna see what's keeping our composite guy," Phillips said with a quick glance at Maggie before walking out of the room.

Can't stand to see a grown man cry? she wanted to call after him, but kept the comment to herself.

Her heart clenched as she watched the play of fear and guilt on Biggins' face. There was nothing to joke about here. Nothing funny at all.

"You said the gunman was a teenager," she went on. "Had you seen him before? Maybe he was a student at the Special School?"

"No."

"You're sure about that?"

"Yes...no...I don't know." He squeezed his eyes closed again. His hand felt clammy in hers, and Maggie released it, resting her palm on the metal rail. "I'm not sure anymore." The pitch of his voice sounded like a child's whine, underscoring his confusion. "I keep trying, but I just can't focus on him clearly. I can't say for sure how old he was, just what he was wearing."

"Do you think this has to do with Reeder Leasing?"

Biggins blinked. "Why would you say that?"

"I don't think this was random," Maggie told him. "We spoke with your employer, and we heard about how Reeder was shut down. Had you gotten any threats, Mr. Biggins? Anything at all that would make you think this was payback from a Reeder driver who lost his job?"

"No." The sallow skin turned vaguely gray, and Biggins rolled his head on the pillow. "No, nothing like that. I didn't have anything to do with Reeder going under. No one could've blamed me."

Maggie nodded. It had been a long shot. "Did you notice anything else that morning, anything that was different. A strange car parked on the street, anyone else hanging around?"

"I don't know," he whispered. "Nothing seemed any different than it normally did."

He swallowed hard, his throat undulating with the effort.

"I opened the door, and he boarded. He pulled the gun from under his jacket and fired." His every word rattled. "I felt the sting as he hit me in the leg and the shoulder. I don't think the girls knew what was going on until I fell over and they started screaming." Tears welled again, dampening his eyelashes. "I was down for a second or two. I must've blacked out for a bit. He was gone when I got up. Then I called for help and got Sandy and Sarah off the bus. I saw Pauletta...I knew she was dead."

Phillips reappeared with Officer Patrick at his side, a black laptop in hand. Carl Patrick had been specially trained on the composite-building software called FACES and could work it better and faster than Maggie or John.

Maggie leaned closer to Biggins. She inhaled the scent of him, a mix of rubbing alcohol and sweat. She could see the tiny red veins in the whites of his eyes, the faint downy fuzz on his cheeks and chin.

Her voice was urgent as she told him, "Help us find Pauletta's killer. Think hard and try to remember what he looked like, anything you can recall. A scar, a gold tooth, a tattoo, anything that could help us identify who it was and put him away for good. Can you do that, sir?"

He gave a feeble nod, and Maggie patted his hand.

You're all we've got, she mentally added.

She helped prop up the pillows at his back, though he cringed with every movement he made, and Maggie was half-afraid he'd press his call button and summon Nurse Connie, who'd then proceed to kick them out before the composite was done.

But that didn't happen.

Officer Patrick shifted the tray over Biggins' middle and opened his laptop upon it.

Then he began explaining the program to their only witness, showing with a quick tap of the keyboard how they could mix different features to create a face on the screen until it matched Biggin's memory of the killer.

"Good luck," Maggie said over her shoulder as she headed out, but she didn't think either of them heard.

Phillips followed her from the room, and she leaned against the nearest wall, raising a hand with crossed fingers.

Nurse Connie approached, not looking at all pleased with them. "Your ten minutes are up. I saw that other man go in there. How long will he be? Doctor said our patient needs rest."

"You tell the doctor," Phillips said, stepping in front of the door, his bulk about double hers, "that we'll be here as long as it takes." He folded his arms, bending forward so his breath ruffled her bangs. "We're trying to find a killer, and your patient's our sole witness."

"Well, I...," she started, then clamped her mouth shut. She stood there a moment, apparently weighing her options, before she spun on a heel and stomped off.

It was an hour before they had what they'd come for, and Maggie hoped it was worth the wait.

Chapter Sixteen

They bumped into Mrs. Ronald Biggins as they made their way toward the elevators.

It would've been hard to miss her: a brunette about as wide as she was tall. Her legs looked thick as tree trunks and her heavy belly and breasts strained the confines of a navy blue maternity smock with white collar and bow.

Her otherwise simple face bore lines at the corners of her eyes and mouth, and she had a smattering of reddish freckles across her cheeks and nose. Or were those blemishes?

Her close-set eyes raked over Maggie and Phillips. "You're the two detectives investigating the shooting, aren't you?" she asked, stopping them before they could duck around her. She talked as rapidly as machine gun-fire. "I heard y'all were coming by this morning, and I told Ronnie he better think hard about what he saw, try to remember every detail. Did he do that?"

"He did his best, ma'am," Maggie assured her.

"The doctors said he might have some trouble with his memory, that he might only recall pieces and not details."

"As long as we can fit those pieces together, it's more than we had before. Now if you'll excuse us, Mrs. Biggins, we need to get going."

Maggie was anxious to return to the station to see if anything had clicked with the computer rendering. Maybe it would match up with a description already in the database, someone with a rap sheet and a current street address. Tie the case up for them with a bow like a Christmas present.

"The most important thing is that my Ronnie's alive," the woman said and smiled tearfully. "How's he doin' today?"

Phillips gave her shoulder a pat. "He's doing fine, ma'am."

"Amen to that." Her palms slipped over her swollen belly, fingers splayed. "It's a miracle, isn't it? God saved him for his family."

"That's as good a reason as any," Phillips told her. She bobbed her chin.

"It's just a shame something like this had to happen in Litchfield. I mean, I was scared to death for Ronnie before we moved up here after Luke was born, but I never worried about him once he took this Litchfield route. Now look what happened."

"It's a rough world," Phillips said.

"You're right about that," Mrs. Biggins concurred. "When Ronnie had big trouble with some kids on his bus, I told him that was that. We were getting out. So we did." She gnawed on her lower lip. "But it wasn't any safer here as it turned out."

Her voice trailed off, and Phillips jumped in to reassure her, "We'll find the man who shot your husband. Don't lose faith."

Mrs. Biggins raised her hands. "Praise the Lord," she said. Then without another word, she brushed past Maggie, disappearing into the hospital room.

Maggie looked at John and shook her head.

"That could be any one of a hundred...Christ, a thousand guys in North Texas," Phillips said as he drove them back to the station house.

Maggie stared out the window, seeing the composite in her mind's eye. A face half-hidden by a baseball cap. The eyes neither close-set nor wide apart, the nose equally nondescript. The mouth was in between narrow and full, and the chin defined but not chiseled. So they were looking for a male of medium height who could be in his teens to twenties, probably a light-skinned black or a Hispanic kid, although with the baseball cap pulled so low, how could they be sure? The composite looked like no one she knew and like any one of a thousand young men, just like John said, though she wasn't about to agree with him.

"It just takes one person to ID him." She refused to believe the shooter would get away with murder because their only eyewitness was a little fuzzy on details. "Someone will put it together. A relative, a neighbor, an employer."

Phillips barked out a laugh. "Like our shooter's got a job. Give me a break. Oh, yeah, wait a minute. I think he handed me my Egg McMuffin this morning."

She cuffed his shoulder. "Stop it."

"Just telling it like it is."

"You giving up?"

"Hell, no," he grunted. "If I wanted to quit every time things got tough, I would've turned in my badge years ago."

"That's the spirit."

He made a face at her, but Maggie could see something more in his eyes, and she figured he was thinking about Biggins' wife and what she'd said about moving to Litchfield. Phillips had uprooted his family from Fort Worth for the same reasons.

But Maggie knew as well as anyone that there wasn't a place far enough away from violence to escape to anymore.

"At least now we've got some fish food for the feeding frenzy," Phillips murmured, and Maggie silently agreed.

There were still a good number of media vans clogging up the station's parking lot; but, her partner was right, this time the reporters wouldn't leave empty-handed.

"It's showtime," she said as they got out of the car and headed inside.

The FACES composite had already made it into the system and had been reproduced so that everyone in the station had a copy to study and pin up at their desk.

Overkill

After a meeting with the brass followed by a briefing of other officers, Sarge held a press conference for the waiting newsfolk. Standing before the jabbing microphones, his solid body buttoned up tight in his blue uniform, he exuded control and confidence, assuring all that the investigation was moving along as it should and their perpetrator would most certainly be apprehended soon, so that even Maggie felt the back of her neck prickle as she listened to him. How much she wanted to believe it.

Back at her desk, the phone rang incessantly, the little red light forever blinking.

It was enough to give her a headache on top of the one she already had.

Delores had called from Parkland. Momma was still unconscious, but the EEG looked promising, and the doctors seemed a bit more optimistic about her coming out of the coma than they had the day before.

That news was brighter than anything she had on the school bus shooting, which so far amounted to a sketchy composite, no weapon and no motive. Though they did have a ballistics report from the county lab confirming that the casings and slugs came from .45 caliber made by Colt. The firearms examiners were still comparing the magnified computer photographs of the casings and slugs with the FBI's Drugfire system, trying to locate a match with bullets recovered from other crime scenes in Texas and neighboring states. If that worked, they might be able to trace the weapon.

If, if, if.

Brad Thomas' Colt .45 had been sent off for analysis, but Maggie had a strong sense that would lead nowhere. The fact that he had a similar gun was too coincidental for her taste. The man might be unemployed and overwrought, but she couldn't imagine him making minced meat out of his daughter with his own handgun. He'd threatened to kill his wife the night before, but he hadn't pulled the trigger. And he'd had plenty of reasons to do it.

Phillips had argued that Brad could have hired someone to do the dirty work, even loaned out his gun, but Maggie didn't buy into either explanation. How could he have paid for a hit when he couldn't even afford an attorney? Hell, he couldn't even post bail.

If the computerized ballistics program couldn't help point them toward their killer, then they'd just have to keep asking questions, keep looking until they found him some other way. He couldn't have gone far, she was sure of it. She had no doubt the gunman was still around, probably watching the evening news to catch the latest and getting off on it.

If Dave Gray had his way, the shooter might be so greedy as to turn in his own ass to collect the 100K.

She wished the technomillionaire would've written a six-figure check to the city to spend on extra cops instead of using it to keep their switchboard overloaded. As it was, those on call spent all-too-precious time following up on useless tips.

Maggie had taken dozens of calls already, most asking straight off the bat when they could pick up the hundred grand, then ratting out a friend or relative. Trouble was, so far, many of the names she'd been able to pull up on the system belonged to cons serving time or to dead men. Kind of hard to commit murder when you're behind bars or buried six feet deep.

After a couple hours of this, her shoulders had knotted and her jaw ached from gritting her teeth.

When her phone buzzed yet again, she grabbed at it, snapping, "No, you can't pick up the reward today, not in small bills, installments or a cashier's check, you got me? There's got to be an arrest and conviction, or you don't get a red cent."

"God, Maggie, you sound like a state lottery official with PMS." Mahoney's gentle voice barely contained his amusement. His words rippled, on the verge of laughter.

Maggie wanted to tell him there was nothing remotely funny about this, but grinned regardless and leaned back in her chair. She tapped her pen against her thigh. "So, did you call just to hassle me or do you have an honest-to-God tip about the school bus shooter. And don't tell me it was your mother out gangbanging, because I've heard that one a dozen times."

"Are you kidding? My mom's scared to kill a cockroach. It's the crunch that gets her."

"Lovely." Maggie made a face.

"I'm serious. She's severely squeamish."

"So her son became a medical examiner?"

"I take after my father, I guess. He's a retired Marine. He served in Vietnam and doesn't like to talk about it. But I'm sure he killed plenty of people. You want to drag him in for questioning?"

"I think I'll pass." Maggie couldn't tell if he was serious or not. She rubbed the pen against the curve of her chin. "So what's up, Mahoney? I know you didn't track me down just to let your family skeletons out of the closet."

"I wish I had." His tone turned subdued, and there was just enough dead air between them for her to guess the reason for his call.

"You're ready for Pauletta, aren't you?" The words slipped through her lips.

"Didn't you get my message last night? She's on the table, Maggie. I'm ready to start on her, but I figured you and your partner would want to be here."

"But I..."

He cut her off. "I know you said you weren't interested, but I figured you'd change your mind once you thought it over."

She nearly told him she hadn't, that she wanted to skip the postmortem, but the denial stuck in her throat. Now she wasn't so sure it was the right thing to do. She felt responsible for the girl, felt she owed her being there while Mahoney examined her.

She sighed. "What time?"

"How about three?"

It was well past noon already. "We'll be there."

"You had lunch?"

Maggie wrinkled her nose. What kind of question was that? "You think I should skip it, Mahoney? Are you afraid I'll dirty up your shiny floor?"

Mahoney laughed. "Like you'd be the first. Seriously, I'm only look-ing out for you. I just figured that maybe when we're through here, we could grab a bite."

"After Pauletta's autopsy," she said for him, her voice tight.

"Look, if you don't want to show, it's okay."

"No," she assured him, "I'm fine."

"I'll see you soon then, and we'll talk about dinner, all right?"

"I don't know."

She wondered why her heart was beating so fast.

It was just Mahoney.

"Hell, I'm not asking you to marry me. I thought it might be fun to hang out again. Without your partner keeping watch around like Papa Bear."

She was being silly, reading more into his words than was there. They were friends, weren't they? Colleagues. So what if they went out for something to eat? It didn't have to mean anything at all.

"We'll see," she finally got out, because that's the best she could promise him.

"So it's a maybe?"

"Yeah, maybe," she whispered.

"You're still a workaholic, aren't you?" He sounded so sure of himself, so sure of her. "And I thought that you'd run away from the rat race so you could kick back a little, take some time out for real life."

Take some time out for real life.

Jesus, she got enough of this from Phillips.

"See you at three, Mahoney," she said and hung up without waiting for him to say goodbye.

As soon as she broke the connection, her line quickly lit up again.

"Detective Ryan," she got out, by now on automatic, but only heard the sound of someone breathing. "Litchfield Police Department, hello? Anyone there?"

She heard a click and then the dial tone.

Maggie held the receiver for a moment after.

"Wrong number?"

Phillips leaned on her desk.

Overkill

She shrugged it off, hanging up the phone. "Yeah, I guess."

He held a folded piece of paper and tapped it against her desk. "I called Dr. Abley's office, and his secretary made us an appointment for tomorrow morning at eight o'clock sharp. I'll pick you up if that's okay?"

She nodded. "Sounds good."

"You want to get some lunch?"

"I'm not hungry." Her stomach was tied up in a million knots.

"Heard they got a fresh stock of burritos in the vending machine."

"Ugh."

He rubbed his hands together. "All the more for the big bad wolf."

He turned to leave, and Maggie came out of her chair. "John, wait." She caught his arm, and he looked at her.

"What's up?"

"Mahoney called," she told him. "The autopsy on Pauletta is this afternoon at three. I said we'd both be there."

His gray-flecked eyebrows arched. "I thought you were sitting this one out? You already saw her on the bus. You sure you want to see the body again?"

"Yes." Maggie didn't hesitate. "I want to go. I think I need to go."

"For your sake or hers?"

"Does it matter?"

Phillips set a hand on her shoulder, bending toward her so that his forehead almost touched hers. "Don't let yourself get too caught up in this one, okay? No wonder you checked out of the DPD. Sometimes you act like you're diving in to rescue a drowning baby. You can take it hard, but you can't take it to heart, understand? Pauletta Thomas was not your kid sister. You gotta take a step back."

"Why does everyone feel the need to tell me how I should live my life?"

"Because you're such a good listener," he kidded, but Maggie wasn't in the mood.

"C'mon, John, I'm not a rookie who needs a lecture about working a homicide. I can separate my job from my personal life just fine."

141

"I thought your job was your personal life," he deadpanned, his sun-weathered features stoic, though she caught the glint in his eyes.

"Get out of here." She pushed his hand from her arm and went back around her desk, dropping into her chair and picking up her pen.

As if on cue, the phone rang, and Phillips laughed as he walked away. She wanted to put her hands over her ears and just ignore it.

But she couldn't.

"Detective Ryan," she said for the hundreth time that day, making all the right noises but hardly hearing, her mind on only one thing.

The autopsy.

Chapter Seventeen

The morgue had never been one of Maggie's favorite places. Not when there were so many other nicer spots in the city. She could name any number of them off the top of her head.

The Morton Meyerson Symphony Center, for one, with its curved marble stairs and foyer. There was the Galleria with its skating rink where she could stand and watch little girls in ponytails and bone-white boots slip and slide around the ice, pretending they were Michele Kwan or Tara Lipinski. The canals at Las Colinas were nice, too, lined by eclectic shops and restaurants.

And the Art Museum. Colors everywhere she looked with only the sound of occasional hushed voices and the click of heels on marbled floors. That was a place knee-deep in awe, filled with paintings, small and large, vibrant hues and brooding brushstrokes, all tucked inside gilded frames and marked with shiny metal plaques.

She could sit upon a bench and stare at a panel of Monet's waterlilies for hours, caught up in a world all her own. That's why she'd bought the Monet prints in the gift shop, had them framed and hung them in her condo. To give her that same sense of tranquility anytime she looked at them on her walls at home.

But the medical examiners' office. That was a completely different story. Nothing there put her the slightest bit at ease.

She couldn't imagine even the dead were at peace there, kept in refrigerated limbo until their chance came to go under the ME's scalpel, to be talked about and unable to talk back, to lie immobile while organs were removed and weighed, and tissue, muscle, blood and fat scrutinized in a way they never were in life. It was ironic, the meticulous attention paid to a corpse. Medical care was rarely so thorough in life.

"...I just want to go in my sleep, the way God intended..."

She could hear Delores even now and found herself gently nodding in agreement. To die a natural death meant bypassing the forensics weigh station altogether. Cardiac arrest? No problem. Fairly painless and quick. A few check marks and a physician's signature on the death certificate, and you were good to go. Not a bad plan, if you had any say in the matter.

A chill rushed through her as she led her partner toward Mahoney's office, the hairs on her arms standing on end.

Flashes of other days passed through her mind, too many times that she'd walked these same halls, seen the same faces. As a detective on the Dallas death beat, she'd had far too many occasions to pay this place a visit.

It had made her uncomfortable then, and it made her uncomfortable now.

Some things you never outgrow.

She paused outside Mahoney's office.

The door was open, but she knocked anyway. Her eyes swept across the room before she saw him rising from the chair behind his cluttered desk.

He ran a quick hand over mud-colored curls, his preppy specs perched on his slim nose. His green scrubs still bore the creases from a recent folding, but he sported no blood stains. Fresh from the supply closet, she figured and was thankful for small favors.

For a brief moment, their gazes locked, and Maggie felt him looking a little harder than he should.

Her cheeks warmed, and she glanced aside, thinking of something to say as he came around his desk toward them.

"I see you haven't redecorated," she got out.

"So kind of you to notice."

Books were everywhere. They filled shelves on the walls, sat stacked upon chairs, rose up from the floor like a child's blocks built up into a crooked tower. Files and papers appeared in similar abundance. Boxes filled to overflowing crowded the room like cardboard furnishings. Maggie noted a pair of Nike cross-trainers that he'd kicked off near the door.

So he was still running. He'd once tried to get her into it, but Maggie had told him she'd only sweat that hard if she were being chased.

"I like the place, Doc," Phillips said with a nod, folding his arms over his chest in his best impression of macho. "Has a lived-in look."

"Since sometimes I'm here more than I'm home, I'd say that's a fairly accurate description," Mahoney responded, and Phillips grinned, sharing one of those guy bonding moments with just a grunt and jerk of chin.

Maggie's eyes fixed on the wall behind Mahoney's desk. A framed Dallas Cowboys jersey hung proudly between a handful of diplomas and certificates stamped with gold seals. The jersey was white with gray. Number 22. Emmitt Smith. Autographed and authenticated. The glass shone brightly as polished patent leather.

"Nice trophy you've got there," Phillips said, having obviously noticed it, too. "You get him to sign that for you?"

"Nope, I bought it at a charity auction."

"Bet that cost a pretty penny."

"Practically the shirt off my back," Mahoney quipped. John guffawed.

Maggie rolled her eyes. "Oh, God."

"At least I haven't lost my sense of humor." Mahoney said, too closely watching her.

She quickly lowered her gaze to the bag in her hands and began fumbling inside. "If you're ready, can we get this show on the road? I just need to bring my notebook."

"You can leave your purse here. I'll lock up," Mahoney said, waiting till she'd found her pen and pad. Then they left his office, Mahoney pulling the door shut behind him with a solid click.

Maggie trailed the two men to one of the autopsy suites, shuffling her feet as she walked. Maybe it was her imagination, but she could smell it already, before they even got there.

Death.

The odor of decay, sickly sweet and cloying, tickled her nostrils. She tried to breathe out of her mouth, but it didn't work. It was worse than cigarette smoke and clung to hair, clothes, and skin. Sometimes it took two or three showers to wash off. She told herself to get used to it and to forget the rolling inside her belly.

In the autopsy suite, X-rays of a skull riddled with slugs glowed eerily from where they hung against the light boxes on the wall. Maggie tried to superimpose the school picture of the smiling Pauletta atop them, but couldn't. That girl was no more.

"I've got the clothes bagged and tagged as well as her possessions," Mahoney said as he headed toward his post where the body lay.

Maggie heard a buzzing in her ears as she stared at Pauletta's remains, seeing but not seeing. The room was cold, and she felt her hands tingle. She flexed her fingers to keep them from going numb, hoping she wouldn't drop her pad and pen.

"You look kinda green," Phillips whispered, but Maggie didn't move, didn't turn her head, didn't shift her gaze from Pauletta.

"I'm okay," she said.

A gloved and scrubbed lab tech was there with a camera in hand. He was already taking photographs when they entered the room. Mahoney donned a heavy apron atop his scrubs and large plastic goggles covered his glasses.

"You folks ready?" he asked, and Phillips grunted an affirmative.

"All rightee then." He began to reel off the equivalent of name, rank and serial number, a barely detectible microphone overhead picking up his every word. Maggie could make out the video camera in the room's upper corner. Then, "This is the body of a well-developed, well-nourished 16-year-old white female, measuring five foot two inches in height and weighing approximately one hundred fifteen pounds." His voice was calm and methodical, almost rhythmic.

Pauletta's skin was a gray-blue, but looked smooth and unblemished save for the destruction the bullets had done to her face.

"...there are no scars or tattoos noted," Mahoney was saying, and Maggie clenched her teeth to keep them from chattering.

Overkill

A vent hummed above, rattling every now and again like a child with a cough.

She willed herself to watch, but not to feel, to separate her brain from her emotions.

"...she's not your kid sister. You have to take a step back..."

Maggie tried to focus on Mahoney's words, made her hand move to take notes as the autopsy proceeded. No wounds on her torso. No bruises or scars. An outwardly healthy-appearing sixteen-year-old girl who would never smile again.

The pen scribbled on the page, but it was an automatic motion. Part of her felt miles away, high above what was happening here.

Mahoney's lab tech had since put down the camera and was now standing nearby to take the samples Mahoney handed off to him.

She flinched as he opened up the body cavity, and the stench of the bowels and stomach contents permeated the all too close air in the room. Maggie struggled against lightheadedness, reminding herself that she had done this before, seen this before, and it was no different this time around.

No different.

The vent rattled overhead.

Maggie took notes with a shaking hand.

Mahoney kept up a running monologue about the appearance of each organ that was removed and weighed, interrupted only on occasion by John Phillips asking about signs of physical abuse or the effects of Williams' syndrome on her development, her heart, her brain.

Mahoney was saving the head to examine last, she knew.

The clock seemed to move so slowly, though more than an hour had already passed.

Mahoney's examination moved down to the pelvic area when the smooth flow of his voice suddenly stopped, and he unmistakably uttered, "Hello."

Maggie and Phillips exchanged glances.

"What's up, Doc?" her partner asked.

Mahoney turned away from the tablet and looked at them. "Did you know your girl was pregnant?"

Chapter Eighteen

Maggie sat on her bedroom floor, back against the wall and knees bent to her chest, chin atop them.

Pauletta Thomas had been pregnant.

The angelic-faced, nearly 17-year-old with Williams' syndrome who smiled so guilelessly in her school picture had been sexually active, at least enough to produce a fetus that was perhaps 10 weeks along, according to Mahoney. Under Texas law, not viable enough to charge their gunman with a double homicide, but that's exactly what it was.

She covered her face with her hands and let out a soft moan.

She and John had left the morgue in stupefied silence. He'd obviously been as taken aback as she. This was not a revelation they'd been expecting. Far from it. That they'd both assumed Pauletta Thomas had died a virgin went without saying; though, halfway back to the station, John had not refrained from uttering a few choice words on the state of the world in which he was bringing up his daughters.

"You think they should be worrying about pimples and prom dresses, and instead they're debating whether or not the guy should wear a condom or if they should use a flavored lubricant."

"John, please."

She'd scrunched up her face, not wanting to listen, though he hadn't seemed to notice. His eyes had been fixed on the road, but apparently his mind had stayed back at the morgue with Pauletta.

"Well, it's true. You know what I saw the other night when I couldn't sleep?"

"What?"

"One of those assinine talk shows with some blonde floozy host, looking like she'd gotten a bucket of cow fat injected into her cheeks."

"It's called collagen."

"You say collagen, I say cow fat," he'd countered, his face a heated pink. He'd started on one of his tears, and Maggie had realized it was best to let him go until he ran out of steam.

"The topic was something like 'Teen Sex Secrets,'" he'd ground out, "and there were a couple of twelve-year-old girls talking about their sex lives. Sex lives! Christ!" he'd spat, smacking the steering wheel so hard it had made Maggie flinch. "Can you imagine a twelve year old girl with a sex life? Who's she sleeping with, for God's sake? Bert and Ernie? Barney? Big Bird? You should've seen these girls, Maggie, wearing hot pants and more make up than Dolly Parton, their tiny boobs half out of halter tops. One of 'em bragged about being with thirty or forty guys, and she had a mouth on her like a sailor. They had to keep bleeping out every other word."

He'd shaken his head, the angry flush deepening with each slap of tire on the road. "I don't get it. I just don't get it. Where the crap are the parents? If one of my kids talked like that, she'd be grounded for a month. If she tried to wear hot pants out of the house, I'd lock her up and throw away the key."

"These are scary times," she'd reminded him. "Phone sex, Internet sex, pedophiles coming out of the woodwork."

"But parents have to be responsible."

"Sometimes the parents are the problem."

"Isn't that what I'm saying?" He'd snorted. "Parents either don't do the job or they can't. There's no such thing as discipline any more. You can't spank a kid without Social Services ending up on your doorstep, for Christ's sake. So what's the alternative? Letting 'em do whatever the hell they want or turning a blind eye and letting them be victimized. It's easier to be ignorant than to fight for your kid these days. Hell, look at Littleton."

Maggie couldn't disagree with him there. The parents of the
Columbine High killers had cried ignorance about their sons' involvement
with the Trenchcoat Mafia, their penchant for all things Third Reich, and
the building of bombs in the family garage.

"Or how about JonBenet Ramsey?" John had said with a scowl. "Mom
and Pop supposedly slept like babies while their kid gets sexually tortured
and strangled in their own house?" He'd hit the steering wheel again, setting off a honk of horn this time. "Well, that's what they want the world to
believe, isn't it? Better to be bad parents than killers?"

Maggie hadn't responded, but John's remarks had resonated with her.

Her own mother had seemed oblivious to the fact that her second husband had made nightly forays up the hallway into his stepdaughter's bedroom for years.

Had something similar happened with Pauletta?

Had the young woman been made to have sex against her will? Had
Candy Thomas been so preoccupied with fighting her husband and playing
footsies with Dave Gray that she'd left Pauletta's care to the wrong hands?

*"It's all her fault, don't you see? She's the reason Paulie's dead...her
boyfriend wanted me and Paulie out of the way, and that's what happened..."*

They needed to talk to Candy Thomas again and find out the truth, but
Dave Gray had thrown a wall up around her. She wasn't taking calls at
home or at the office. Maggie had left messages at both places only to be
told Mrs. Thomas was on a leave of absence. She was making arrangements for Pauletta's funeral and, should the police wish to talk to her, they
could schedule an appointment through the law firm of Otis & Otis, Gray's
attorneys.

What the hell?

"It's the O.J. thing all over again," Phillips had grumbled. "Money is
power. You can even buy innocence if you can pay the price."

"You think Brad Thomas is right? That Candy's boyfriend had Pauletta
killed? What about your initial reaction to Brad Thomas, that he could be a
suspect?"

Phillips had shrugged. "What? I can't change my mind?"

Maggie had already changed hers several times.

What she did know for sure was that Candy Thomas had kept secrets from them, and she had the strongest urge to shake the woman until she got the truth out of her. Had she realized Pauletta was pregnant? Did she know who the father was?

Maggie had her own suspicions.

Three months earlier, Candy had kicked Brad Thomas out and Dave Gray's suddenly in the picture. Candy's changing locks and filing restraining orders under the close watch of her "man friend," and the next thing you know Pauletta's dead and pregnant. Or rather, pregnant and dead.

What the hell was she supposed to think?

That it was a coincidence? Like Brad Thomas owning a Colt .45?

She raised her head from her knees and leaned it back until it touched the wall.

She stared into the darkness of her bedroom, seeing the body on the table in the morgue, wondering now as she had then who Pauletta Thomas had really been. Because of the Williams' syndrome, they had taken it for granted that she was not like other young women her age. That she was somehow more naive, more protected from the real world and its evils.

Now Maggie wasn't so sure.

Had Pauletta ever smoked a cigarette? Had she tried booze or pot? Had she done all the things that the average teenager did?

She'd had sex.

There was no doubt about that. But had the sex been consensual? Or had she been forced? Did she even have the intellectual ability to make that decision?

Mahoney had seen no evidence of trauma, nothing to indicate she'd been assaulted. Not that it was out of the question, but it would be hard to prove.

Matthew Prentice had said Pauletta was good with words, could communicate well for a disabled person, but how much did she really understand?

If she'd been forced, Maggie had a feeling she would have at the very least exhibited behavioral changes. Neither her principal nor her teacher had noticed anything like that.

Somebody has to know something, she was sure of it. How could the carefully monitored teenager have gotten pregnant without anyone finding out?

Who'd had the opportunity to be with Pauletta alone?

She realized she was grinding her teeth and shifted her jaw around, trying to relax.

Still, her mind kept working even as she focused on deep breathing. She couldn't let Pauletta go.

When was Pauletta by herself? Her mom saw her onto the bus in the mornings, her teacher even walked her to the high school in the afternoons for classes there, then accompanied her back to the LSS. What about after school? If Candy worked regular hours that meant Pauletta would come home to an empty house, which would explain the key around her neck. Could Pauletta have invited someone in? Would her mother have ever known?

Maggie rubbed the back of her neck, her muscles so tense they felt like knots beneath her fingers.

What if her parents' separation had left Pauletta feeling so confused that she'd turned elsewhere for guidance, for understanding, for affection? What if that had led to a sexual relationship?

"She could not add two and two, Detective. She was frighteningly unprepared for the real world."

"There are moments when I found myself forgetting why she was here. Then I'd remark about something abstract, and she'd stare at me like I was speaking Swahili."

The phone rang, and she turned her head at the interruption, the high-pitched chirp dissolving her train of thought.

She got up slowly, stretching her legs and her achy lower back, catching the receiver just after the third ring.

"Mag, it's Terry."

Overkill

"How'd you know I needed to talk to a therapist just about now?" she said, only half-teasing.

Terry could read her moods as well as anyone and understood her better sometimes than was comfortable for Maggie. She worked with troubled kids everyday, saw into places most people didn't want to acknowledge existed. Dirty places, scary places, purely evil places.

Places Maggie still revisited in her nightmares.

"You holding up?"

"I'm okay."

"How's the investigation coming?"

Maggie dropped down onto the bed and reached out to turn on the tabletop lamp. "Things just got more complicated."

"More complicated than someone shooting up a Special Ed bus?"

"The victim...the sixteen-year-old with Williams' syndrome...she was pregnant."

"My God." Terry sounded truly shocked.

"It'll be in the autopsy report, so the press'll know soon enough."

"Was she raped?"

"No signs of trauma on postmortem."

"How far along?"

"Approximately ten weeks."

Terry whistled softly. "What a damned shame."

Maggie couldn't have agreed with her more. "Are you familiar with a clinical psychologist named Abley?" she asked, sure that she was. If someone worked with kids in the State of Texas, Terry Fitzhugh doubtless knew about him.

"Francis Abley?" Terry seemed to be choosing her words carefully, "We've never personally met, but, yeah, his name's familiar. He used to advocate zero tolerance, as he called it. But he's since moved into more of a touchie-feelie type therapy."

"What's zero tolerance?"

"Basically, the moment a kid acts out, he's tossed into solitary confinement. A closet will do, if that's convenient. No contact with anyone for a period of at least 15 minutes but up to an hour or more in some cases."

Maggie recalled the gray cubicle in Matthew Prentice's classroom, imagined being a child left there alone for hours. "Sounds harsh."

"You're not the only one who thought so. He took so much flack about his methods that he shifted gears awhile back." Terry's laugh was dry. "Abracadabra, he was a different man, suddenly a proponent of hugging and touching. Was he seeing your girl?"

Maggie removed her loafers. "Apparently he visited the Special School twice a month and Pauletta saw him as often as possible. Her parents had separated and were engaged in World War Three. The father had moved out a couple months earlier."

"That's a lot for any child to absorb, more confusing still for someone who's disabled."

"My thoughts exactly."

"Wow, she really was pregnant, huh?" Terry asked in a rush. "Her mother must've been under a lot of pressure already. The stress of raising a handicapped child is enormous, not to mention doing it alone. Then to find out there was a baby on the way."

"Enormous enough to make a parent snap?"

"Snap how?"

"Murder."

Terry was silent for awhile. "You did hear of the parents who dropped their son off at a hospital at Christmas and left him there? He had cerebral palsy, and they couldn't—or wouldn't—keep up his care."

"But that's not the same as killing him."

"No, it's not. But it's a desperate act."

"Desperate," Maggie repeated the word. "The perfect description of Pauletta's father. As we speak, he's being detained for assaulting his wife. He defied a restraining order and held her at gunpoint in her kitchen last night."

"You've got to be kidding?"

"I wish I were." She hesitated before tacking on, "The gun in Brad Thomas' possession was the same type as the one used in the shooting."

"You think he did it?"

Overkill

"No." Maggie had already gone over this in her own mind, and it just didn't fit. She didn't buy it, even if Phillips could entertain the idea.

"Mag?"

"Yeah?"

"You know I'm here if you need me?"

"I know," Maggie said quietly, meaning it. She trusted Terry like she did few others, and that in itself had taken time. She was everything that Momma never had been: a strong woman with a husband who was her partner, a son she cherished, and a normalcy Maggie hoped would someday rub off on her. "Kiss Andrew for me, would you?"

"Will do."

She hung up and sat there for a moment, pressing her eyes tightly closed, her thoughts so fiercely rumbling in her head that it sounded like the whistle of a speeding train. It shook the floor beneath her, drowning out the drumbeat of her heart, pounding and pounding.

Pounding.

Someone was knocking.

Beating on her door.

She opened her eyes.

The roar of the train disappeared, and the room came still around her.

She walked from the bedroom in her socks, a muffled voice audible now as she moved through the living room and approached the front door.

"Maggie, you in there?"

She paused in the small foyer, catching sight of herself in the mirror above the table on which she'd earlier dropped her mail and car keys.

Her heavy hair tangled upon her forehead. Her eyes were shadowed beneath. Her mouth was pulled tight, her nose pinched.

She pushed a hand up to her brow, brushing the waves from her face and tucking loose tendrils behind her ears. She breathed in deeply.

"Maggie?"

Slowly, she turned away from her reflection and put a hand on the door knob; with the other, she unlocked the deadbolt and steadied herself before she opened up.

She knew who was there. She had recognized his voice.

Even in the dark, she could see Brian Mahoney's eyes flicker over her from behind his glasses. He looked worried.

"You were gone by the time I changed out of my scrubs. I thought you said you'd have dinner with me," he started in on her, his normally boyish expression replaced by that of a disappointed man. "I figured maybe you were sick or something."

He lifted his hands, then let them drop, finally sticking them into the pockets of his corduroy barn coat. It was a funny shade of purple. He had on khakis that looked soft from washings and a tan crewneck sweater with cables. He'd always dressed like a refugee from L.L. Bean. And he smelled of cologne. Something subtle and clean, a little citrusy.

"We were supposed to have dinner," he said again. "You stood me up."

"No, what I said was 'maybe.'"

"Doesn't matter." He rubbed his hands together. "Since you don't appear to be ill, you can eat with me now. Food's on its way as we speak."

"Mahoney," his name slipped out in a breath of frustration. She was tired. She just wanted to shower and go to sleep. She couldn't think clearly much less share a meal and make small-talk with him.

"C'mon, Maggie." A hopeful smile played on his lips. The over-grown Eagle Scout who never took no for an answer. "I ordered a pizza. It should be here any minute. And don't tell me you've already eaten, because I know it ain't so. I saw your face during the postmortem. You probably had a Coke and a bag of chips for lunch. Am I right?"

"Just a Coke," she corrected him.

He put a hand over his heart. "My God, woman. How do you do it? Your blood sugar level must be shot to hell."

"Mahoney..." she wanted to tell him to leave, that it wasn't a good time. She had too much on her mind, not just the Pauletta Thomas case and Brad Thomas' arrest, but Momma at Parkland, the pressure from Delores to be there.

She swallowed hard, feeling the urge to run. But it was her house. She had nowhere to go.

Overkill

"Well, are you gonna let me in?"

God, how she wanted to say no.

"Mahoney, I..." she tried again, "it's just that I'm so tired. It's been a long day."

He squinted, worry lines on his brow. "You do seem pretty beat. Your partner says you're taking this girl's murder really hard."

Her back stiffened. "So now you and Phillips are talking behind my back?"

"He's concerned about you, Maggie."

"Well, he shouldn't be. I can take care of myself just fine." She shivered suddenly, a combination of the chilly temp and her fatigue.

"You're cold," Mahoney said, putting a hand on the door to push it wider. "Let's go inside."

Hello? Had he not heard a word she'd said?

"Mahoney...," was all she got out, when a Jeep with a lit-up Pizza Hut delivery sign hanging from its window careened through the parking lot and screeched to a halt in front of her unit.

He turned away from the door and waved to the guy, who jogged up the walk with the pizza box in hand, snugly wrapped up in an insulating sleeve.

Mahoney paid the kid, who in turn slipped the pizza from its nylon cocoon and handed it to him with a pat on the arm and a "Thanks, dude."

Maggie knew that to resist was futile, but she did warn him, "We eat and then you leave, you got that?"

"Got it," he said, inclining his head toward the burned out bulb overhead. "Your light's out."

"I know."

She moved back and waved him in.

"You got beer?"

"I've got Coke."

"Diet?"

"Real."

"Hell, Ryan, why don't you just inject the sugar?"

"You want to stay or not?"

He quickly stepped into the tiny foyer, asking "Kitchen?"

She pointed to it.

He took off with the pizza in hand, leaving Maggie to lock the door and follow after him, the scent of hot crust, meat and cheese filling her nose, making her stomach growl despite everything.

How'd he remember her weakness was a specially ordered pizza with barbecued chicken?

Damn him.

Chapter Nineteen

They sat on the sofa, Maggie at one end and Mahoney at the other.

Paper plates with the remains of the pizza and two cans of Coke littered the coffee table. She hadn't realized just how hungry she was until she'd taken that first bite. Now she felt as overstuffed as the furniture.

Mahoney's corduroy jacket hung over the sofa's arm. He had his long legs outstretched and his head propped against plump pillows, looking as cozy as a bear in hibernation.

She fiddled with the fringe on the chenille throw neatly folded between them, casting sidelong glances at him.

He seemed an alien presence in her familiar room of soothing dark greens, soft sands, and blurry Monet prints, and his nearness unsettled her more than she thought it would. With every breath she took, she inhaled the scent of him, the mix of maleness and lime-tinged cologne with just a hint of the spicy chicken.

The TV was on, but turned low, so that she could make out only moving lips and body language. They had not said much as they'd eaten, Mahoney mostly commenting on the Cowboy's lackluster season and chitchatting about people at the DPD she used to work with, though Maggie didn't really care about any of them. So long as he didn't bring up something that mattered. Like why she'd packed up and left the city without an explanation. Why she'd never said goodbye until she was gone.

Now the quiet seemed awkward.

She was tempted to reach over and grab the remote to turn the sound up. Way up. She didn't mind the silence when she was alone, but now it resonated like an echo.

"You want to talk about the case?" Mahoney asked, as if reading her thoughts. Or maybe he just felt awkward too. "You seemed real surprised your girl was pregnant."

"I was."

"You know who the father is?"

She shook her head, pulling a tweedy green pillow onto her lap and hugging it against her belly. "We're still trying to figure that out."

"Did she know she was pregnant?"

She raised her eyes to his. "We're seeing one of her doctors in the morning. Hopefully, he can shed a little light on the subject. But, yeah, in my gut, I think she knew."

"So the family must've wanted to keep it quiet, huh?" He lifted his glasses to rub his eyes, and she saw the pink indentations on either side of his nose. "Otherwise, they would have been upfront with you."

"The father had moved out three months ago and was being kept away from Pauletta, so I don't think he had a clue. But her mother...she's a different story." She realized how critical she sounded, but she didn't care. Pauletta was her only concern.

"We've got fetal tissue samples for testing when you need a comparison."

She stared at him.

"Well, you're looking for the father, aren't you?" He pulled his long legs up and leaned toward her, his thigh catching part of the chenille throw beneath. His arm settled onto the back of the couch, his fingers dangling, almost touching her.

"Can we change the subject?" Her head was so full of suppositions about Pauletta and her baby, she could hardly keep them straight.

"Okay, I've got a question for you." He pursed his lips and looked hard at her. "Why'd you bolt from Dallas two years ago?"

Maggie's heart stopped for a second. She couldn't come up with a fast answer. She squeezed the pillow tightly, resting her chin on it, hoping her voice did not betray her. "I was burned out, that's all."

"You sure?"

"Yes," she told him, but she couldn't look him in the eye when she said it.

"Do I make you nervous, Maggie?" She nearly jumped as his fingers came off the cushion and brushed against her cheek. Light as a butterfly, he stroked her skin, ran his thumb across her lips. "I thought we were heading somewhere once, and I miss that, you know? I've missed you."

She closed her eyes. Her body quivered.

His mouth came softly down on her own, sweetly, as though he were afraid his kiss might hurt her. A moan emerged from a long-forgotten well down deep inside, and she felt herself responding to him, tasting him again, breathing him in until she felt herself drowning, falling out of control.

Something pulled inside her chest, like a bowstring tightening, setting off a rawness in her belly that she didn't want to feel.

Fire couldn't have made her draw away from him any faster.

"I think you'd better go," she whispered hoarsely, rubbing the back of her hand across her mouth, slightly dizzy, her voice raw and unsteady. "Phillips is coming by early to pick me up, and I need to get to bed."

He stared at her for a moment, then blinked and glanced down at his wristwatch. A klunky thing with nylon straps. "It's barely ten."

"Brian, go." She could hardly hear herself for the rush that filled her ears.

"All right, I'm gone."

With a sigh, he withdrew his arm from the back of the sofa and got up, gathering his corduroy jacket from the rolled arm. A rash of heated pink suffused his cheeks, and she could read his disappointment like a flashing neon sign. "Guess I should thank you for having dinner with me after all," he said. "I'll see you around then?"

She nodded and stood up unsteadily, still hugging the pillow against her.

He headed toward the door.

She didn't follow.

Instead, she lamely called after him, "Bye, Mahoney."

He hesitated, one hand on the doorknob, turning toward her with a shake of his head. "Not goodbye, Maggie. Just goodnight."

Then he left.

She stood there, not moving, her eyes on the door. The scent of him lingering. She sucked in a deep breath, putting the pillow aside, and went to the door to lock the deadbolt. There, she hesitated, fingers on the metal, still a bit warm from his touch.

"Why'd you bolt from Dallas two years ago?"

"I was burned out."

Liar, liar, pants on fire.

It wasn't the whole truth. She knew it. And if Mahoney hadn't realized it before, he knew it now.

She switched off the light in the tiny hallway and padded into the living room to shut off the television. She picked up the plates with the pizza crusts and the empty soda cans and took them to the kitchen.

"Do I make you nervous, Maggie?"

Her palms were sweating, and she rubbed them on her slacks.

Did he unnerve her?

No, Brian, she'd wanted to tell him. You just get too damned close.

She awakened in a sweat.

Heart pumping, breaths quickened.

Eyes wide, she glanced at the bedside clock, the numbers glowing green.

Three-thirty.

She gulped in a deep breath, blinked into the black of her room, and forced herself to remember the dream that had shaken her out of sleep.

The girl had been sitting at the piano, pale fingers dancing upon ivory and ebony keys. She could only see the back of her head, the dark hair, curled above the Peter Pan collar. But she could hear the voice, the lovely voice that soared above the music. Like a dove, it was borne into the air, spreading its wings and soaring sweetly, magically.

She was an angel...

Then the music stopped.

The voice stilled.

The shadowy form of a man came up behind her and touched her, gently at first, then violently he threw her to the ground.

She screamed from beneath him, his body so heavy on her own. He had his hands around her neck and he was choking her.

She couldn't breathe.

Couldn't breathe.

Maggie sat up, sucking in air.

Stop it, she told herself. Settle down. It was just a dream.

She exhaled slowly, turned on the light and got out of bed.

She headed for the shower, stripping off the t-shirt she'd slept in, stepping out of her panties. She got in and stood with her face uptilted, hot water pulsing down hard as hail, willing herself not to think about Pauletta or Brian Mahoney or Momma or anything at all.

Chapter Twenty

She was ready when Phillips honked his horn in front of her condo at a quarter to eight.

When she wasn't on a case like this, she was a fitful sleeper at best. Until they closed this one, she knew she'd probably get little rest at all.

Even her dreams were of Pauletta.

She wanted answers, wanted the truth. She only hoped Francis Abley could help fill in some of the gaps.

His office was across from Methodist Hospital in the adjacent professional building.

Maggie figured they'd check up on Ronald Biggins afterward, see if he'd remembered anything else that might help them track the shooter. So far, the composite had not brought them any closer to their killer.

Even at five minutes to eight, the parking lot at the hospital campus was full save for spaces so far away it seemed half a mile between them and the building. Phillips groaned when he slowed at the first available, bypassing it with a spurt of the accelerator.

Despite Maggie's protests, he pulled his old Ford into a handicapped space in the shadows of the facade. "There's plenty of these open," he insisted, but Maggie let him have it.

"I hope you get a ticket," she told him, grabbing up her purse and opening the door.

"Who's gonna ticket a cop?"

Overkill

"I would."

She got out and slammed the door, walking a few steps ahead before she turned around to wait for him. She saw him hanging one of those disabled plastic tags around his rear view mirror, and she stared, incredulous.

"What the hell is that?" she asked as he caught up with her.

"I've got bad knees," he told her with a straight face, smoothing a hand over the tufts of hair the wind had blown awry. "Old football injuries. Just ask my orthopedist. He's talking total knee replacements not far down the road. Plastic joints. It gets worse every year."

"Give me a break." She snorted as automatic doors parted before them. "You're just exercise allergic, Phillips, admit it. You'd rather take the elevator than a flight of stairs any day, and it has nothing to do with bad knees."

"I am not allergic to exercise. I just don't do it. It hurts."

Their shoes clicked against the tiles of the lobby as they headed around a circle of seasonal plantings toward the elevators.

Maggie pressed the fourth floor, giving him a sideways look. "You don't care for it because it hurts?" she echoed his words. "You ever heard of no pain, no gain?"

"You want to leave the nagging to my wife?"

The doors of the nearest lift pinged open, and Maggie stepped inside, Phillips on her heels, neither of them saying anything more.

They were all business as they entered the office of Dr. Francis Abley.

Phillips rapped on the glass reception window, and it slowly slid open to reveal a white-haired woman with half-glasses balanced on the end of a pointy nose.

"Detectives Phillips and Ryan, Litchfield P.D.," John said, and the lady glanced at a computer screen, punching a few keys before she seemed satisfied. She peered over her specs at Maggie and John, the expression on her face not changing an iota as she told them, "Take a seat, please. I'll let Dr. Abley know you're here."

The frosted glass closed twice as fast as it had opened.

Maggie raised her eyebrows at Phillips, who shrugged and headed for the nearest empty chair.

The door into the inner office came open with a click before her partner even had a chance to pick up a magazine.

"Come with me," the woman said crisply.

Maggie noted Phillips was on his feet pretty fast for an old football jock with bad knees.

She followed the slender woman in gray skirt and gray blouse down a slim carpeted hallway, the walls a nondescript beige and bare of any hangings whatsoever. Maggie contrasted it with Terry's office on Harvest Hill where framed finger paintings in vibrant hues dressed up cranberry-colored walls. From what Terry had told her about Abley, he sounded wishy-washy, changing methods of therapy to suit the trends. Probably couldn't decide what color would be in vogue next, so he opted for neutral.

They passed a kitchenette with a coffee pot gurgling, and Maggie inhaled the smell of freshly brewed, though White Hair made no move to offer them a cup.

About ten more paces forward, then the receptionist paused at the only door at the end of the hallway. She knocked twice briskly with a bony hand, then pushed it in.

"Dr. Abley, Detectives Phillips and Ryan," she announced, each syllable as sharp as the chop of a lumberman's ax. She was gone from the room without further ado, though she left the door wide. In case Dr. Abley needed to yell for her help? Maggie wondered.

"Good morning, Detectives." Abley rose from behind an imposing desk in the room's far corner. It looked as though it weighed more than her Mazda and was decorated with a Tiffany lamp with daffodils on its stained-glass shade. If real, Maggie wagered it was worth near as much as the mortgage on her condominium. She'd caught *Antiques Roadshow* a time or two.

Unlike Terry's office with its homey atmosphere of needlepoint pillows and stuffed animals, there were few signs that children came here. The glass coffee table had sharp corners, the requisite sofa and side chairs were of creamy wool, and crystal collectibles gleamed from an antique tea table, shot through with the light spilling into the room from an unshuttered window.

Overkill

Maggie wondered if Abley did most of his counseling at the schools themselves and did little of it in his far from kid-proof digs.

"Nice place," she heard Phillips say and nearly laughed. He'd said the same thing about Mahoney's cluttered space.

She took a deep breath, detecting a slightly sour odor, a little like spoiled milk.

Book cases abounded, the same dark wood as the desk, filled with leather-bound tomes. Framed certificates stamped with important-looking gold seals hung on the walls behind where Abley stood, instant reminders of an expensive education.

Dr. Abley was equally impressive with his head of neatly-combed white hair and beard. He seemed a cross between a college professor and Santa Claus in a white turtleneck, blue crew-necked sweater and sharply-creased gray trousers. Did Santa shop at Abercrombie & Fitch?

He came around the desk with hand outstretched and addressed Phillips first, nodding and repeating his name as if that helped him to remember it.

He approached Maggie next, his hand dry, barely a brush of skin against skin with little pressure to it.

She didn't quite trust a man who couldn't shake her hand like he meant it.

"Please, sit down," he said, returning to the high-backed leather chair behind the mammoth desk, clasping his hands neatly atop a green blotter and what looked like a single manilla folder. "I spoke with Dr. Candor when I returned from Austin last evening. She told me about the death of Pauletta Thomas." His forehead wrinkled. "What a horrible tragedy. She was a delightful young woman. It's just senseless. Senseless."

He shook his head in a "tsk, tsk" manner. "This is what comes to pass when we neglect our young ones. Broken families and working mothers...it all adds up to disaster. Kids need to be listened to and embraced, otherwise they're little more than empty vessels filled up by violent video games and movies."

"Is there something wrong with working mothers?" Maggie asked, but the doctor ignored her comment.

"On the other hand, some children are pampered and spoiled to the point of numbness, especially those with disabilities." Abley turned away from Maggie and aimed his monologue at Phillips. "If we coddle them too much, then they don't see themselves as capable of functioning in our society. They become totally dependent on others for their every need."

Maggie braced her arms on her knees. "But aren't some of the disabled actually incapable of caring for themselves? Don't they have the right to be coddled if that's the case?"

Abley rubbed at his beard, slowly turning to address her. "Some handicapped people are unable to care for themselves, that's true. But many of them don't fulfill their potential because they have been taught to conform to the stereotypes we've placed on them. I try to break through that wall, to understand each child individually, and proceed to boost their self-esteem through whatever means necessary."

"You feel touching is the way to do that?" she asked candidly. "Isn't that taboo in schools this day and age?"

"I don't advocate that teachers embrace students."

"What do you advocate?"

"Special needs children are different." He seemed to wave off her ignorance with a wiggle of fingers. "What's best for the children is all that matters. Contact is so important in people whose brains don't function normally. I encourage the parents to hold their children often, to hug them when anger strikes and speak in soothing tones until the tantrum passes. Only so many mothers and fathers are too busy with careers to give their young ones the time and attention they require."

"As a matter of fact," Phillips cleared his throat and remarked, "I was just saying the same thing to my partner."

"Oh?" Dr. Abley's bushy white eyebrows peaked.

"'Where are the parents?' I was asking her. Doesn't anybody keep tabs on their kids anymore? Seems to me they're left to their own devices too much. They don't have any boundaries. Pretty soon they don't know good from evil, and they end up on drugs or in gangs." Phillips was using his hands now, waving them in the air, rashes of pink staining his cheeks. "Next thing you know, they're mowing down their classmates with semiautomatics and feeling no remorse."

This time, it was Abley doing the nodding, stroking his beard with manicured fingernails, his eyes narrowed on Phillips, his concentration as intent as if he were hearing about a cure for cancer. "You must have children, Detective?"

"Matter of fact, I have two girls."

"Ah, I guessed as much."

Maggie cleared her throat to remind them she was there. "Dr. Abley, how often did you see Pauletta Thomas?"

He folded his arms over his broad chest, squinting at the ceiling for a moment. "Let's see, I visit the Litchfield Special School twice a month, and Pauletta was always worked into my schedule."

"Was this ongoing since she enrolled at the LSS two years ago?"

He steepled his hands, tapping his fingers together. "No, only for the past three months, though I'm not at liberty to divulge our conversations, you understand."

Maggie shared a knowing look with her partner, before turning her attention back to Abley. "Your client is dead, Doctor."

His mouth softened into a smile, but his tone was patronizing as he said, "But her parents are not, Detective, and the child was a minor. Her records are privileged."

"We could have them subpoenaed," she reminded him, unwilling to let him have the upper hand.

"Of course you can." He leaned back into the plush confines of his chair, the leather softly creaking. "And when you do, I'm sure the school will provide you with a copy."

Every muscle in her body tightened, tensing like a tiger ready to attack. This was not what she'd expected, not what she needed.

"Are there any questions you would be willing to answer about the victim?" she asked directly only to see his eyes narrow.

"Such as?"

"Did she discuss being afraid of anyone?"

"Most children are afraid of something," he answered evasively. "Of the dark, of monsters, of abandonment."

Maggie held her voice steady. "I'm asking about Pauletta Thomas specifically, not all children. Did she mention an individual she was frightened of? A classmate? A teacher? A family member?"

"I can't discuss that."

"Can't or won't?"

"Now, Detective..." he bent over his desk, shaking his head, the soft-lipped smile reappearing. "You're boxing me into a corner."

"Boxing you into a corner?" Maggie heard her voice rise and steadied herself, forcing a calmness to her tone she did not feel. "There's a killer out there, Doctor. He shot Pauletta to death on her bus 48 hours ago. She took four bullets to the head. Am I getting through to you now?"

He frowned at her. "There's no need to be graphic. I realize how ugly it must have been."

"Do you?" she asked.

"Of course."

"Then help us out."

"Detective Ryan, I would like nothing more than to see this man caught, but there are professional boundaries I must observe."

Maggie jumped all over that. "What do those matter with Pauletta dead?"

Abley reddened. "There are other children and parents whose trust I must consider."

Phillips dove right in. "Look, Dr. Abley, to be honest, we're hitting the wall when it comes to motive. Pauletta Thomas seems to have been right there behind Mother Teresa on the short-list for sainthood. There must be something you know about her that can point us in the right direction."

Abley opened his mouth, but John cut him off with a raised hand.

"You don't have to break any confidentiality. Give us hypotheticals if you have to."

Maggie wanted to shout at the top of her lungs, "Dear, God, forget about the effing client privilege and tell us everything you know!" But she managed to squash that urge. If she couldn't pry the truth out of Francis Abley, maybe Phillips could in his own unique fashion.

"We're clearly aware that her parents have split," Phillips was saying, "and that there's a lot of animosity between the Thomases, especially since Brad Thomas moved out. We know about Candace Thomas' close relationship with her boss at Cybercytes, and we know that Pauletta was caught in the middle of this triangle."

Abley's eyes registered the mention of Dave Gray with a passing flicker, but he made no comment.

"We understand the situation took a toll on the girl, and she was a sensitive child to begin with. Maybe even hypersensitive. Would you agree with that much at least?" Phillips asked him.

"I will agree that she was troubled by her parents' separation, as any child would be," Abley responded, and Maggie half-expected him to add, "theoretically."

She watched the doctor's face, but remained silent. She realized full well that this had turned into a man's game. No women allowed.

"We know Pauletta had Williams' syndrome and her disability caused some problems in the marriage," Phillips continued, and Abley at least did not refute him. "The cost of Pauletta's medical care was a burden. On top of that, she had to be tested over and over until a proper diagnosis was established. Then the family moved to Litchfield to enroll her in the LSS. All of this caused a strain on their relationship, perhaps even led to their splitting up. That much you can verify, can't you, Doctor?"

"You seem to know the situation fairly well," Abley said simply.

"Dr. Candor gave us a basic definition of Williams' syndrome and the so-called cocktail party personality that goes along with it." Phillips cocked his head. "I'd assume then that Pauletta was probably more gullible than the average young woman. Am I on the right track?"

Abley tugged at the cuffs of his sweater. "People with Williams' don't see danger as something concrete. The concept is too abstract for them to grasp."

"We've been told Pauletta would walk up to strangers and hug them without a second thought. This tells me she would have been easy prey for a sexual predator, am I right, Doc?"

"Unfortunately, such would be the case with many children."

Another safe answer, Maggie noted, feeling increasingly irritated by Abley's evasiveness.

"Is it possible she may have been a victim of sexual aggression and not even realized it?" Phillips pressed. "That she might have misinterpreted the act as affection?"

Abley shifted in his seat, face closing up, the bushy white brows converging atop his nose. "Let me make one thing very clear to you both. If Pauletta Thomas had been assaulted, causing her physical pain, there would have been repercussions."

"What repercussions?" Phillips asked, and Maggie concentrated on Abley's face as she awaited his answer.

The doctor bent forward, hands clasped atop the file, the skin at his mouth tightening, his eyes narrowed, unflinching. "Pauletta had a good awareness of her life as she knew it. Though emotional issues may have confused her, she could comprehend being hurt."

"So, if she'd been attacked, she would have communicated that to you?" Phillips said.

"Should anyone come to me and report an act of violence committed against them, I take it very seriously. If I believe a minor has been abused in any way, I would be derelict morally and professionally if I did not report it to the proper authorities. After all, the child's welfare is of the utmost concern."

"And you didn't do that in Pauletta's case?" Phillips followed up, obviously wanting to pin him down on this one.

"No," Abley admitted. "I did not."

Maggie instantly registered the significance of those words. Pauletta likely had not been raped or else she would have told Abley somehow or another, and he would have contacted the authorities.

"Could she have willingly engaged in sex?" Maggie asked aloud what she'd been wondering. "If people with Williams' don't understand the abstract, such as being in love, could she have made such a decision voluntarily?"

"The issue is confusing." Abley kept his gaze on Phillips as he answered Maggie's question. "While Pauletta could certainly have been a willing partner, she could not legally have consented to sex because of her IQ. Under the law, she did not have the intellectual capacity to do so."

Maggie nodded to herself, her understanding of the matter perfectly clear.

"Can you tell me anything about Pauletta's relationship with her father?" Phillips forged onward.

Abley shook his head. "I'm sorry."

"Was she afraid of him?"

The doctor gave him a guarded look and said, "There was no evidence of that, though I would suffice to say that Pauletta had a stronger bond to her mother. Her father's presence in her life seemed negligible."

"How about Matthew Prentice? Anything unusual happen between the two of them? He told Detective Ryan he had a close relationship with Pauletta. He was the one who took her to the high school every afternoon. Did their bond go beyond that of student and teacher?"

"Detective, please," Abley protested, but Phillips kept right at him.

"And how about her mother's boyfriend, Dave Gray? Brad Thomas seemed to think he wanted Pauletta out of the way. What was her relationship with him?"

Abley frowned. "You're treading on extremely thin ice here."

Phillips took a slight change in direction. "Did Pauletta ever mention the name of a man she was involved with?"

The doctor pursed his lips tightly, obviously unwilling to answer.

"Did you discuss Pauletta's health with her?" Phillips asked next, as undaunted as she'd ever heard him.

Maggie knew where he was heading.

Dr. Abley sniffed. "Of course I was aware of her health conditions. I don't imagine it's breaking a confidence to tell you that she went for routine monitoring with medical specialists. She had a congenital heart condition that required careful attention."

"Did you know she was pregnant, Doctor?" Maggie spoke up, unable to sit still a moment longer while Abley hemmed and hawed. That was the crux of the investigation—the baby—she felt certain of it.

Abley's eyes met hers, and she saw something in them, a perceptible widening of the pupils, before they narrowed again, his face closing off.

"I've told you all I can," he uttered and stood with a squeak of chair springs. "I have an appointment in another fifteen minutes and must review some notes beforehand."

Maggie looked at her partner, not so eager to take off just when she felt they might be getting somewhere.

But he nodded, and she didn't protest.

Abley had given them as much as he was willing to. If they wanted more, they'd need that subpoena.

Phillips pushed out of his chair with a grunt, and Maggie got up too.

John approached Abley's desk and extended his hand, which Abley clasped fleetingly. "We appreciate your time, Doc," he said, and Maggie turned to find the loyal Eleanor hovering by the door.

"I'll see them out, Doctor," she intoned, and Maggie wondered at her abrupt appearance. How had she known the interview had ended? Had she been listening outside the door?

Maggie forced a smile. "Don't worry about us. We can see ourselves out."

But the woman made no move to go anywhere. Instead, she waited for them to exit Abley's office, then chaperoned them on the return trip down the hallway, out into the reception area, even holding wide the outside door for them to pass through.

Maggie kept her anger in check all the way to the elevator and down the four floors. She even made it through the lobby and out the glass doors.

A pair of smokers huddled on a wooden bench in the sun, neither talking, just puffing away like needy nicotine junkies.

Maggie got to the parking lot before she lost it.

Overkill

"The arrogant bastard!" All the frustration and anger she'd bottled up so tightly in the past few days spewed out. "A girl is dead, and he won't give us diddly. He knew so much more than he admitted... hell, he had her chart right in front of him." She exhaled a shaky breath, raising a fist as she finished, "My God, how I wanted to just beat the truth out of him."

Phillips reached for her clinched hand and wrapped his fingers around it. "We got plenty, Ryan. Think about it."

"Plenty?" She snatched her hand from his.

But Phillips reminded her, "He didn't deny that he knew Pauletta was pregnant."

She raised her eyes to his. "Yeah, he knew all right." She ran nervous fingers through her hair. "Jesus, maybe there is something in his notes...hell, he could have our killer's ID in that file he held under our noses."

"We'll subpoena her records."

"Damned right we will."

Chapter Twenty-One

Maggie didn't bother to put on her seatbelt for the ride across the mammoth parking lot to the hospital, just kept her hand planted firmly on the console in front of her to protect her from sudden stops.

Thankfully, a gleaming silver Cadillac the size of the Titanic was pulling out of a spot not too far from the main entrance to Methodist, and John homed in on it with the Ford. He plucked his plastic disabled tag from the rear view mirrow and stuck it back under his seat.

Maggie hoped she never had to see it again.

Bum knees.

More like bum cop.

Nurse Connie was nowhere to be seen on the Surgical Recovery Wing this time around, and Maggie surely didn't miss her.

A skinny guy in pink scrubs whose name badge said, "Larry O'Kane, RN," told them that Biggins was truly out of the woods, his vitals were stable, there were no signs of clots or infection, and he was expected to make a complete recovery without complications. He might even get to check out sometime early next week if his luck held.

"Unless his wife sits on him and puts him back in ICU," the guy said out of the side of his mouth, and Maggie gave Phillips a warning look as he laughed aloud.

She caught his arm and drew him alongside her up the corridor toward Biggins' room.

Overkill

"Jokes about overweight pregnant women are not funny," she told him. But his eyes twinkled. "That one was."

The door to Biggins' room was propped open, but Maggie knocked lightly on it as she entered. The second bed was still empty, but Ronald Biggins was in his.

"Can we come in?" Maggie asked, though, in fact, she and John were already inside.

Biggins had raised the head of his bed so he was propped up about halfway to sitting. A morning paper was folded upon the brown rolling table pushed to his side as well as the remains of his breakfast tray.

The television set was on, the sound coming from a cabled box in Biggins' left hand. He switched it off as they approached.

He smiled hesitantly as Maggie came to stand at the foot of the bed. "I hope you've got good news," he said. "Is that why you're here?"

"We just thought we'd check in on you, son," John told him, pausing to fiddle with the curtain that cut the room in half.

"You look better today," she said, and she meant it. There was at least a hint of color to his cheeks, not the bloodless white of yesterday. And, though his limp hair seemed desperate for a good washing, his eyes appeared far less groggy.

"I feel better," he said, glancing sideways toward the pole from which IV bags dripped into tubes that snaked their way into his right arm. "It's amazing what pain meds can do."

Maggie grinned. Her heart kicked in her chest, so glad was she that the shooter had not killed this man. Maybe the good guys did win sometimes.

"We ran into your wife yesterday," she said for no reason other than it came to mind.

Biggins' blinked blond-lashed eyes. "You did?"

"As if we could've missed her," Phillips said under his breath, though Maggie heard him. She hoped Biggins had not.

She quickly asked, "When's she due?"

Biggins exhaled. "Eight weeks."

"I'll bet you're even more excited about it now, huh?"

177

He teared up, his voice tight as he replied, "The birth of a baby can be a great blessing. It's truly a miracle that I'm alive to see our second son come."

He was still wrapped with gauze across his chest and shoulder, the bandaged thigh no more than a hump beneath the white sheets.

Maggie understood the implications of what he'd said. By all rights, he should have been dead. Surely the gunman had intended to kill him, too.

She pushed the thought from her mind and moved around the bed toward the window, peering out the blinds that slanted up to keep the sun from glaring in.

She could see halfway across Litchfield from here, could even make out the flagpole that rose in front of the high school. Just a football field beyond it sat the Special School.

She let the blinds snap shut and turned away.

"They said I might go home before too long if my vitals stay strong and the wounds show healing without infection."

Maggie smiled at Biggins. "That's definitely good news."

"Bet you're tired of Jello already," Phillips cracked, and Biggins grimaced.

"I'm just plain tired," he said.

Maggie turned her head, catching sight of the headline on the folded copy of the Dallas Morning News. "Gunman Kills Stu—" was all she could make out, but, like a game of hangman, she could figure out the missing letters. They'd also run a small photograph of Pauletta, and it grinned up at her in black and white.

She touched the face with her fingertips.

"Did you know she was pregnant?"

Who else was aware of that fact besides Francis Abley?

"The birth of a baby can be a great blessing...."

When it's wanted, Maggie mused. But what about when it's not?

She covered the photo with her hand.

Was that it, Pauletta?

Overkill

Was that the reason she was killed?

She wondered, too, what part Pauletta's parents had played in all this? How about Dave Gray? She didn't trust the man as far as she could spit.

Had someone been afraid for the news to leak out? Had Pauletta been killed to keep her silence?

"Have you tracked him down yet?" Biggins asked, and she turned to find him watching her.

"Did the composite help?"

They'd gotten the computer rendering out as fast as they were able and still there were no matches coming in, no leads that could finally put this one to rest. The Dallas news stations had been showing the face on every broadcast since, but no arrests were forthcoming, despite the pressure they were getting from the top brass to make one soon.

"Detective Ryan, has anyone identified the man?" Biggins asked again. "Do you even have a name?"

"No," she said though she wished she could tell him otherwise. "Not yet."

"Not yet?" Biggins repeated, clearly unsettled. "So you're saying you're still at ground zero? You still have nothing?"

"We have to give it time," Maggie tried to reassure him. Jesus, she realized, he had to be scared as hell. The guy who'd shot him twice, who'd killed Pauletta, was out there somewhere, and Biggins was the only reliable witness to the crime. Was he afraid he was still a target? Did he think the guy would come after him again?

"You're safe here in the hospital," she told him, wondering as she said it if they should get someone pulling duty on his door.

"I just want this to be over," he whispered. Tears glistened on his eyelashes.

"We'll find him, Mr. Biggins, and he'll be put away for good, you don't have to worry about that. But let us do our job, okay?" Maggie said, glancing at her partner for help. "It's only been two days, which isn't unusual for a case of this type. It's still early in our investigation."

"Early?" Biggins winced. "But doesn't it get harder to catch someone

179

as more time goes by?"

"Hell, son, we only got the composite out yesterday, so we can't expect too much too soon," Phillips reassured him, and Maggie saw Biggins relax. "We have to give it time, like Detective Ryan said. We're fielding tips like crazy. Don't worry, it'll happen any time now."

"You really believe that?" Biggins turned his head to Maggie, and she nodded.

"You just rest easy and think about getting better, all right? That's all you have to do." Phillips stepped up to the bed, and he patted Biggins' arm.

A sudden, persistent shriek rent the air, and Maggie nearly jumped out of her skin.

Biggins' eyes went wide, and even John started at the sound.

"It's okay." Maggie realized what it was and grabbed at the beeper hooked on her waistband, quickly silencing it.

"Christ, Ryan, you almost gave the guy a heart attack," Phillips chided.

Biggins' skin appeared near as white as the bed linens.

"Sorry," she said to him for the second time that morning. She scanned the number on her pager. It was the station. "Mind if I use your phone?"

He shook his head, rolling it against the pillow. He closed his eyes with a moan, and she wondered if he were in pain or had just had enough of his visitors.

She edged between the bed and the window ledge, shimmying around the rolling table with the folded paper and his half-finished breakfast.

An ancient-looking phone sat on a bedside table. She picked up the receiver and propped it up against her shoulder.

"I'll make it quick," she promised.

She shifted around in the cramped space, trying to face away from Ronald Biggins as she dialed the number on her beeper.

The dispatcher answered at the first ring.

"Litchfield Police Department."

"Susie? It's Maggie Ryan. You paged me?"

"Oh, God, Detective, I'm glad you got back to me so fast." The dispatcher sounded breathless. "You had a call earlier. We were going to try to patch it through, but we didn't know where you were, and I didn't think he'd wait besides."

"What call?" The first thing that came to her mind was Momma. Had her condition worsened? Had she passed away? Had Delores tried to find her to break the news? She made herself ask, "Who was it?"

"Someone with information about the school bus shooting."

Maggie released a held breath.

The school bus shooting.

It wasn't about Momma.

"Detective Ryan?"

Maggie groaned. "You paged me to tell me another crackpot's looking to cash in on the reward?" She had come to hate that word in the past two days. "So why didn't you just forward the call to another detective. Wasn't Leonard or Washington around?"

"This particular tipster would only talk to you, ma'am. And the reward wasn't even mentioned."

"Didn't mention the reward?" She glanced over her shoulder and saw both her partner and Ronald Biggins had their eyes on her. "Did you get a name?"

"No."

"A number."

"No."

"He sounds like a crank if you ask me."

"I'm not so sure, Detective. I've got a weird feeling about this."

"Why would he only talk to me?"

"Saw your name in the paper as one of the lead investigators and you were the only woman."

Maggie wasn't sure what to make of that. Susie wasn't the only one who had a weird feeling about their anonymous tipster. "What else did he tell you?"

"It was kind of hard to hear. The connection wasn't great, and the voice was really vague and breathy. When I said you weren't in, I was afraid I'd lost 'em. But they said they'd give you another chance."

Maggie's mouth went dry. "You don't think it's a hoax, Susie?"

"No, Detective."

"How am I supposed to reach this person if I don't have a name or number?"

"I was told you'd get another call at the station in an hour, and that was about ten minutes ago."

"You try to trace it?"

"Dead end," Susie said. "All we came up with was a phone booth at a service station on West Jefferson."

West Jefferson was in southwest Dallas.

Maggie's pulse went into overdrive.

What if this was for real? What if Susie's instincts were right? She couldn't take the chance of missing the second call.

"I'll be back in ten flat," she said, then banged the receiver down with a clatter.

"What the hell was that about?"

She turned to her partner, fighting hard to keep from shouting. "We've got a tip about the shooter," she told him as she came around the side of the bed.

Phillips croaked, "What?"

"Take me back to the station, all right? Whoever it was said they'd call back in about forty-five minutes. I have to be there, because this tipster apparently won't talk to anyone else."

"You're shitting me?" John stared at her, hands on hips, hardly appearing convinced.

"No."

"It's not a gag someone's pulling?"

"Susie thinks it's legit."

"Christ Almighty."

"What's going on?" Biggins asked, his face a puddle of confusion.

Maggie paused at the foot of the bed and looked right at him. "We have a tipster who says he can ID the man who shot you and killed Pauletta. If

we can catch a break, maybe we'll have an arrest made before you check
out of this place."

"You've caught him?"

"We will," she told him, getting a rush like she hadn't felt in awhile.

Something was about to go down.

Chapter Twenty-Two

Back at the station, Maggie could hardly keep still, though she was afraid to leave her desk for an instant. God forbid the tipster should call back and catch her in the john.

She tried to work on her reports, but her efforts were pretty sloppy. More typos than typing, and she'd run out of correcting tape to boot.

She dug in her top drawer in search of a bottle of Liquid Paper, managed to find one with a light layer of crust around the cap. When she finally got the thing unscrewed and pulled the brush out, a spray of white spattered on her navy trousers.

Shit.

She stared down at the mess, knowing if she rubbed the stain she'd only make it worse.

She felt her eyes burn and bit hard on her lip.

"You okay, Ryan?"

Phillips stood over her, a can of Coke and a Snickers bar in his hands.

"I'm fine." She dumped the bottle of correction fluid into her trash can. White smears stained her fingers. "Just had a fight with some Liquid Paper."

"And it threw up on your pants," he cracked, pointing the Snickers at her thigh.

"Very funny."

She yanked a couple of tissues out of the box, added some spit, and went at the stuff on her skin.

Her extension lit up, the line ringing, and she forgot all else. She grabbed at the receiver. The damp tissues sank to the floor.

"Detective Ryan," she got out.

"Honey? It's Delores."

Maggie nearly screamed with disappointment.

John mouthed the words, "Is it him?"

She shook her head. "Delores, I'm kind of busy right now."

Phillips put the Coke and candy bar on her desk, then perched on the edge, listening to her end of the conversation.

"I know how busy you are, baby, and that's why you haven't been back to the hospital or returned my calls, but we've gotta talk a minute about your mother." The ever-smooth drawl had a weary edge to it, and Maggie felt the familiar pangs of guilt take fire in her belly.

She checked her watch. The tipster wasn't supposed to call for at least twenty minutes. "Okay, but I have to make it fast."

"I understand."

"Is Momma doing any better?"

"I swear she squeezed my hand this morning." Delores laughed. "Can you believe it? The doctor said her EEG is looking better, that the swelling in her brain is going down, and they think she's on her way back." There was a momentary quiet; Delores gathering her thoughts. "The truth is she'll need more care than I can give her whenever the day comes that she can leave Parkland. She'll need therapy and qualified people to tend to her night and day."

"A nursing home?"

"They call them extended care facilities."

Jesus. She couldn't deal with this now. "Look, Dee, I have to go. I'm waiting for an important phone call."

"I see."

And this isn't important? She could hear the question Delores left unsaid, but she couldn't worry about hurt feelings. Not now.

"I'll be at the hospital as soon as I can, and talk about everything."

"Sure, baby, sure," Delores agreed without inflection, then she hung up.

Maggie held the receiver a moment after, before she put it down in the cradle.

"Bad news?" Phillips asked her.

She avoided his eyes. "Nothing I can't handle."

"Shit, Ryan," he said, shaking his head. "You're like a broken record. If there's something going on, and you need a shoulder..."

"Drop it, all right?"

He threw up his hands.

"Thank you."

She felt his eyes on her as she turned back to the papers on her desk, the typed reports, the preliminary copy of the post mortem results faxed over from Mahoney, ballistics, the crime scene photographs, the collection of interviews, and the handwritten notes that added together to equal nothing.

No solid leads. No arrests.

No prime suspect.

She pushed the papers away, frustrated by this whole mess. Why the hell couldn't she see through it? Where were her instincts on this one? Did her sixth sense need a tune-up?

"Spill it, Ryan."

She sighed, glancing up at him. "He's right under our nose, and we can't find him."

"You think so?"

"She was shot in the face, John. He fired five shots at her and four hit their target. Mahoney even called it overkill. She didn't look human by the time he was done with her. Someone had a personal score to settle with her."

The photograph of Pauletta from the crime scene was right there in front of her—in front of them both. So ugly it didn't seem real.

Phillips put his hand down over it. "Stop focusing on how she died."

She snapped, "What the hell else should I focus on?"

"Why?"

"Hell, that's all I've been thinking about." She ground her teeth, pressing her fingers to her temples. "I keep going over possible motives again and again until I think my skull's about to split."

"Then stop thinking." He tapped two fingers to his chest. "Tell me what's in here. What your gut's telling you?"

"My gut's not making sense either."

"Maybe you just haven't been listening to it," he told her, his face lined with intensity. "I can look in your eyes and see your brain going a hundred miles a minute. Throw the brakes on for a second, all right? Then tell me the thing that's been gnawing at you on the inside. Spit it out, right off the top of your head."

This was crazy.

She turned away from him, sighing with frustration, and her eyes fell on the fax from Mahoney. The words "approximately ten weeks IUP" jumped out at her like they were on fire.

"The baby's the key to this whole thing," came out before she'd considered what she was saying. It was the one thing she couldn't shake. It had nagged at her since the autopsy. Night and day.

"So she was killed because she was pregnant?" John asked, doing his good cop-obtuse cop routine.

"It's my guess, yes."

"That's assuming she knew it herself and that whoever killed her knew it, too."

"Abley knew," she told him.

"When we get that copy of her records we'll be sure of that."

"He knew," she said again, as certain as she was when she saw Abley's face in his office.

"You figure someone didn't want this baby born?" Phillips egged her on further, and she nodded, recalling something Matthew Prentice had said.

"There's a fifty-fifty chance it would have had Williams'," she told him. "If the father assumed the baby would be born retarded, maybe he couldn't handle it. Maybe he couldn't risk her giving birth at all. Sooner or later, someone would find out the truth, and he didn't want it to be public knowledge that he'd had sex with a student from the Special School."

"Okay, what else, Maggie?"

"Could be he didn't want a retarded kid or a kid at all for that matter, and he sure as hell didn't want to get caught and prosecuted for diddling with someone who's IQ made it nonconsensual."

"You figure he was a grown man not a student?"

"It doesn't fit any other way, not that I can come up with," Maggie admitted, looking sideways at him. "He's definitely an adult. Maybe he's in a prominent position. An authority figure most likely. That would fit, don't you think? I mean, what if she's glad that she's pregnant? Prentice said she wanted to be a mother. What if she tells the guy, and he panics. He realizes he's screwed up royally and that his career could be ruined...hell, his whole life could be destroyed if he's prosecuted for statutory rape."

"She could've had an abortion," he countered.

Maggie shook her head. "I have a feeling Pauletta would've resisted that option."

"So why didn't Mrs. Thomas go to the police to press charges once they found out Pauletta's condition?" John kept up his role as devil's advocate. "Why didn't she get on the horn the minute the stick turned blue?"

"I think she may have known her daughter was pregnant, but either she didn't know who'd knocked her up or didn't want to believe it."

"She's protecting someone?"

"Could be."

"You're thinking Dave Gray?" Phillips asked.

Maggie wondered how he did that. "Maybe," she said slowly, suddenly hearing Brad Thomas' angry voice in her head: *He wanted Paulie sent away...so he could have Candy all to himself...Guess he finally got what he wanted, didn't he?*

Candy had tried to make her husband sound like a man out of control, insensitive to his daughter's problems, centered only on his own needs.

But what if Brad had been telling the truth?

What if Dave Gray had a reason for wanting Pauletta sent away? What if he'd gotten desperate when he realized Candace had no intention of packing Pauletta off to Minnesota?

Overkill

"Let's take it in another direction entirely." John screwed up his face. "What if the guy wasn't so stand-up after all. Maybe he had a record," he tossed out. "Maybe he was a fuck-up to begin with, so it wouldn't be such a stretch for him to get his hands dirty again."

Maggie tried to picture it. "So he gunned her down on the bus with the driver sitting there and two girls as witnesses?"

"The girls had Down's Syndrome. They couldn't have ID'd Colonel Sanders in a line-up with the Jackson Five."

"How'd he know that?"

"Shit, they were on the Special Ed bus, weren't they? He probably figured if he took out the driver, he was home-free."

"But he only injured Biggins. Even if he knew the Potter girls wouldn't be reliable witnesses, he left us a competent adult."

"An accident." Phillips raised a hand, fingers cocked like an imaginary gun. He squinted as if staring down its sights and pulled the trigger. "Bang, bang. Two shots into the driver, and he keels over. There's blood on his clothes and kids screaming. His adrenaline's pumping. He goes for Pauletta. You think he's gonna stop and take the driver's pulse? Hell, no. For all intents and purposes, the vic on the floor with all the blood on his shirt and pants is a goner."

Maggie felt a twinge between her eyes. They had too many "what ifs" to suit her.

She needed caffeine. Her tank was beyond empty. She popped open the Coke and chugged enough to get her blood moving again. Then she wiped the back of her hand across her mouth and tried to wrap her brain around Phillips' scenario.

"Okay," she weighed her thoughts aloud, "so the shooter assumes he's left no credible witnesses. He figures he's gotten away with it. But who is he exactly? Maybe your fuck-up with a record who pulls the trigger is not the baby's father."

John squinted at her. "So we're back to the idea that there are at least two players in this game?"

She met his overbright gaze, feeling surer by the minute that they were on to something. "What if Pauletta's stand-up lover paid your fuck-up to do the hit?"

He wagged his fingers at her. "Keep going. You've got my attention."

"It's just that Candor and Prentice seem so sure no one at LSS or the high school had anything against Pauletta. And there's no evidence that her mystery man was a classmate or a neighbor. Someone would have known that, would've seen them together at some point. No, this guy made damned sure no one could link them up in a romantic sense."

She tapped a finger against the soda can. "If Pauletta's so-called boyfriend were just another kid from the LSS, it wouldn't have come to this. Hell, a teenaged student probably would've been bragging about it to his friends. What happened to Pauletta isn't a natural reaction. It's extreme. Somebody's panicked."

"So where'd our gunman come from? Thin air?"

"From the city," Maggie said confidently.

Phillips crossed his arms, tipping his head as he heard her out. "So he drives in from Dallas bright and early in time to waste our girl after the bus picks her up, then he disappears back into the woodwork?"

"I can't see it happening any other way." She ran a finger through the sweat beads on the red and white can, her suspicions chasing each other like a game of tag. She pushed the can away. "I just think if the gunman was from around here, we'd have a line on him by now. Litchfield's a molehill. Someone would know who he was. On the other hand, Dallas is a mountain. People don't even know their next-door neighbors."

Phillips gave a slow nod. "Not a bad theory."

"Not bad?" she shot at him. "You got a better one? Would you rather go back to believing it was a random act of violence? Does the idea of a paid hit on a Special Ed student sound too cold?"

Phillips threw up his hands. "Hey, I didn't say I didn't buy it. Anything goes these days, right? Too cold? Nah. More like it freezes my ass off. Life doesn't have value anymore, not even a baby's." He scrunched up his face. "People dump their newborns in trashbins, throw 'em off bridges, bury 'em in the backyard. Look at that pro ball player from Carolina who shot his own girlfriend in a drive-by when he found out she had his bun in her oven. He was already paying child support for one mistake, right? Why dole out more green for a second kid he didn't want?"

He tugged at his shirt collar, turning red from the neck up. Maggie wondered how high his blood pressure was about now, and she'd bet the numbers weren't good.

"Christ." He shook his head, his tone bitter. "If that kinda thing can hit the national news any day of the week, why wouldn't I believe some schmuck from Litchfield had a hired gun make sure Pauletta never gave birth?"

Maggie stared at him. "So you're with me on this one?"

"Hell, yes." He snorted. "Christ, I'm telling you that I don't think it's far-fetched to assume a mentally disabled 16-year-old was executed because she was pregnant. And I'm not real proud of the fact that it's so easy to digest. In fact, it's damned scary. Next thing we'll hear is some five-year-old's shot up his kindergarten class for their cartoon trading cards."

"Not funny," she said, poking his shin with a loafer.

"I'm telling you, it'd be safer just to teach 'em in preschool how to bet on the horses than let 'em spend their allowance on..."

Her phone buzzed before he'd finished. Her extension light blinked red.

She snapped up the receiver.

"Ryan," she said.

"You're on, Detective. I'll put the call through, and we'll trace it again," Susie told her, sounding nervous, and Maggie waited, listening to the clicks that followed, expecting a voice.

Instead, there was dead air.

"This is Detective Ryan," she spoke clearly into the receiver, worried that somehow the caller had been disconnected or gotten scared and hung up. "Hello? Anyone there?"

Phillips came off the corner of her desk, hovering above her like a shadow.

Then a soft voice said, "I need to talk to you, Detective."

"You called earlier, right?" she asked, just to reassure herself. She could barely breathe. "You saw my name in the paper?"

"Yes."

The hair on her neck prickled. "You said you knew something about the shooting? Did you recognize the gunman from the composite?"

There was no answer.

"Hello? Are you still there?"

"Yes."

"Do you know something? Can you help us out?"

She had to strain to hear the whisper.

"I know who killed her."

Chapter Twenty-Three

Maggie's heart stopped mid-beat. "You know the gunman?"

"Yes."

"Why'd he do it?"

"Someone paid him."

"Who?"

"Not on the phone. I have something to show you."

"Give me names."

"Are you taping this?"

"Can I meet you somewhere?" Maggie asked, sensing she was losing him.

"I'll let you know," she heard, then it was over that quickly.

When she put the phone down, her hand was trembling so that she had to cover it with the other to keep it still.

Phillips shook her shoulder. "What the hell did he say? What's going on? Shit, Ryan, spit it out before I wet my pants."

She looked up at him, meeting his eyes as she told him, "The caller knows the shooter and said he was paid to kill Pauletta."

John put his hands on his head, his mouth open. "Christ Almighty." He pounded a fist on her desk. "It's like we thought. A hired hit. The son of a bitch. Well, what're you waiting for? Give me what you got so we can get moving on this. What's his name for starters? Where can we pick him up?"

Maggie hated to knock the wind out of his sails. "I don't have any names yet."

"Huh?"

"The caller was scared, John. Really scared. He wants to meet in person."

"When?"

"I don't know," she admitted, not liking it any better than he did.

The flush in his cheeks faded. "You don't know?"

"We didn't exactly set anything up."

"What the hell's going on, Ryan?"

"He said he'd let me know."

"Let you know?" Phillips barked and stared at her as if she should've been wearing a straight jacket. "That's all he said?"

"He has something to give me," she explained, "but he wouldn't say what that was either."

"Ryan." He shook his head. "I don't like it. It ain't kosher..."

Her extension buzzed. It was Susie, telling her they'd gotten the call on tape and traced it to a phone booth on South Hampton.

"The call came from the city."

"I don't like it," Phillips kept repeating. "I don't like it at all."

"It's out of my hands," she told him, not feeling any better about the situation, but knowing she didn't have a choice. She wanted the information on Pauletta's killer, and she'd take it any way it came.

"He wants you alone."

"Like I said, he's scared."

Phillips didn't seem at all reassured.

"I can handle it." She summoned up a smile, one he did not return. "When I know when and where he wants to do a face-to-face, you can wire me. I'll aim for somewhere public. It'll work out fine, you'll see. Trust me on this one."

"It's not you that I don't trust," he muttered.

She pushed her chair back, away from him and got up on her feet. She pulled her jacket off its back and shrugged into the sleeves.

Overkill

"Let's talk about this later, all right?" She grabbed her purse out of her bottom drawer. "I've got to go."

"Where?"

"To see Candy Thomas."

He caught her by the arm. "I'm coming with you."

"No."

"No?"

She patted his hand. "Not this time, okay? You'd only get in the way. I need to appeal to Candy's maternal side, talk to her woman to woman."

That did the trick.

He let her go.

"Maybe you could head over to the high school and interview Pauletta's teacher. See if she agrees with Matthew Prentice about Pauletta having nothing to fear from any of her classmates there." She picked up the Snickers he'd brought her and peeled down the wrapper. She took a bite, telling him as she chewed, "Oh, and page me when you see any sign of her medical records or the ballistics report on Brad Thomas' gun."

He didn't seem any too happy, but managed to nod.

"I'll check in with you later," she said, walking away while she still had the chance, before he changed his mind and decided to follow.

He called after her, "You watch your back, partner."

She waved at him over her shoulder.

A thin layer of clouds scudded across the blue, partially blocking out the sun. The wind was picking up, an icy edge to it, plucking yellowed leaves from trees and tossing them about.

Was a cold front pushing through?

She hadn't kept up with the weather reports. It had been the last thing on her mind the past few days.

I know who killed her.

The caller's words kept rolling around in her head. Was it a lie? A way to throw them off track? Was she putting herself at risk, like Phillips had suggested? Was it some kind of trick? Was this caller playing games with them?

Didn't she owe it to Pauletta to find out?

Besides, she believed it. For some damned reason, she didn't think it was a scam.

She had to trust her gut. Phillips always told her that. And her instincts were saying it was no gag. The caller had sounded afraid, scared to talk above a whisper. And no mention of reward money had come up. Not this time, not the time before, according to Susie.

Hell, whoever it was had been so careful. Finding her name in the paper. Wanting only to speak with her. Calling twice from different pay phones, one on West Jefferson and another on South Hampton.

Both were in South Dallas. In fact, they intersected.

Something about the streets nagged at her.

What was it that she wasn't seeing?

A fat leaf blew straight at her windshield, splatting flat against the glass, and she blinked, startled, afraid at first she'd hit a bird.

She ran her wipers, knocking if off.

You're too damned jumpy, she told herself. *Take a deep breath and chill.*

Yeah, right.

Maybe when this case was put to bed.

Two vehicles were parked in front of the Thomas house, one a van from a glass company and the other a white Toyota.

At least she didn't see a red Porsche.

Maggie pulled her Mazda behind the Camry and cut the engine. Glancing into the rearview mirror, she brushed the dark waves off her forehead and silently went over what she would say to Pauletta's mother.

She headed up the front walk, noting how peaceful the house seemed this afternoon. No terrified screams or gunshots or red and blue strobes. She guessed the glass man was at work around back. She could see that the front doorframe had been repaired already. Maggie had no doubt Dave

Overkill

Gray had made sure of that. Maybe money couldn't buy love, but it could sure as hell get you at the top of the list when you needed a plumber or a new kidney.

She pressed the bell and waited, hands shoved into her jacket pockets, fingers crossed that the white Toyota in front didn't belong to one of Gray's lawyers, though she somehow doubted it.

The lock clicked open, the door parting as far as a chain would allow it.

Narrowed blue eyes peered at her. Or rather, one eye, a nose and a slice of mouth.

"Yes?"

"I need to talk to Mrs. Thomas," she said. "I'm Detective Ryan from the Litchfield Police. It's about her daughter."

"Just a minute."

The door shut, and Maggie felt the candy bar she'd scarfed down in lieu of lunch do a cha-cha in her stomach. She hoped like hell the woman hadn't been instructed not to let her in. She needed to talk to Candy alone, not under the watchful eyes of Dave Gray and his lawyers.

She heard a rustling, and then the door again came open, this time minus the chain.

"Come inside, Detective."

Her knees nearly buckled with relief. "Thank you."

"I'm Jeri Berkley, Candy's sister," the woman explained as she led Maggie toward the living room from the foyer. "I drove down from Little Rock as soon as I heard. Candy doesn't have anyone else."

She has Gray, Maggie wanted to correct, but said instead, "I'm sure she's glad to have you here."

"It's a terrible thing, isn't it? You don't hear of things like this happening in Little Rock."

"We don't normally have things like this happen in Litchfield either," Maggie replied, but Jeri Berkley didn't seem to be listening.

She was walking toward the floral sofa, toward the woman who sat upon it. Dozens of photographs littered the coffee table.

"How're you making out, Sissy?" Jeri asked draping an arm around

197

Candy's shoulder. "Have you picked out the photo you want to use tomorrow."

"I can't do it," Candy moaned, shaking her head. "I can't."

"Hush, sweetie," Jeri cooed, drawing Candy's head against her hip and petting her pale hair. "Maybe you should take a break for a bit, how's that sound? There's someone here who needs to talk to you besides. Detective Ryan."

Candy pulled away from her sister and turned her head to spot Maggie standing in the doorway. Her mouth fell open, but not a sound emerged.

"I'll go check on the repairman," Jeri said and smiled sadly at Maggie. "If you need me, give a holler."

Then she left the room.

Maggie took a few steps further inside.

"What are you doing here?"

Candy stared at her, and Maggie was startled by her appearance. She wore no makeup, not a lick. Her skin was ashy and drawn. Only a sliver of eyebrow curved above each undressed blue orb, her lashes invisible around them. The effect was stark and revealing. There was a vulnerability to Candy now, a nakedness. She was the grieving mother who had no reason to pretend anymore. One who maybe even felt a little guilty.

"I shouldn't be talking to you, not without someone here," she said, sounding more nervous than angry. "Dave wants everything to go through the lawyers."

"Please, Mrs. Thomas." Lawyers were exactly what she wanted to avoid. "Just give me a few minutes, then I'll go."

Candy raised her hands to her face, palms together, as if in prayer.She closed her eyes for a moment, inhaling deeply, then slowly opened them. Her fingertips touched her chin.

"Her funeral's tomorrow morning," she said bluntly. "The judge is letting Brad come, did you know that?"

Maggie shook her head. But she was glad to hear it. No matter what he'd done, what kind of person he was. He was Pauletta's father. He should be there.

Overkill

"Have you thought about dropping the charges against him?" she dared to ask, then wished she hadn't.

Candy blanched. "He held a gun to my head in my own home and nearly shot me."

"He wasn't himself," Maggie said cautiously, remembering all too well what she'd seen that night. "He lost you, then he lost his daughter. He was out of his mind."

"Well, he should have thought about that before he broke in here and threatened me."

Maggie winced, wishing she'd kept her mouth shut.

Candy's hands dropped to her lap and fiddled with the hem of her shirt, a blue button-down that looked man-size. One her husband had left behind? Or one of Gray's? Either way, she was swallowed up in it. "I don't imagine you came here to talk about Brad. So, please, sit down, Detective Ryan, and let's get this over with."

Maggie settled into a side chair, slipping her bag to the floor. Her gaze fell on all the photos of Pauletta spread out on the table just beyond her knees.

It was as if Pauletta were watching them, listening. Maggie's mouth went dry.

Oh, hell. There wasn't any easy way to ask what she needed to ask.

"Mrs. Thomas, do you have any idea if Pauletta was seeing someone before she died?"

Candy avoided her eyes, fiddling with the photographs. "Pauletta wasn't dating, if that's what you're asking. She had friends at school, of course, but no one special. And our neighbors are mostly retired folks or families with younger children, so she didn't have anyone around to play with."

"She'd never brought a boy home to meet you?"

"No."

"Was she alone in the house after school, before you returned from work?"

"Pauletta knew the routine, Detective. She had a house key with her at all times. She let herself in, then phoned me at Cybercytes. She might've called later some days than others, but she always called. It was the one thing she seemed able to remember. She stayed late at school on Wednesdays for The Eagle Club, which was Dr. Candor's way to get the kids to socialize outside the classroom," she explained. "But the bus always brought her home afterward."

Okay, this wasn't going anywhere. Maggie took a deep breath and asked point-blank, "If your daughter had no social life outside the school, Mrs. Thomas, then who was the father of Pauletta's unborn baby?"

Candy looked as if she'd been slapped.

"The autopsy confirmed that your daughter was pregnant. It's in the preliminary report, though the information hasn't been made public yet. She was about 10 weeks along. You did know, didn't you?"

"I can't talk about this," Candy murmured. "Please don't make me talk about it."

Maggie edged forward in her seat, trying not to raise her voice. "Mrs. Thomas, you have to. We think it's the reason your daughter was killed."

"No." The blond head shook violently. "No, I won't believe that."

"We've subpoenaed Pauletta's medical records," Maggie informed her, knowing she couldn't back off even if she'd wanted to. "We've spoken with Dr. Abley and we'll get his records from the school as well. If there's anything in there...like the name of the man...we'll find it. It can't remain a secret anymore."

Blue eyes widened, terrified. Slender shoulders shook. "That's not right. Those sessions are private. Anything Pauletta said to the doctor is confidential."

"Your daughter is dead."

"Do you think I've forgotten that? I lay down on her bed last night and cried myself to sleep, knowing she'd never be back, that I'd never see her smile again except in a picture." With that, she grabbed a fistful of photographs from the coffee table and held them up, shaking them in the air. "This is all I have left, Detective. All I have of my baby."

"Then help me," Maggie urged. "Stop hiding the truth, whatever it is. Whoever you're trying to protect isn't worth it. Someone arranged for

Pauletta's murder, Mrs. Thomas. Don't think you're helping him by lying to us."

"Arranged for her murder?"

"Yes."

Candy opened her hands, and the photographs drifted down, one sailing to the floor near Maggie's feet.

"You think I'm lying to protect Pauletta's killer? You think I know who shot my child? How dare you..."

Maggie interrupted her righteous indignation. "I believe you know more than you've told us."

"For God's sake, I would have told you if I'd known anything more. I would have told you."

Maggie fought not to let the stricken face get to her. This woman was playing games, side-stepping unpleasantries like they were dog doo on her front lawn, and she was losing her patience.

"I don't think you understand the reality of keeping secrets from the police, especially when they could lead us to your daughter's killer."

"I'm burying her tomorrow," Candy snapped back, wiping snot from her upper lip, "how much more real does it get?"

Maggie didn't flinch. "Who's the father?"

Candy shook her head. "I can't tell you that."

"Can't or won't?"

She didn't answer.

"What was the nature of Pauletta's relationship with Dave Gray?" Maggie bluntly asked. The thought had preoccupied her ever since she'd learned Pauletta was pregnant. Had Candy's "man friend" been the one to take advantage of the girl? Had he established her trust, encouraged her affections when her mother was not around, then tried to send her away when he realized the consequences?

Maggie certainly had no reason to trust him any more than she trusted Candy.

"Pauletta was two and a half months pregnant," she continued when Candy said nothing. "Your husband moved out of this house three months ago, and Gray was suddenly in like Flynn, advising you about how to keep your husband at a distance. According to Brad, he was even telling you how to deal with your daughter, suggesting that you board her at a group facility out of state. Three months ago this all started up. It fits the time frame..."

"Stop it," Candy said sharply. Her chin quivered. In fact, her whole body shuddered.

"Did Dave Gray have sex with your daughter?" Maggie pressed, long past worried about being indelicate. "Maybe it happened only once and he knew it was a mistake, but, by then, it was too late."

"Get out, Detective," Candy hissed. "Get out of my house and don't come back."

Like hell she was leaving now.

"Is Dave Gray the father, Mrs. Thomas?" she repeated yet again, frustration making her eyelid twitch. "Pauletta may have been able to name dinosaurs you've never heard of, but she had no street smarts, no common sense. She couldn't discern the difference between right and wrong, between sex and love."

"No more, please." Candy was holding her hands over her ears, her fingers trembling so badly she couldn't keep them in place.

But Maggie wasn't finished. "Did Gray get her pregnant and then panic? Is that why he's taken such an interest in her murder, even offered the reward, because he's so sure he won't get caught?"

"Stop it, I said."

"Why the hell are you protecting him? If he's involved, you have to tell us. You owe it to Pauletta, if nothing else."

"He didn't do anything!" She came off the sofa, raising clenched fists. "He didn't touch Pauletta, not that way. I know he didn't."

"So they weren't ever alone?"

"I trusted him with her!"

Maggie glanced around her, at the floral print sofa and drapes, the framed reproduction oils, the television and wall-to-wall carpeting. Even potted plants without yellow leaves. It was Barbie's dreamhouse in middle class suburbia. Picture perfect. Only she knew better. Things were rarely as they seemed.

"I know Dave. He wouldn't have hurt Pauletta, not in any way. Not intentionally. They got along well at first, and then maybe"—Candy bit her lip—"maybe he lost his temper a time or two. He'd tell her to fetch something from the kitchen, and she'd come back without it. She'd forgotten what he'd sent her off to do. I tried to explain to him that it was part of the Williams'. He did try. But he was used to people doing what he wanted, and sometimes Pauletta didn't understand. They did spend time alone, but he wouldn't have taken advantage of her. I trusted him with her life. With my own."

For an instant, Maggie felt as if she were looking at Momma, at pale eyes without guile, blinded by trust; at the willingness to stand by her man no matter the cost. It was so easy to turn away from what was ugly and pretend it didn't exist. Only somebody had to take responsibility. Someone had to take the blame for this.

Anger surged through her, blasting through each limb until she couldn't contain it.

She banged her shin as she stepped around the coffee table to take Candy by the arm. "Jesus, don't you get it? If he's guilty and you protect him, you're an accomplice after the fact in your own daughter's murder."

Candy's eyes flickered, frightened as a doe. Tears pooled above her pale lashes, one after another, then coursed down her bare cheeks and dropped onto blue cotton. She was breathing hard, shivering, and Maggie feared she'd gone too far.

She felt suddenly sick to her stomach.

With a sigh, she let Candy go and walked away, picking up her bag from the floor. "If he's the father, we'll find out, you know. We'll get a court order for a blood draw. And if his DNA matches the fetus, then I'll know you were lying. I'll come after you, too."

She started to walk away, but only got as far as the open arch into the living room.

"Wait."

Maggie stopped.

"It wasn't Dave," Candy said, sotto voice. "I don't know who it was...who the father was. Pauletta wouldn't say. She'd never kept a secret from me before. I wasn't even sure that she knew how. But she kept this one locked up tight. When we learned about the baby, she said she told him and he would marry her. It was like she was repeating his words back to me, his reassurances. She couldn't have come up with them herself."

Maggie turned around.

Candy had picked up a photograph and was cradling it against her breasts. Her cheeks glistened wet.

"When did you know for sure?"

"About two weeks ago when I took her for a check up. She wasn't feeling well. She'd been nauseous, had some diarrhea, which happened now and again. They took her blood and urine. They had the lab run a whole slew of tests, and one of them came back positive. The pregnancy test." Her chin fell, and she closed her eyes, moaning loudly. "Oh, God, I didn't know what to do. I never imagined she'd been involved with someone that way."

"She was nearly seventeen."

"But she wasn't like other teenagers."

"She was a human being," Maggie reminded her. "She had feelings and needs."

Candy rubbed a sleeve against her eyes. "I wanted her to have an abortion before it was too late, but Pauletta was dead set against it. She was dead-set on keeping this baby. I knew she didn't understand, that she imagined it like playing with dolls. But she seemed so happy about it. Truly happy."

"Her teacher mentioned how close you were," Maggie told her. "He said she wanted to be a mother, too."

"Oh, God...oh, God." The tears started up again, though they'd never really stopped.

"No one at school admits to seeing her with a boy there. And Prentice denies she had anything going on with a high school student."

"I don't know who it was," Candy insisted. "I don't know who he might have been. But it wasn't Dave. I swear it wasn't Dave."

Overkill

Maggie sighed. This woman would have made Tammy Wynette proud as all get out. "Like I told you already, a simple blood draw will tell the tale."

"That won't be necessary." Candy avoided her eyes, her chin falling. As she talked, she stared down at the hands in her lap. "Dave had prostate cancer several years ago, Detective. They saved him with surgery, but they made a mess of his sex life. Even Viagra can't do the trick. He couldn't have made Pauletta or any other woman pregnant. And if you don't take my word for it, you can always subpoena his medical files, can't you?" She slowly lifted her head, eyes hard as pebbles. "Now will you go away and let me alone to grieve?"

Dave Gray was impotent?

Maggie didn't know what to say.

Jeri took that moment to pop back into the room. "Is everything all right? I could hear you all the way back to the kitchen. What's going on?"

"Detective Ryan was just leaving."

Maggie fumbled for words, but could only come up with, "Forgive me."

Candy turned away.

She heard their voices rise behind her back as she headed to the door and let herself out.

A rush of freezing wind blew out of nowhere, whipping the fallen leaves upon the grass into a frantic dance as she hurried to her Mazda.

When she shut herself inside, she was trembling. Her fingers fumbled with her keys.

She could hardly function.

Could only think of one thing.

Gray was impotent.

In three words, Candy Thomas had just toppled the delicate house of cards Maggie had constructed.

She started her car, cursing herself for seeing what she'd wanted to see, blaming the man she most wanted to blame.

It would've been so easy for her to lock up Dave Gray and throw away the key.

Chapter Twenty-Four

She kept driving, not really thinking about where she was going, just knowing she couldn't go back to the station, not yet.

Frustration gripped her fiercely, squeezing her chest so that it hurt to inhale deeply. Maybe she was having a heart attack. Maybe Phillips wasn't the only one who should be worried about blood pressure.

So it wasn't Gray, she told herself. Deal with it and move on. Going out on a limb was part of the job. Sometimes you had to circumvent a few roadblocks before you could get where you were going.

But if Dave Gray wasn't the one, who was?

She had to focus on that, not on what might have been.

Her gut told her Pauletta's lover was an older man, someone who had a certain power over her, who had the opportunity to be with her alone, who had convinced her imperfect brain there was a future together when there never had been.

She wasn't wrong about that. It was the only scenario that made sense. Even Phillips agreed with her there.

If only Candy had been straight with them sooner. They could've eliminated Gray if they'd known he was impotent. It was a no-brainer.

Gray was a jerk, a pompous egotist who controlled the people around him like puppets.

But she couldn't blame him for what had happened to Pauletta.

C'mon, Pauletta. Give me a sign. Something.

Overkill

She wrapped her fingers hard around the steering wheel. Her foot pressed down more heavily on the gas. As if the car could take her mind in the right direction if only she drove faster.

Okay, so start from the beginning.

What did she know?

She was sure now that Brad Thomas had not been lying. Gray had indeed wanted Pauletta out of the way. He may have tried to get Candy to send her off to some facility in Minnesota, but he hadn't killed her.

So where did that leave things?

Who'd spent time with Pauletta? Who had inspired her confidence, her love?

Francis Abley?

Certainly Pauletta would have trusted him. Maybe she saw him as a protector or father figure.

But sex?

Maggie made a noise of disgust. She couldn't begin to picture Pauletta doing it with that Santa Claus clone. That didn't mean it wasn't possible, unless Abley was a member of the Erectile Dysfunction Club, along with Dave Gray and Bob Dole.

What about Matthew Prentice?

The melancholic face slipped into her head, and Maggie frowned, not liking that image any better. Pauletta's teacher had clearly been distraught at her death. He'd worked closely with Pauletta since she'd enrolled at the Litchfield Special School, admitted she was special to him.

Maggie had seen his agonized expression, the way he stared off into space when he talked about the girl.

Could he have done such a thing? Could he have betrayed her so cruelly?

She didn't want to believe it.

Headlights from behind struck her rearview, blinding her for an instant, until the vehicle changed lanes and the burst of white disappeared.

From up ahead, the reflectors on the overhead signs glinted at her, the tiny winks urging her toward the path to take.

She cruised into the city limits, heading for the North Dallas Tollway. She took it south; her gaze fixed on the patches of gray pavement, on the white lines her headlamps unveiled. She listened to the hum of her engine shifting gears, to the gentle whump of her tires turning round and round, to the steady thump of her heart in her ears.

She retraced the drive she'd taken two mornings before, the tollway exit to Wycliff Boulevard and then to Harry Hines.

To Parkland Hospital.

To Momma.

Guilt drove her there.

That and avoidance.

She parked at the first space she could find in the lot across from the main building and crossed the street at a jog.

She blinked against the overbrightness of the interior lights as she entered, the fluorescence making faces she passed look harsh and tired and older than their years.

A nurse in scrubs was coming out of Momma's room in ICU, and she smiled at Maggie. She looked familiar, but Maggie couldn't remember her name. She tried to glance at the tag at her breast without seeming obvious, but the woman was apparently aware of what she was doing and fingered the plastic strip, holding it at a tilt so Maggie could better read it.

Brenda Harris, R.N.

"Your mother's off the respirator as of an hour ago," she said brightly.

"Which means what?"

"She can breathe on her own."

"Can she go home soon?" Maggie felt a rising tide of panic. She wasn't ready for that. Wasn't near ready.

"Oh, no, I doubt it." The round face puckered. "She has a long road ahead of her. With the head injury and the Alzheimer's, it's not going to be easy."

Easy? When had things ever been easy with Momma?

Maggie steadied herself, put her emotions in neutral. She unplugged herself like Momma from the ventilator. "Can I see her?"

Overkill

"For a few minutes, sure."

"Is Delores around?"

"Mrs. Oliver?" Nurse Brenda's expression softened. "She went home for awhile. Poor thing. She's been here day and night ever since Vi was brought in. I told her to get some sleep and come back in the morning."

In the morning?

But she needed to talk to Delores now.

Maggie nearly turned around and left.

She's your mother, a voice nagged at her. No matter what she's done, she's that. Go sit with her a minute, hold her hand.

Can't you forgive her now? When she's like this? When she can't even answer your questions? Can't tell you the truth? Can't say she didn't know?

Dammit.

She walked into the room with its curtained dividers. The blinking lights and buttons and eery green numbers flashed at her from behind Momma's bed. Though this time there was no loud hiss and pump of the respirator, just the noise of other voices, the vague hum of machines, and the movement upon the white sheets.

Momma's fingers twitched.

The jerks were spasmodic. Without rhyme or reason.

Was that some kind of reflex? Or was Momma trying to gesture?

Maggie went slowly to the bed and stood there, hands curled around the metal bar.

"Momma?" she said. "It's Maggie. Can you hear me?"

The eyelids fluttered, but did not come open.

A soft moan filtered through chapped lips.

"It's Maggie, Momma," she repeated. "How're you feeling? The nurse said you're doing better."

The withered face stayed still as stone.

Momma might be breathing on her own, but that's about all she seemed able to do.

She has a long road ahead of her.

Maggie stared at the fragile-looking woman lying in the bed with IVs running into her arms, tubes in her nose, her skin purpled with bruises, mottled with age spots. Her neck was patched with gauze and tape.

When she was a kid, she'd thought Momma would be young forever, that she'd never grow old.

She saw that woman suddenly, the one from long ago. A made-up face in the mirror, painted to perfection. Red lips. Rouged cheeks. Hair as glossy as new kitchen linoleum. Never mind the creases at her eyes, the slight sag beneath the chin. Suddenly he came up behind her, nuzzling her neck, making her laugh. And Maggie stood paralyzed in the doorway, just watching, fascinated by the sight. Revolted by it. Because she knew it was all lies, even then.

"Your mama's the prettiest woman in Dallas and I'm the luckiest man. Ain't that right, Magpie?"

She shivered.

Jesus.

She shouldn't be here, shouldn't have come at all. It just added to the pretense, didn't it?

Sometimes, the charade was easier than others. Tonight it was too hard.

I'm sorry, Delores.

"I've gotta go, Momma, but I'll try to get back some time when you feel more like visiting."

Momma's left hand twitched again.

But Maggie didn't touch it.

She just got the hell out.

She took the stairs down, pushed out the lobby doors, ran to the parking lot and crawled into her Mazda.

She drove south instead of north. Further into the city instead of toward home.

Past the downtown lights, the skyscrapers that reached for the moon, the glow of Reunion Arena.

Past run-down buildings, litter blowing across cracked concrete, empty lots, mesh metal fences.

Past gas stations, fried chicken joints and Mexican buffets.

Overkill

Past Lamar and Industrial.

Onto West Davis, then to South Hampton and finally left on West Jefferson.

Less than five miles from Parkland.

We traced the call to a public phone on West Jefferson.

The second call had come from a public phone on South Hampton.

Her foot hit the brakes, and she pulled the car over to the shoulder.

Dear God.

It was right there in front of her.

On West Jefferson just beyond where it intersected with South Hampton.

Sunset High School.

That's what had been gnawing at her. That's why the streets had tugged at something in her brain.

Her old days on the south city beat.

Tough neighborhood.

Tough kids.

Was her anonymous caller a student?

Was their killer?

What was the connection between this place and Litchfield? Between a high school in South Dallas and a school bus shooting on Elm at Fifth in a far north suburb?

The killer lived around here.

Her beeper went off, and she started at the interruption.

She looked at the backlit number.

Phillips.

It was dark out, pitch black, and her heart was pounding in her ears.

She radioed into the station that she was on her way back. She wondered what her partner had found out at Litchfield High, wondered if any medical records had come across their desks and what they'd prove.

But most of all she wondered about the connection between Pauletta Thomas, her murderer and Sunset High School.

Chapter Twenty-Five

She stayed at the station with Phillips until almost midnight. Her partner had taken a call from the county lab while she'd been gone. Ballistics could not match Brad Thomas' Colt. 45 with the evidence found at the crime scene.

His gun had not killed Pauletta.

Maggie had known all along that he hadn't been involved with his daughter's murder.

A few of Pauletta's doctors had already messengered over her records, everything from pediatric vaccinations to gastroenterological studies diagnosing problems with her digestive tract. There were cardiology reports, detailed blood pressure monitorings and endless listings of current and past medications.

A visit with the gynecologist around the first of October listed a slew of laboratory results, including the one that mattered most: the positive level of chorionic gonadotropin. Or, as Phillips so archaically put it, the rabbit had gone paws up.

There was a handwritten note about doing an ultrasound, but Maggie could find nothing indicating whether it had been performed. Candy Thomas hadn't mentioned it, and she wondered if the doctor had intended to schedule it on her next visit. A prescription had been written for prenatal vitamins.

"I wanted her to have an abortion before it was too late, but Pauletta was dead set against it."

Overkill

Pauletta had wanted the baby.

It seemed more clear now than ever to Maggie that her lover had not.

Maggie had gone over the scenario in her head a million times already. There was no other motive. Nothing they could come up with but Pauletta's pregnancy. No other reason for her death.

They still waited for Francis Abley's notes. She had to believe his records would provide clues to the identity of Pauletta's lover, especially now that her theory about Dave Gray had been shot down.

If there was a chance Pauletta had mentioned the name of the father during her sessions with Dr. Abley...my God, they'd be an inch away from closing the case.

Unless Abley himself was involved.

It wasn't unheard of after all; a therapist getting emotionally entangled with a patient and crossing the line physically as well.

Phillips gave her a funny look. "What're you thinking now?"

"That maybe Abley put us off because he's scared for himself."

John drew back. "You think he dipped his ladle in her well?"

"It would explain his complete reluctance to cooperate."

"Whoa." Her partner expelled a slow breath. "If he screwed the kid, I doubt he jotted that down in his notes."

"We've got fetal DNA," she reminded him. "We can request a voluntary blood draw."

"And Abley's probably got his lawyers on-call already. If we don't have some evidence that it was him, they're not gonna let us waltz in and take a pint."

Maggie hated when he was right.

Jesus, but this case was like riding a roller coaster. Every upturn seemed to go nowhere but down.

They needed proof. Something solid. More than just an educated guess, a supposition.

She changed the subject. "So the remedial English teacher at the high school confirmed what Prentice told me, that Pauletta wasn't having problems with any students or faculty there?"

"Nope. Mrs. Evers said Pauletta was a happy kid, positively glowing."

"Glowing, huh? Well, you know what they say about pregnant women."

"Yeah, their feet swell, they need the air conditioner turned up full blast, they cry at the drop of a hat, and they blame it all on men."

Maggie swatted at him.

"Look, Evers confirmed that Prentice went everywhere with Pauletta, even walked her to the little girls' room when she had to go. No one would've had a chance to stalk her or threaten her life, 'cuz this guy stuck to her like toilet paper on her shoe."

"It was his job to see that she mainstreamed smoothly. I got the impression he loved his students like they were his own kids." She tapped a pen against her chin. "Teaching isn't just his occupation."

"It's his obsession," Phillips remarked.

Maggie shifted in her chair. "Are you implying something?" The butterflies took off in her stomach. Phillips was going right to the place she'd been avoiding.

He looked hard at her. "Should I be?"

"You think Matthew Prentice had sex with Pauletta?"

"Hey, I'm just trying to cover all the angles."

Maggie didn't say anything. Matthew Prentice was one of the good guys, wasn't he? A man who'd devoted his life to working with children whose futures were limited; kids who likely would never go on to college, who'd be lucky if they could find a job and a little independence.

"You can't tell me you haven't considered the idea?" Phillips asked.

No, she couldn't tell him that. Prentice had certainly spent plenty of time with Pauletta. Her gut just told her it was all wrong. He had loved the girl, Maggie had seen that in his eyes. The thought that Prentice had betrayed Pauletta in the most brutal way possible seemed incomprehensible even to her. And she knew brutal firsthand.

She dropped her pen on the desk and rubbed at her temples. "Can we not talk about this tonight? There's nothing we can do at this hour besides."

"You got a thing for the guy or something?"

Overkill

Maggie glared at him. "No, I don't have a thing for Matthew Prentice. I just don't happen to think he had anything to do with Pauletta's death," she asserted, though she didn't feel too sure of anything at the moment. She'd had enough disappointment for one day, and she was ready to pack it in. "Hey, isn't it way past your bedtime?"

With a noisy shuffle, Phillips put aside the copies of the records they'd both gone through twice already. He glanced down at his Timex. "Christ, you're right. Time flies when you're having fun, huh? The wife was gonna keep something warm for me, but I have a feeling everything's already gone cold by now and I mean everything, if you get my drift."

If he'd spelled it out any more clearly, Maggie would've felt obliged to blush.

"Go ahead. Take off," she said.

"What about you?"

"I'm not spending the night if that's what you're afraid of."

"Good." He nudged the papers into a fairly orderly pile, then shoved them into his top drawer. "I didn't want to have to drag you home by the hair. If you go willingly, you'll save me the hassle."

"Does your wife know she married a caveman?"

"Who d'you think polishes my club and takes my fur suit to the cleaners?"

"Jesus, John," she groaned and pushed back the chair she'd pulled up to his desk. She stood slowly and arched her back, trying to work out the kinks in her muscles.

Her legs wobbled beneath her, and her head dully ached. Every nerve was raw. She felt strung out and wired, exhausted and anxious.

"You need a ride?" Phillips said.

"I've got my car," Maggie told him over her shoulder as she headed to her own desk and grabbed her jacket off the back of her chair.

"You sure you'll be okay?"

"Yeah."

She flattened the leather collar and tugged at the cuffs. Phillips was watching her with that look in his eyes.

"Promise you won't be taking any detours?" There it was, that Father Knows Best tone of voice, low and brimming with concern. Mahoney was right. Her partner worried about her. And she had a good guess what was uppermost on his mind.

"I'm going straight home," she assured him. "I have no plans to rendezvous with anonymous callers in dark alleys tonight. Girl Scout's honor."

"Were you really a Scout?"

"I was a Brownie for two weeks." She'd been kicked out for using a pair of pinking shears to cut off the braids of a girl who'd teased her about her secondhand uniform.

"You're not pulling this old man's leg just so I'll have sweet dreams?"

"I wouldn't pull your leg, John," she said and added with a straight face, "I might aggravate your bum knees and then you'd have to roll around on a walker."

"Smart ass."

"Old fart."

He blew her a kiss before he took off.

Maggie hung back, smiling to herself, breathing slowly, oddly calm.

The bay was quiet. That shift's patrols were already on the street, and, despite the reward offer, the phones had died down in the last 24 hours. The Dallas media had apparently shifted focus to a triple homicide in Garland, and most reporters had taken to calling the station house for updates instead of camping out in the parking lot with microphones and ready-cams.

Maggie was thankful for the reprieve.

She could almost pretend things were back to normal if she hadn't known better.

She could almost imagine the toughest case on her desk was the mayor's missing lawn jockey.

Almost.

She sensed the momentary calm was like the eye of a hurricane: deceptively placid before another wave of violence.

The clock on the wall read 12:15.

She sighed wearily.

Overkill

The effects of the caffeine from chain-Coking had been flushed from her system with her last potty break.

Phillips was right. It was time to head home.

She collected her bag from her bottom desk drawer and called it a night.

Chapter Twenty-Six

The lake appeared black in the darkness. Clouds veiled the moon so not a beam glinted off the glassy surface.

The lights in the center fountain that normally illuminated the water after dark had been shut off hours before. Country Club Acres had tucked itself in for the night. The code of conduct provided each new year to tenants and owners strongly advised that, once the big hand struck twelve and the little hand ten, large appliances were not to be run, stereos were to play quietly if at all, and slamming of doors was to be kept to a minimum.

Curfew for grown-ups.

The orangish glow from the widely-spaced street lamps brightened select pockets: a clump of landscaped shrubs here, a bit of parking lot there, a slice of the nature trail where a lone jogger pumped along with reflective shoes and vest.

Another woman burning the midnight oil.

Up ahead, a small figure clad in bathrobe and slippers stared in the other direction as her leashed puppy squatted on the grass.

Maggie smiled at the tableau.

Headlights filled her rearview as another car turned into the complex and settled in behind her, and she averted her eyes to avoid the glare.

She took a right onto her street, hoping she'd get lucky and find an empty space in front of her unit. She scanned the row of cars lined up as snugly as teeth on a zipper.

Overkill

Damn.

Though tempted to double-park behind a Saab with paper plates and the Beamer anchored nearest her door—it would serve them right—she gave up and looked further down, finally sliding her Mazda between a pair of yellow lines half a block away. She locked up, then followed the sidewalk home, her steps brisk. The night air dragged its icy fingers across her cheeks.

Porch lights glowed against the pitch, though her own front door was dark.

Damned burned out bulb.

You should've had Mahoney replace it last night when he'd pointed it out, she told herself, only regretting now that she hadn't.

She held her keys close to her face, picking out the right one using touch more than sight.

A dog barked, its cry hanging on the crisp air, sad and soulful. The wind snapped at tree branches. A car door slapped shut.

Maggie pushed her key into the center of the deadbolt and twisted left until she felt it give.

Blindly, she thumbed at the doorknob for the groove in the center, then jammed the key in.

When they mass produced night vision goggles, she planned to buy herself a pair.

The knob turned in her hand, and she gave the door a push. She heard the shuffle of footsteps on the walk behind her and stiffened at the sound of her name.

"Detective Ryan?"

The voice sounded soft and uncertain, the raspiness striking a cord in Maggie's brain. Where had she heard it before?

Oh, God.

She turned her head.

Her anonymous caller stood not four feet away, face veiled in shadow, though Maggie could plainly make out the silhouette: small shoulders and slender build, short spiky hair and backpack. A too sweet smell filled her nostrils. The scent of freesia.

The tipster was a woman.

Maggie let out a held breath.

"What the hell are you doing?"

"I n-need to talk to you alone," the girl stammered. "While I've got up the nerve."

"How'd you get here?"

"I drove."

"How'd you know where I live?"

"It wasn't hard."

"Did you follow me from the station?"

The bright light in her rearview. The car had been tailing her, and she'd been too tired to realize it.

"Look, does it matter? I mean, don't you want to hear what I have to say about the girl who was killed? This is already hard enough, don't you get it? I'm taking a real chance coming here."

She glanced around her, clearly nervous. Even in the darkness, Maggie caught the glisten of wide eyes, the shift of her shoes on the concrete.

She looked scared all right.

"Can we go inside?" the girl pleaded.

"*Watch your back, partner*," Maggie could hear Phillips warn her, even though she didn't feel the least bit threatened by this waif.

She fingered her keys. "How about we go to the station," she suggested, "so I can take a formal statement..."

"No," the girl cut her off, fast as a heartbeat. "I can't do that. He'd find out, you know? Can we just go inside for a minute?" She glanced behind her at the sudden glow of headlights as a car turned onto the street. "C'mon, don't make me stand out here where anyone can see."

Maggie felt herself give in. "All right." She slipped her keys into her bag then held out her hand. "Give me your knapsack."

"For what?"

"I'll return it to you when we're done."

The girl slowly shrugged out of the straps. "You think I've got a gun or something?" she asked as she passed it over.

"You'd better not," Maggie said and gave the door a shove. It opened with a creak, and she reached inside to flip on the lights. A couple bills and a grocery store flyer littered the floor. She ignored them, motioning the girl inside.

She saw her face then clearly as she passed into the light. Cropped hair too red to be real, an earring through her eyebrow, a few pimples on her cheeks, a bruise on her neck—or was that a hickey? She wore the universal uniform of youth: a hooded sweatshirt with "GAP" emblazoned on the front, faded bluejeans with holes in the knees, and chunky black boots. Maggie guessed she wasn't more than seventeen or eighteen tops.

She closed the door behind them, locking the deadbolt, and set the knapsack on the floor.

The girl walked into the living room and stopped, looking around.

Maggie removed her holstered .38 from her handbag, unsnapped it, slipped it out and tucked it beneath her jacket in her waistband. The cold metal against her back felt reassuring, and her guest was none the wiser. She followed the girl into the living room, turning on the table lamps.

"Go ahead and take a seat."

"I'd rather stand."

Maggie folded her arms over her chest. The girl's back was to her, head tipped and spiky hair infused with fire by the soft lights. She was eyeing the countless colored spines on the shelves in front of her. "What's your name?" Maggie tried.

"Do I have to say?" The girl turned away from the wall of books. Her pointed chin quivered. "You don't understand. He'd probably kill me if he found out I was ever here. If I tell you who I am, someone'll find out, maybe even the papers or the TV news. I can't let that happen."

"Who's this guy you're so afraid of?" Maggie asked, because that's all she really wanted. The name of the shooter, his gun for a ballistics match, his ass in prison with no chance for parole. "How d'you know him?"

"He's my boyfriend."

"And he killed Pauletta Thomas?"

"Yes."

"He confessed this to you?" If she sounded a little skeptical, it's because she was. Although she was damned willing to be convinced.

"Yes." The girl toyed with the hem of her sweatshirt, seemingly unable to keep her hands still. "He bragged about getting paid two grand to off a retard on the Litchfield Special School bus. He said it wasn't really murder, since she wasn't all there, if you know what I mean."

Maggie did, and it made her cringe inside and out. "So that made it okay?"

"You gotta understand," the girl pleaded in her breathy voice so that Maggie had to concentrate to hear. "Jason's into this neo-Nazi thing, swastikas and Hitler and all that crap. He's scary sometimes. He can be violent if anything riles him up." She waved her hands dismissively. "But he wasn't always like that, not until his freshman year when his mom died. Then he fell in with these tough dudes, you know? A bunch of rednecks who went to gun shows and beat up fags. He dropped out last year. If he hadn't, he probably would've been expelled for good."

Maggie had heard similar stories a hundred times before. The state prisons were filled with guys who blamed their woes on dead mothers.

"Where'd he get the .45?"

"I shouldn't say," the girl murmured, rubbing her hands on the front of her sweatshirt.

"Is it registered?"

She scratched at her red hair. "Look, I think it's stolen. Jason and his friends...sometimes they break into people's cars, maybe a house every once in awhile. They take the electronics stuff mostly, but I know they've gotten guns, too."

Maggie stared at her. "And this doesn't bother you?"

"No, no, it's not that." The girl blushed. "But I didn't know what to do. I love him, you know? Him and me, we've been together, like, since we were eleven."

Love wasn't just blind. It was deaf and dumb to boot.

It made Maggie sick to her stomach. Gut-wrenchingly sick.

O v e r k i l l

A stolen semiautomatic weapon in the hands of a neo-Nazi high school dropout who burgled houses and beat up gays for kicks, and this girl hadn't bothered to look for help until he'd actually committed murder?

Two thousand dollars to kill a retard.

A noisy rush filled her head, an anger intermixed with impatience. She wanted to shake this girl until the dirty secret fell out all at once instead of in bits and pieces.

"What's Jason's last name?" Without it, this girl wasn't going anywhere.

"Carson," the wispy voice reluctantly volunteered.

"What's his address?" She was gritting her teeth. She couldn't help it. That or scream.

"Shit, I can't tell you that." The girl wriggled like she would piss in her pants.

"Is he Hispanic?" Maggie asked. "A light-skinned black?"

"No." The girl reached into her back pocket and pulled out a folded paper. She smoothed it open and took a few steps forward to drop it on the coffee table.

Maggie went over and picked it up.

It was a photograph.

"See," the girl said. "He's white. That description on the news doesn't look much like him either. He's got his head shaved, but you couldn't tell that if he was wearing a hat."

Maggie's eyes were glued to the face in the photograph. An unmistakably Caucasian man with a lumpy bare skull wearing Army fatigues and holding a rifle. The grin on his bulldog's face was ear to ear.

Her first impulse was to crumple it into a ball and toss it, but instead she re-folded it and slipped it into her back pocket. As she did, her fingers grazed the metal of the .38 at her waistband, and a rising fury rushed up.

Jesus, if Jason Carson were here right now, what she wouldn't do to him....

Settle down, Maggie, she told herself. Settle down, or you're going to lose this girl. You're gonna scare her off if you push too hard, understand?

223

"How about you tell me who paid Jason to kill Pauletta Thomas?" she managed to get out in a fairly level tone.

"It was an older guy, a white dude, he said."

"What's his name? Did he tell you that?"

She shook her head, biting her lip with crooked teeth.

"How did Jason find Pauletta's bus?"

"The guy told him where to be at."

"How could he be sure the bus would stop and let him on?"

"I guess the guy said it would."

"You guess? Your boyfriend climbed on a Special School bus to blow away a 16-year-old girl, and you aren't sure how he knew it was her?"

"Two s-seats behind the driver," she stammered. "He said she'd be two seats back."

"Did he want him to shoot the driver, too, or was that Jason's idea?"

"I don't know."

"Did he realize the girl he blew away was ten weeks pregnant?"

"Oh, God, no." She clasped her fingers over her belly, her mouth slack with surprise. "No, he couldn't have known that. He didn't."

Maggie felt like she was pulling teeth. "How'd this man find your boyfriend?"

"He came around to his house when his dad was at work."

"Just out of the blue?"

The girl shrugged. "Yeah, I guess."

"You guess?" She fought to keep her voice down, but it rattled nonetheless. "Did the guy just pick him out of the phone book? Did he just assume Jason of all people would do a hit for two thousand dollars? C'mon, they must've had some connection?"

"He knew Jason from his freshman year. Jason caused him some trouble." When Maggie just stared at her, she lifted empty hands. "What do you want me to do? Make up something?"

"I want the truth."

"I'm not lying."

Maggie squinted at her. "Yeah, but what aren't you telling me?"

Overkill

"There isn't any more, I swear!" The pale eyes flooded with unshed tears.

Maggie wanted to drag this girl by her ear, shove her into the car, and take her down to the station house. Throw her in the tiny interview room with its carpeted walls. Let her sit there alone for a few hours and think about what mattered. Maybe she'd get straight answers then.

"Let's do this right, okay?" She'd had enough. She reached for the telephone on the sofa table and picked up the receiver. "Let's call your parents and have them meet us at the station."

"No!" The girl violently shook her head. "No, I can't...I can't do it. I've told you enough already," she said and took off for the door.

Maggie put down the phone and went after her. She reached out and grabbed her sweatshirt.

"You can't keep me here." She was crying now, her whole body shaking.

But Maggie didn't let her go.

She forcibly turned the girl around, gripping each arm and giving a firm shake. She got in her face, hardly able to keep her anger contained. "This isn't a game, don't you get it? A girl is dead. A man is lying in the hospital with two bullet holes in his body. You owe it to them to be straight."

"What do you want from me?" She was sobbing, but Maggie was way past the point of feeling sorry for anyone besides the victims.

"Who paid your boyfriend to do the hit? Give me something more than an older white dude or you will be going with me to the station even if I have to cuff you to do it."

The girl nodded, tears splashing onto her thin cheeks. "He...he was someone from school, that's all Jason told me, I swear." Her voice sounded even smaller than before, if that were possible.

"He knew him from school?"

"Yes."

"Sunset High?" Maggie asked, and the girl's eyes went even wider. "How'd you know?"

"Your calls were traced to public phones on South Hampton and West Jefferson. Sunset's not far from where they intersect."

"You traced my calls?" Panic filled her thin face. "Are you gonna follow me when I leave? Get my license plate and track me down? Oh, fuck, you're gonna blow this whole thing. He's gonna find out." She struggled to break free of Maggie; batting at her with clenched fists. "This was a mistake...a huge mistake."

Maggie released her, and she backed away, brushing at her cheeks with a sleeve. "I've gotta go before he realizes something's wrong," she said and spun around to snatch her knapsack from the floor. She made a grab for the knob, but it wouldn't turn. Both hands yanked, but the door only rattled.

"Let me the fuck out!" she yelped, clearly panicked.

"Take it easy, okay?" Maggie walked over and unlocked the deadbolt, then pulled the door wide.

The girl darted out like a wild bird set free, running for the sidewalk.

Maggie crossed the threshold onto the tiny porch, tempted to go after her, afraid she'd disappear forever if she didn't.

She started to step down to follow her to her car and take a peek at her plates.

Headlamps from across the street flashed on, illuminating the girl at the curb and trapping her in its beams; the lights so powerful and overbright that Maggie froze where she stood, unable to move forward without stumbling from the stoop. She put a hand up to her face to shield her eyes and ducked her head. It was like staring at the sun.

"Hey..." she tried to call out, but the words stuck in her throat.

She heard a loud pop and then another and another in split second succession.

Jesus Christ.

She had no time to think, just to move.

She dropped to the ground hard, the world exploding around her: shattering glass, a horrific cry, a car alarm whooping at an ear-splitting decibel.

Throwing her arms over her head, she pressed her face to the gritty slab, body twitching at every sound.

Overkill

As abruptly, the shooting stopped. An engine gunned and tires squealed on asphalt.

Now, Maggie's brain screamed, and she scrambled to her feet, grabbing behind her back for the .38 in her waistband. Her legs felt like rubber beneath her. Her ears rang, throwing her slightly off-balance.

By the time she stumbled from the stoop to the street, all she could see were a pair of brake lights, winking at her in the pitch.

In seconds, the shooter had sped away before she could get off a shot.

Lights came on all around her. Doors popped open, frightened faces peering out. "What's going on?" people shouted to each other as the car alarm continued hooting and screeching. Barking dogs added to the God-awful racket.

Maggie tucked her weapon back into her waistband. She wiped at the dirt on her cheek with a sleeve, gritting her teeth against the clamor that filled her ears as she looked around. Her eyes blurred, and she squinted hard to concentrate.

Where was the girl?

She picked her way between the Saab and the Beamer, the rear windshields of both shattered. Shards of glass crunched beneath her heels as she moved toward the curb where she'd last seen her standing.

There on the ground lay a dark figure, curled up like a wounded dog.

Maggie quickly crouched beside her, reaching for the pale head and cupping it in her hands.

The girl moaned.

"Stay still," she said. "Don't move."

She felt the damp on her skin and cursed.

"Call 9-1-1," she started shouting at the top of her lungs, while inside her head a voice screamed even louder: *Don't let her die. Please, don't pull this on me now.*

Chapter Twenty-Seven

The street in front of her condo swarmed with people and squad cars with flashing strobes. The ambulance had come and gone minutes before. She'd watched them load the gurney with the girl into the back before they'd taken off with siren whining.

Lacy Hurley. Her name was Lacy Hurley.

Maggie had found the girl's ID inside her knapsack along with some school books, a brush, a pack of Camels, and three crumpled dollar bills.

Her driver's license picture was as bad as a mug shot, but there was no question it was her.

And now she was in a fight for her life, headed for emergency surgery at Litchfield Methodist. She'd taken a bullet to the face.

Maggie cursed under her breath.

It wasn't fair. It just wasn't.

Lacy might've been a mixed-up teenager whose character left a lot to be desired, but she'd tried to do something right in the end.

She'd come forward to tell a horrible truth: that her boyfriend had been paid two thousand dollars to kill Pauletta Thomas. It had taken a lot of courage to do what she'd done.

So what was the moral here? No good deed goes unpunished? Is that how the saying went?

Well, it sucked.

Maggie had used the address on the driver's license to track down

Overkill

Lacy's mother at home. She'd been on her way out the door to work the late shift cleaning on the house staff at the Adam's Mark downtown. She thought Lacy was spending the night with a friend from school; she'd had no idea what her daughter was involved in. Now the woman was on her way to Litchfield Methodist Hospital to wait and see if Lacy came out of this, and Maggie could only stand on her front stoop and stare down the sidewalk at the puddle of blood marking the spot where Lacy went down.

Crime scene tape marked off an area nearly to her door. The boogey man had come that close, but he wouldn't get away. This one had a name.

An APB had already been issued for Jason Carson, and the photograph of him that Lacy had given her was already in the process of being copied and distributed to law enforcement agencies throughout the state. DPS turned up a license and registration for a 1989 Ford pickup and an address on Marvin Avenue, not far from Sunset High School. Leonard and Washington had been called back to the station and were digging up any priors. Maggie would bet they'd find more than a few if Lacy was right about the burglaries Jason and his friends had committed. If he was sloppy enough to brag about killing Pauletta, then he'd probably been stupid enough to get picked up in the past for one of his break-ins.

Now they just had to find the son of a bitch.

"He'd probably kill me if he ever found out I was talking to you..."

She had no doubt that Carson was the one who'd gunned down Lacy in her parking lot. But how had he known his girlfriend had intended to talk to Maggie about the murder? What had tipped him off? Had he been so paranoid that Lacy would rat him out that he'd kept tabs on her whereabouts since he'd told her what part he'd played in Pauletta's death?

Did it even matter?

All that did count was Lacy. Maggie only hoped she would live to testify against him.

If she couldn't—if she died—he'd have two counts of first degree homicide hanging around his neck. If the law were different, it would be three.

You can run, but you can't hide, Mr. Carson, she thought grimly.

The pieces were finally fitting together. Now they were only missing one.

The man who had ordered the hit.

An older white dude.

Someone from Sunset High School, so Carson had told Lacy. Someone Jason had known back when he was a freshman, about four years earlier.

But who?

The butcher, the baker, the candlestick maker?

C'mon, Maggie. Think.

What older man could Jason have come in contact with at school? A teacher?

"I used to teach remedial English classes in the public schools before I came here, so the curriculum is old hat..."

Had Matthew Prentice taught at Sunset High School? Was he there when Jason Carson was a freshman?

What about Abley? Had he ever seen any students from Sunset? Did he know Jason Carson? Was there a chance he'd counseled him in the past, realized the kid was turning into a monster, one he felt he could call on to violently extricate him from a reputation-ruining affair?

"Hey, Ryan, you all right?" Phillips hurried toward her in his shuffling gait, emerging from the parking lot, now a carnival of cars and cops setting up barricades and interviewing neighbors. "I got here as fast as I could. Christ Almighty, you're bleeding. Were you hit?"

Maggie looked down at her turtleneck now splotched with rust-colored stains. She turned over her hands. The skin of her palms was encrusted in dirt and dried blood. But the blood wasn't hers.

"I'm all right," she told him, rising to her feet, though her legs were so unsteady she nearly did a nose dive into the bushes. Would have if Phillips hadn't been there to steady her.

"They check you out?"

"Yeah. I'm okay, John. Just a headache."

One of the EMTs had quickly looked her over, even though she'd protested. Physically, she was fine, just a little fuzzy upstairs. But the guy had threatened to sit on her until she cried "uncle," so she'd acquiesced. She was too damned shaken up to pick a fight with anyone.

So her pupils were a tad dilated and she had some scratches on her palms and cheek from kissing the concrete when the gunfire started. Hers were hardly mortal wounds.

It was Lacy who'd taken the worst of it. She and the shattered windows of the BMW and Saab parked right out front. Maggie had seen the owners emerge from their condos to take stock of the damage done. The way they'd howled, she would've thought they'd taken the bullets themselves.

They're only cars, she'd wanted to yell at them, but it wasn't worth it. She needed her energy for other things.

"What the hell happened here?" Phillips' eyes flickered back and forth, taking it all in, no doubt wondering how he could've left his partner at the station less than an hour ago only to find out she'd been shot at on her doorstep.

Maggie explained in a detached monotone: "She followed me home, John. She was too scared to talk at the station, and she wanted to give me his picture. She was so afraid he'd figure out what she was up to if she didn't do it on her own terms." Her gaze dropped to her hands. "Somehow, he knew anyway."

"Goddammit, I had a bad sense about this whole deal. It didn't feel right to me from the beginning, the way you were being singled out. Hell, this shouldn't have gone down." Phillips slapped a hand against the porch post. "I should've driven you home and slept on your couch. We could've handled this thing together, made the girl go to the station."

"No," she told him. "No way."

"Hell, Ryan, this wouldn't have happened if I'd been here."

"You don't know that."

"Like hell I don't."

He was blaming himself, she realized. Pinning it on his own ass that she'd been put in danger. No matter that there was never anything he could've done about it, except try to shadow her until they'd closed the case. And she was too damned old for a babysitter.

231

"The shooter was her boyfriend," Maggie spelled out, not sure how much he knew already. "She was scared as hell of him. She figured he'd stop her permanently if he found out what she was up to. I think that's why she couldn't do this on the phone. He was keeping tabs on her. She'd told her mom she was staying with a friend tonight, probably fed Carson the same lie. But it looks like he didn't trust her."

"You figure he was aiming at you, too?"

She shook her head and pulled apart from him, finding her legs stable enough to stand on without a crutch. "He wanted to silence Lacy. If she was out of the picture, he'd be home-free, right? But if I got hit when he sprayed the parking lot with bullets, he wasn't gonna lose sleep over it, I'm sure."

"What else did she tell you?"

"Just that Pauletta's life was worth a measly two grand on the street."

"You get her on tape?"

"No," Maggie admitted, wishing now that she had. It had all happened so damned fast and she'd been so unprepared. "But I remember everything she said. Every word." She would never forget it.

"You didn't see the shooter beforehand?"

"No." She felt as if she'd let him down. Let Lacy down. She should have seen something. She should've sensed it coming. That was her job, right? To serve and protect? She'd for sure messed up this one.

She squished her eyes closed, trying to think, trying to envision the moment when Lacy had come up behind her on the sidewalk. Had there been a car turning onto the street? Had she picked up on the crackle of tires on the asphalt? The glimmer of headlights turning their direction?

But she couldn't picture anything but the brights in her eyes right as the shooting started.

She shivered and crossed her arms, rubbing them. "I've got a hunch he showed up just in time to see her go inside with me, so he waited until she was leaving to take her out." Her chest tightened, and she flinched as she relived those few seconds again, the loud pops, the percussive beats that still rang in her ears. "I should've listened to her, John. She was afraid this would happen. I should've have protected her somehow, and I didn't."

232

Overkill

"How bad is she?"

Maggie met his eyes. The blue and red of the strobes flickered in his pupils. "She looked real bad." The words were hard to say.

"Shit."

Shit was an understatement.

"So you checked the casings? It was a .45?" Phillips asked, sounding no less angry than she. He stared ahead at the sidewalk, and Maggie turned to see what he was looking at: a pair of blues setting down numbered cards where casings had fallen on the street. "You think he used the same gun to shoot Pauletta?"

"I do." Maggie had no doubt that ballistics would find a match.

There was unmistakable relief in Phillip's face. "Thank God you had enough sense to hit the dirt. God knows I would've gone after the son of a bitch myself if anything had happened to you." He put his hand on her shoulder and squeezed.

Maggie felt tears come to her eyes and held them back with all her might.

She would not break down now.

They had too much to do.

"We've got to get a warrant for Carson's house," she said, ignoring the catch in her voice and the ache she felt in every inch of her body, "and we'll need to subpoena the bank records for Francis Abley and Matthew Prentice, see if either one of them withdrew two thousand dollars from their accounts in the recent past. I want to talk to someone in human resources at the DISD headquarters, find out if Prentice worked at Sunset High School or if Abley had any affiliation when Jason Carson was a student, and we have to get blood draws from both men to compare to the fetal DNA..."

"Hey," Phillips cut her off. "We're gonna get him, okay? Nobody's getting off on this one."

Maggie nodded, her eyes on the bloodstained curb.

Chapter Twenty-Eight

The funeral service for Pauletta was scheduled to start at eight-thirty.

Maggie had arrived half an hour early. For the past twenty minutes, she'd stood at the edge of the street with her arms crossed over her chest, her eyes on the arched wooden doors of the First Methodist Church of Litchfield, just watching people arrive all gussied up in their most somber clothes. She'd only seen one outfit yet that wasn't jet or navy.

Black and blue.

The perfect colors for mourning.

Even she had to admit she felt more than a little beat up by the past three days.

Ten minutes before, the curtained hearse from the funeral home had arrived with Pauletta's casket; it had pulled around back to unload.

Like a superstitious child, Maggie had found herself holding her breath as it passed.

She tried not to think of the cargo it carried. Tried to focus instead on the image of the smiling girl in the school photograph and found herself wondering which picture Candy had picked to set upon Pauletta's casket.

Cars filled the parking lot and lined the street. People kept arriving, though it seemed the whole population of Litchfield was already inside, Matthew Prentice and Dr. Francis Abley among them.

Maggie curled her fingers to fists in her pockets.

After a long night spent at the station giving a formal statement about

234

Overkill

the shooting in her parking lot and meeting with Sergeant Morris and their lieutenant, going over the evidence they had so far, both circumstantial and from Lacy's confession to Maggie, a search warrant had been issued for Jason Carson's house. The Dallas police who'd executed it had found a cache of rifles and handguns stashed under his bed, White Supremacist propaganda, and recipes from the Internet for making bombs. Jason's father had been detained, but claimed to know nothing about his son's activities.

Go figure.

Maggie had called the hospital herself this morning and talked to a nurse in ICU. Lacy had come out of surgery and was doing okay.

Things must be going their way, right?

And, if all went well, by this afternoon they'd have the court orders for the blood tests they needed to ascertain if Prentice or Abley was the father of Pauletta's child, as well as the subpoenaed bank records and files from the HR department at the Dallas ISD.

Once they had those answers, they'd have their man.

It was that simple, wasn't it?

Maggie shifted on her feet, feeling uneasy and not certain why. They were so close. She should've felt solid, sure, but she couldn't quiet the voice in her head that told this wasn't finished.

She flipped up the collar of her jacket and pulled her chin down to warm her ears.

Is this it, Pauletta? she silently asked, wishing there were some way the girl could answer, reassure her they were on the right track.

Phillips seemed convinced enough with the evidence at hand. He'd gone into the church not long after Abley and Prentice. He'd told her he wanted to stand on the sidelines, to see their expressions as Pauletta was eulogized. "You can read guilt a lot more plain on a face when a choir's singing 'Amazing Grace,' you ever notice that?"

Maggie couldn't say that she had.

She had declined to join him, instead remaining outside.

It made her too angry.

She couldn't bear to see all the tears. She couldn't stand to hear all the bittersweet words about Pauletta's too short life. It didn't matter how often she'd gone through it before, it still cut out a piece of her heart every time she listened to a child being eulogized. It wasn't the natural order of things. Yet it happened everyday. Much too often.

She checked her watch.

Eight twenty-five.

Where was Pauletta's mother?

Just as the question came to mind, a black stretch limo pulled slowly up the drive and stopped before the church doors. It looked bleak as a large crow silhouetted against the dying grass. The thick overhang of gray clouds reflected in its tinted windows.

A uniformed driver emerged from the front and opened a rear door with a sweep of his arm. A man was disgorged, his face half-hidden behind sunglasses, despite the gloomy morning. Maggie recognized Dave Gray by the peacock stance, chest forward and shoulders back; his trim form nattily attired in a tailored charcoal gray suit.

Candy shimmied out next in a black dress and pearls. A ribboned hat hid all but a sleek blond ponytail. She took Gray's arm and, head ducked, leaned against him as he walked her around to the doors of the church.

Neither he nor Candy so much as glanced in her direction.

A shiver shot up her spine.

She wondered what the pair would think when they spotted Brad Thomas inside with a corrections officer escort. He'd be unshackled for the service, or so she'd been told, and she hoped he was kept at a distance from his estranged wife. At least he wouldn't be armed this morning.

Ashes to ashes, dust to dust.

The one tenuous string that had bound them together was now gone. It was time for them to let their daughter go in peace.

The wind picked up, blowing across the church yard like a heavy sigh, and she flicked her hair from her eyes and turned her head to catch sight of something colorful in the distance. A spot of yellow on this gray day, and it was growing larger, coming closer.

Overkill

A school bus rolled up the street toward her with a rumble of gears and pops of exhaust.

The black letters on its side read, "Transportation Management," and, on a square of white near the door, "Litchfield Special School."

She started to walk across the lawn toward the vehicle as it rounded the drive in front of the Methodist church. Once it had stopped, a darkly-clad women emerged, then children, one after one, until a dozen gathered at the base of the stone steps.

As Maggie got closer, she heard a familiar voice, sharp and clipped as a metronome.

"...stay with me, do you understand, and no loud sobbing, please. Pauletta's parents do not need to hear you boo-hooing your lights out. They need you to be strong."

Maggie recognized a few faces she'd seen at the Litchfield Special School. The messy-haired boy with glasses, a teenaged girl with red hair, a broad-shouldered blond boy with earrings.

Candor ceased her instructions and looked up at Maggie.

"Doctor, could I speak with you a minute?"

The principal hesitated, but then told her charges, "Wait here," before she stepped away from the cluster of them toward Maggie.

"Please be brief, Detective, we're late as it is, and I'd like to get them inside before the service starts. Several of our teachers are inside already, and hopefully they've saved us a pew."

"I saw Mr. Prentice enter the church at least ten minutes ago," Maggie told her.

"Good." Candor nodded, her eyes shifting toward the heavy wooden doors as a pair of black-clad late-comers pulled them wide. For an instant, the sound of an organ escaped, and the slow and sweet dirge-like notes carried over on the wind to wrap around them.

Then the doors quickly shut, and the music was gone.

"We're close to finding who did this," Maggie said, her hands stuffed into the pockets of her leather jacket. "We've got an APB out on the shooter, and we're working on finding out who was behind it all."

237

"Behind it?" Candor's dark eyes narrowed, her weary brown face further creasing. "You make it sound as if Pauletta's death was a conspiracy."

"It was."

The skirt of Candor's black coat-dress flapped, and she reached down to still it. "Detective, I really must get the kids inside. I don't want them catching cold."

Maggie didn't waste another moment. "Do you recall if Matthew Prentice worked at Sunset High School before he began teaching at LSS?"

Gray-tinged eyebrows knit together. "Are you implicating Mr. Prentice in this conspiracy of yours?"

"I'm just looking for answers, Doctor."

Candor's voice was cross. "He wouldn't have hurt Pauletta, I'm sure of it."

"Did he work at Sunset?" Maggie tried again.

"What if he did? It doesn't prove a thing."

"What about Dr. Abley? Did he ever make visits to or take occasional referrals of children from the Dallas School District?"

Candor frowned at her. "I'm here to attend Pauletta's funeral, Detective, not to undergo an interrogation. Now if you'll excuse me...."

"Just one more thing, Doctor. Can you tell me a little more about a group called The Eagle Club that stayed after school on Wednesdays? Was that a supervised group, or were the kids left alone?"

Candor paused, then shook her head. "Of course we supervise the kids, but, honestly, I don't know why you're even asking about that. What could the club possibly have to do with the murder?"

Maggie pushed wind-blown hair from her face. "Mrs. Thomas said Pauletta participated."

"Well, she was wrong. Pauletta hadn't attended a meeting for at least two, maybe, three months. Please, Detective, I really must go."

Maggie stood there as Candor strode back toward the children, huddling together against the gusty wind. The principal promptly shepherded the bunch up the stone steps of the church and inside without so much as a glance behind her.

Overkill

As the doors hung open for each child to enter, the organ music filtered out again, this time accompanied by the swell of voices.

Amazing Grace, how sweet the sound that saved a wretch like me...I once was lost, but now am found, was blind but now I see....

The hair at her nape prickled.

She had to get out of here.

Phillips could stay and watch for guilt on people's faces.

Maggie crossed the grass toward her Mazda as the wind picked up suddenly, plucking dying leaves from trees and sending them swirling around her.

She got in her car and started the engine, but didn't move for a moment. Just sat and thought about everything, tried to assimilate all the thoughts that ran round and round inside her head.

Something nagged at her, chewed at the inside of her belly, and it wasn't going to stop until she figured out what it was.

Jason Carson had been paid $2,000 to shoot Pauletta on her school bus. He'd been instructed where to stand on the curb, how to flag down the bus, and where Pauletta sat, two seats behind the driver.

Some older white man who used to work at Sunset High School had contacted him because they'd had a run-in back when Carson was a freshman.

This guy had obviously known where Carson lived.

He'd known a lot of things.

Like where the bus picked Pauletta up so that she was sure to be there when the shooter boarded.

He'd known when to find her alone, say when her mother was at work those few hours after school.

"...She had a house key with her at all times. She let herself in then phoned me at Cybercytes. She stayed late at school on Wednesdays for The Eagle Club, Dr. Candor's way to get the kids to socialize outside the classroom, but the bus always brought her home afterward."

Only that wasn't the case, according to Candor.

"Pauletta hadn't attended a meeting for at least two or three months..."

Three months.

Maggie's mouth went bone dry.

Is that when it had happened? On a Wednesday afternoon?

Had she spent the time with Prentice? Or had she been with someone else entirely?

Someone they hadn't looked at because he'd been a victim, too?

Oh, God, was it possible?

But it would make sense, wouldn't it?

"*...the bus always brought her home...*"

What had Lacy told her?

"*...he said she'd be two seats back...*"

"*...did he want him to shoot the driver, too, or was that Jason's idea?*"

"*I don't know.*"

"*...that description on the news doesn't look much like him either....*"

Goosebumps rose across Maggie's skin.

Oh, shit.

Could it be true?

She got on the radio to the dispatcher.

"Hey, Susie, can you do something for me?"

"Sure, Detective. What's on your mind?"

"Would you page Phillips and leave a message for him to meet me at the hospital?"

"Will do."

She signed off, took a deep breath, then put the car into gear and pulled away.

Chapter Twenty-Nine

The elevator bumped to a stop and Maggie waited impatiently as the doors took their time sliding open.

She stepped out to find nurses in pink scrubs running up and down the hallway in a panic.

Had someone had a heart attack or something?

A security guard with walkie-talkie at his lips bumped her shoulder as she turned to head for Ronald Biggins' room.

She caught his arm with one hand and reached into her jacket with the other. She felt the lump of her gun in the shoulder holster as she withdrew her ID. "Detective Ryan," she said as he stopped and looked at her. "What's going on?"

Tiny eyes nearly lost in the folds of wrinkled face visibly brightened. "We've got a patient who's MIA. Unhooked his IVs and disappeared from his room a couple minutes ago, and no one's seen him since."

"What's his name?"

"Ronald Biggins."

Biggins?

Jesus.

Her heart slammed into her throat.

She took off running up the hallway, fingers grabbing at the doorframe as she careened into Biggins' room, her loafers skidding on the tiled floor.

A very pregnant Mrs. Biggins sprawled out in a chair by the window, her large belly heaving as she sobbed hysterically while a nurse held her hand to take a pulse.

"What the hell happened?" she got out in a breath, and Mrs. Biggins stopped bawling long enough to raise her mascara-muddied gaze.

"You're Detective Ryan?" she asked as the hovering nurse frowned. "You're the one I met in the hallway the other day?"

"That's right." Maggie took a few more steps in and glanced around her.

The top sheet on the bed had been thrown back, there was an empty dent in the middle of the pillow, and a clear plastic IV tube dripped a puddle onto the nearby floor, but there was no sign of Biggins.

"Where's your husband, ma'am?"

"I don't know," she wailed, her splotched cheeks turned mottled shades of red and purple. "I took a phone call from a reporter who'd heard you'd found out who shot Ronnie." Her eyes rolled upward, thoughtfully before she blurted out, "Jason Carson, that's it. I told my husband the good news, but he didn't look so good all of a sudden and he asked if I'd fill his pitcher with ice water." Her lipstick-smeared mouth trembled. "So I went up the hallway to get some ice from the machine and water from the fountain, but, when I got back, he was gone."

"Did he say anything else?"

Mrs. Biggins rubbed her hands on her belly, tears coursing down her cheeks. "Just that he loves me and our babies. That's all."

"Now, ma'am," the nurse in pink patted a plump hand and bent over her shoulder. "You shouldn't get yourself worked up like this. I'm sure it's nothing. He'll show up soon. Probably just went to stretch his legs."

With an injured thigh? Maggie wanted to scream, but kept her mouth shut.

She blinked, trying to clear her head, but flashed on Biggins lying on Elm Street, white with shock, blood soaked through his shirt and pants even as a uniform pressed towels hard against them.

"Oh, God, it was my decision, my mistake..."

"...if I just hadn't been so careless, it wouldn't have happened, would it?"

Confessions from a guilty man? Was his mistake, not in opening the bus door, but in having sex with Pauletta? Had he assumed she couldn't get pregnant? Had he been too careless to use a condom, figuring her Williams' syndrome had made her barren?

Maggie stared at the tan phone on the bedside table, the one she'd used to return her page the day before.

"What's going on?"

"We have a tipster who says he can ID the man who killed Pauletta..."

Biggins had been right there, listening. He could've been the one who'd warned Jason Carson that someone was about to turn him in.

Jesus.

They hadn't considered him a suspect because he'd been a victim. He'd taken two bullets himself. Had that been part of the plan? Did he have Carson plug him twice just to divert suspicion?

"It's just a shame something like this had to happen in Litchfield. I mean, I was scared to death for Ronnie before we moved up here after Luke was born..."

"Ronnie's got a three-year-old son and his wife's about to pop out number two..."

"...he had big trouble with some kids on his bus, and that was that..."

Hadn't Biggins worked the city schools before coming to Litchfield? Had he driven for Sunset High School four years ago? Did he have some run-ins with Jason Carson and his gang of thugs?

Is that how he'd known where Jason lived?

It had to be. It made complete sense. And it would explain why their composite didn't resemble their suspect.

Maggie felt as if she'd been smacked upside the head with a frying pan.

"Detective? Detective!"

She turned her head.

The security guard stood in the doorway to the room. A grim smile further creased his face. "Someone in the parking lot spotted a guy on the roof in a hospital gown."

Maggie told the guard, "Keep everyone down, you hear me? And put a call into the P.D. now. Tell them to send backup."

He nodded dumbly.

She pushed on past him, rushing toward the nearest door marked "Exit" and grabbing it open. Her feet clanked loudly on the metal steps as she threw herself up the stairwell, taking one turn and then another, reaching the third floor and the fourth floor, then finally the door to the roof.

There, she paused to catch her breath and to remove her .38 from her holster.

She slowly turned the knob and inched open the door to the outside.

The wind rushed at her, batting her hair in her eyes as she scanned the gravel-covered roof, but she could only discern the metal boxes of the air conditioning equipment and the round silver exhaust fans.

She cautiously stepped through the door and swiveled left, her weapon leveled in both hands.

There he was.

He stood barely a foot from where the roof ended, the flat edge of the world from which ships would drop off into oblivion.

His back was to her, the opened flaps of his hospital gown blowing madly in the wind. He was otherwise bare save for a pair of white briefs and the gauze wrapped around his right thigh and shoulder. She saw plenty of skin.

He had to be cold. The brisk air cut through her leather jacket, chilling her so that her teeth began to chatter.

The sky was lead gray, so thick with clouds she knew the rain was coming. It was only a matter of time. She had to get him down first.

"Mr. Biggins," she called out and started walking toward him, taking measured steps, careful not to slip on the gravel. "Please, move away from the edge. There's no reason for this. Let's go back inside and talk this over, all right? Your wife's worried about you. Don't do this to her or your kids."

He turned slightly, just enough so that she could see a tinge of brown against the white of the bandage on his leg. He held his right arm at his side. She wondered if the trip up had done any damage, if he'd torn any stitches.

Overkill

"You know, don't you? You found Jason, and he told you what I did. Oh, God, he told you," he moaned, his voice so soft against the angry wind. His pale hair swirled around his face. Even from where she stood, she could see his tears. His cheeks were slick with them. "It had to happen, didn't it? That you'd find out about me...the evil that I've done. My wife is better off without me...her and the kids. I don't deserve them, not after how I've sinned. So go ahead and shoot me," he cried out. "Go ahead!"

He suddenly wobbled like a drunk, weaving against the push of the wind and, for a moment, she thought it would topple him right off the building.

"Steady now, Mr. Biggins," Maggie called out and fumbled beneath her jacket with the shoulder holster, strapping in the .38 so she'd have both hands free. He was more a danger to himself than to her. "Let's talk this over, okay?"

"Talk it over?" He raised his left hand to the sky. He lifted his chin and stared into the clouds. "The murderer rises in the dark that he may kill the poor and needy, and in the night he is as a thief. The eye of the adulterer also waits for the twilight, saying, 'No eye shall see me;' and he disguises his face."

He lowered his head and looked straight at her. She stood at least twenty feet away. "Job 24:14-15. Do you know it, Detective? Can you even understand what I've done? I've committed adultery...I've murdered an innocent." He spat out each word. "Don't you even want to hear why I did it? Why I threw everything away because of Pauletta and how she made me feel just for a little while every week?"

Maggie did want to know. She felt near to bursting with an urgency to hear. "Why don't you tell me. Why don't we go back to your room, and you can tell me everything. Let's do that, Mr. Biggins. I'll listen to you for as long as it takes."

She took a step closer, and he reared his head, screaming out, "Don't!"

"The wind is so loud up here," she told him, but he wasn't buying it.

He shook his head, then glanced over his shoulder, toward where roof met air. "I'll do it," he said. "I will jump if I have to."

Maggie wrapped her arms around herself, helpless as she'd ever been, trying to figure out a way to get him down and at the same time wondering if it wouldn't be better for everyone involved if he did take a flying leap. Save the taxpayers money. Save him a life sentence. Save his wife the pain of seeing him for what he truly was. Save his children from visiting their father in prison.

She didn't know the Bible as well as he did, not enough to quote it, though she did know the part about an eye for an eye. Castrate the rapists, hang the killers, stone the child beaters. As far as she was concerned, retribution wasn't such a bad idea.

Before she could stop herself, she asked him, "Did you love her?"

Biggins faced her fully. "What?"

"Did you love her?" she repeated, shouting to the wind. "Because she believed you did. She wanted to keep the baby. But you must've known that, too. You had to make sure she never gave birth. Either way, your life was screwed, right? Divorce would've been the least of your worries."

"You don't understand. You can't." He stared at her, his expression a grimace of pain. "My wife's a Christian woman, Detective. She is a perfect child of God, and I am not worthy of her. I was confused and insecure, and I let the devil creep in, filling my mind with ugly thoughts and desires I should have been able to control, but I couldn't."

"So you took up with Pauletta Thomas?" Maggie made a noise of disgust. "She wasn't even seventeen, and you're, what? Nearly thirty?"

"I'm thirty-five." His face softened, a faint smile appearing. "Pauletta was the sweetest thing. So uncomplicated and undemanding. She listened to me when I talked. She would leave the bus last and give me a hug, hold me so comfortingly. For nearly two years, I didn't let myself respond. I don't know why it happened, but it did, and then I couldn't turn back. I didn't see a way out."

"You were with her on Wednesdays, weren't you? She stopped going to the Eagle Club, but didn't tell her mother, and you took her off somewhere in the bus for an hour or so before you brought her home. Where did you go with her?" Maggie tightened her hands to fists, watching him and

Overkill

waiting for his answer.

He looked away, off into the rushing clouds. "The old depot where the tracks are overgrown with weeds. Nobody goes there anymore. It's as isolated a spot as I know, surrounded by brush and trees. No one could see us. We were free to do as we pleased. Mostly we just talked."

Maggie shook her head. "You're right, Mr. Biggins, I don't understand. I can't imagine that you could cultivate a relationship with a girl whose life was entirely dependent on other people and take advantage of her..."

"That's not how it was." His face reddened. "She was so bright in many ways. She knew words I've never heard before."

"But she likely didn't even understand them all, for God's sake," Maggie cut him off. "Pauletta didn't have the ability to make decisions. She was completely vulnerable, and you knew that. She trusted you...hell, she didn't know what it meant to distrust anyone. So you spent time alone with her, had sex with her and murdered her when you found out she was pregnant."

"You make it sound so cold!"

"You're right," Maggie told him. "She thought you would marry her and instead you had her killed. That's beyond cold, Mr. Biggins."

"No," he sobbed. "No, no, no!"

Jesus Christ.

How she wanted just to run at him now and push him over the edge and be done with it. All in one fell swoop.

"No, no, no," he howled like a wounded animal.

Then he dropped to his knees on the gravel just as the rain started up.

She felt a splatter on her face and then another, until it fast became a downpour.

"Mr. Biggins?"

She could hardly see him through it, could just make out a pale blur on the ground. Within seconds, her hair clung to her head, and leather jacket was as good as ruined. It already smelled like a wet cow.

"Biggins!"

She walked toward him, the gravel slick and unsteady beneath her shoes.

247

He huddled at her feet, drenched and quivering, and she bent down to put a hand on his shoulder.

"Let's go inside," she said through the noise of the rain and helped him stand.

Chapter Thirty

Maggie sat on the vinyl waiting room chair, a towel wrapped around her, and she shivered, teeth chattering. She'd spread her leather jacket out on the arms of the chair to her left and glanced at it glumly. Maybe a dry cleaner could save it.

"Here you go. Fresh from the vending machine."

Phillips held out a cup of coffee, and she greedily reached for it. She clasped the warmth between her hands and sighed. "It's not decaffeinated, is it?"

"Are you kidding?"

"Good boy."

The chair at her right elbow squeaked as Phillips took a seat. "You sure you don't want to change into the scrubs that nurse offered? Hot pink'd look good on you."

"Says you." She closed her eyes, just breathing in the steam from the cup. Her insides were settling down. The incident on the roof now seemed more like a dream than reality. If only her clothes weren't still soggy, she might've convinced herself she'd imagined it.

"Biggins tore open his leg wound, but he's fine otherwise. If we're lucky, maybe he'll catch pneumonia. Sarge put a uniform outside his door and he'll remain under house arrest until he's well enough to check out. Too bad you didn't just let him jump," Phillips said, and she opened her eyes to find him watching her. He had the look in his eyes, in his expression, that fatherly concern that tugged right at her chest. "Christ Almighty, I can't believe he really did it. The son of a bitch."

Maggie took a slow sip of coffee, the brew so hot it burned her tongue. She blew on it before she took another. She didn't mention that she'd had the same thought, of letting Biggins just take the plunge.

He cocked his head. "You okay?"

"Yeah, I'm fine." She lowered the cup to her knees. "How's Mrs. Biggins?"

"Still in labor." He grunted and leaned back in his seat. "Eight weeks premature isn't that big a deal these days, but it's still not a good thing when a baby comes too early."

Nothing about any of this was a good thing, she thought.

"You hear anything about Carson?" she asked.

He shook his head. "APBs still out on him. They'll get him sooner or later, probably sooner if you want my opinion. He's an eighteen-year-old skinhead with nowhere to go. That two grand'll run out fast, if he hasn't already spent it."

She knew he was right. Carson wouldn't last long out there on his own. He wasn't that clever. He couldn't even finish off Lacy, and he'd taken enough shots. The bullet that hit her in the face had gone through her cheek and exited her skull, missing her brain entirely. She'd need some plastic surgery, maybe speech therapy, but she'd live to testify in court against her boyfriend and Ronald Biggins.

And Maggie was going to do her damnedest to see that Lacy got that reward Dave Gray had offered. Every shiny penny. Even if she had to turn the man upside down and shake him until she'd emptied his pockets.

Now that was a pleasant image.

She raised the cup to her lips and drank until the warmth spread through her veins, from her fingers to her toes. Still, her hands were shaking.

When she had drained every last drop, she crumpled the cup and tossed it onto the veneered table covered with magazines. Then she lifted the towel from her shoulders and wiped at her hair.

Overkill

"I wish I'd known what you were up to," her partner said, not for the first time since he'd shown up at the hospital to catch her bringing Biggins down from the roof. It had been quite a scene with the security guard, a matching pair of uniforms, and the nurses all crowded around, mouths open. The worst was Mrs. Biggins' reaction, a cry as painful as any Maggie had ever heard and then her water breaking.

Phillips went on, "You should've come into the church and dragged me out. I'm supposed to watch your back, Ryan. So, if it's not too much to ask, I'd appreciate it if you'd let me do that every now and then instead of pulling a solo act."

She stopped patting at her damp mop and smiled at him. "Hell, Phillips, if I'd known for sure what I was getting myself into, I would've sent you up on the rooftop instead, bad knees and all. Then you'd be the one looking like a drowned rat."

"Smart ass." He chuckled softly, but his laughter quickly faded. Without a word, he reached for her hand and wrapped it firmly in his fingers, and he held on tightly for the longest time before he released it. "Just don't do it again."

Chapter Thirty-One

They had Momma propped up and had extubated her so that she appeared slightly more human and less like an old woman lying on her deathbed.

She was still hooked up to IVs that ran from bags on metal poles into her arms and she had oxygen clips at her nostrils, but her eyes actually followed Maggie as she walked into the room. Her mouth struggled to say her daughter's name.

"Mar-gat" emerged instead of Margaret.

She has a long road ahead of her.

"How're you feeling, Momma?" Maggie forced herself to wear a smile she did not feel. She went to the bed and reached over the rail to clasp a fragile hand. Momma's skin felt like crepe paper. Cool and dry and almost weightless. "You look much better today than when I last saw you."

"Whe...where?" she heard her mother gasp, but Maggie knew what she meant.

"You're in Parkland Hospital, Momma. They brought you here four days ago. You were in an accident."

"Ax-dent?"

"You were hit by a car."

"Don' memer."

"No, I'm sure you don't. You were unconscious for almost three days," she tried to explain, but the pale eyes merely watered and the wrinkled face

252

Overkill

filled with panic.

"Wan home...wan home."

"You can't go home," Maggie said as tears rolled down the deeply creased cheeks and her mother started making horrible noises, pitiful sounds.

"Ow," she moaned. "Ow."

Maggie couldn't tell if she were in pain or just wanted to get out. Jesus Christ, what was she supposed to do? Where was her doctor?

"Hush, Momma, hush." She touched the white fluff of her mother's hair, smoothed it down with her fingers, but none of that did any good.

"Owww."

A nurse hurried into the room and went to Momma's side, checking IV leads and the green and red numbers lit up on the machines. "If you don't mind, I think she needs her rest."

Maggie didn't mind at all. She backed away from the bed and made a quick exit. She hadn't wanted to come in the first place, had wanted to be anywhere but here, but Delores had kept calling and she'd ended up at Parkland despite everything.

She ran into Delores just outside the door.

"Have you got a minute, baby?" The dark face seemed to have aged in the past few days. Always thin, she looked suddenly frail.

Maggie didn't have the heart to tell her no.

"What's up?"

Delores made no move to sit down, though the waiting room wasn't far away. She dug into her straw handbag and pulled out some papers, pushing them into Maggie's hands.

"These are from a few of the extended care places I've been checking out," she said. "We've got to pick one fast and get your mama on the waiting list, or else she might not have a room when they discharge her from here."

Maggie didn't know what to say. She stared at the brochures till her eyes blurred. "Do we have to do this right now? Can't we take some time to think about it?"

"Sometimes it takes a month to get a person into these facilities," Delores told her, weariness further softening her drawl. "And we need to think about putting the house up for sale. Her care's gonna be awfully expensive."

"But she has insurance."

"What she's got isn't enough. It never is."

"What about you?"

"I've still got my condo, honey. I've just been leasin' it since I moved into your mama's house to help her out."

"What about Momma's things?"

"We'll sell what we can, then donate the rest."

"All of it?"

"You can keep what you want, baby." Delores rubbed at the creases in her brow. "You'll just have to take time to get over to the house and pick out whatever you'd like to have."

Go back to the house, go through Momma's things, his things, see it all again in her head, relive what she was fighting so hard to forget?

Maggie felt herself shutting off, shutting down. She was too worn out from the Pauletta Thomas case, too damned tired to think about anyone but herself.

She shoved the pamphlets into her bag. "I'll look at these later, okay? I promise, I will. Then we'll talk about the rest. I won't let you down, Dee."

Delores opened her mouth only to close it, pursing her lips tightly as she nodded.

Maggie tried to summon up a smile and sorely failed. Instead, she reached for Delores and held her tightly. "Thank you," she whispered. It wasn't much, wasn't near enough, but it was all she had.

"I'll call you," she threw over her shoulder before she fled, bypassing the elevators and taking the stairs down, running every step.

She had been running all her life.

And she was nearly out of gas.

Overkill

She didn't see him there until she'd pulled into the parking lot.

The man sitting on her front stoop, huddled in a purple barn coat.

She got out of her car and shut the door.

Mahoney turned his head, and their eyes locked. He slowly came to his feet.

"Hey," he said as she walked toward him up the sidewalk. "I was in the neighborhood, and I thought I'd...oh, hell"—his hands rose, only to fall to his sides a second later—"okay, so I wasn't in the neighborhood until I drove out here, but I needed to see you. I want to set things straight..."

He stopped. Something shifted in his face.

"God, what's wrong? Hell, Maggie, did someone die or something?"

Her teeth were chattering. She felt her body shake.

"Ryan?"

"Just hold me, okay?"

She saw his eyes widen, but he didn't hesitate. He opened his arms to her and wrapped her inside.

Maggie closed her eyes and dared to breathe.

Other Books of Mystery or Suspense by Mayhaven Publishing

Murder at the Strawberry Festival
Warren Carrier

An Honorable Spy
Warren Carrier

Waltz With the Devil
Paul Fouliard

And Then She Was Gone*
Susan McBride

A Family Possessed
W. L. Stevenson

A Broken Reed*
Ron Miller

And introducing our first true-crime:
Lena
Murder in Southern Indiana
Christine Righthouse

*Winners: Mayhaven Awards for Fiction